Peacemaker

C. S. Clifford

First published in Great Britain 2023

ISBN: 9 781739 080198

Printed and bound in the UK

A catalogue record of this book is available from the British Library

Edited by Clive Clarke

Cover by Laura Wilde

www.csclifford.co.uk

Other C. S. Clifford books for older readers:

Navajo Sprit Part 1: Acceptance
ISBN: 9 780993 195754

Navajo Sprit Part 2: Quest
ISBN: 9 780993 195761

Navajo Sprit Part 3: Detour
ISBN: 9 780993 195785

Navajo Sprit Part 4: Penance
ISBN: 9 781999 361143

Alone
ISBN: 9 781739 080136

Still Alone
ISBN: 9 781739 080143

Exclusion Zone
ISBN: 9 781739 080129

Did You See Me
ISBN: 9 781999 361181

Chameleon Origin
ISBN: 9 781999 361167

Chameleon Dawn
ISBN: 9 781739 080150

Potential is determined only by
opportunity, courage, and
determination.

To Violet

Best Wishes

For those who strive to improve

themselves and others.

Prologue:

Among the melee of inhabitants dwelling the Earth, only one currently prospered. Mankind. Man's population was expanding at an extraordinary pace; their demands for land increasing exponentially. Their quest for it, frequently resulting in bloodshed as they attempted to vanquish other species from it.

Three such species guarded their lands under a veil of magic. The Dwarves, High and Wood Elves lived secretly from the rest of the world. Dwarves and Elves locked in a war spanning several centuries.

All species, except Mankind and Dark Elves, suffered from a sickness, contraction of which was ultimately painful and deadly. Thought to have been contrived by a powerful witch, her premature demise prevented the cure becoming known. It is widely believed a Dark Elf held a cure, but had not offered it to any species.

The Wood Elves and Dwarf numbers were decimated by war and sickness. Both species held less than two-thousand individuals remaining. The High Elves were particularly prone to the sickness, their population reduced to a few hundred. At the current rate of decline, all three species would become extinct within a few short sun-cycles, the High Elves probably sooner.

Change was of paramount importance. There was little to prevent Mankind pouring into the unknown, and the likelihood of a combined force of species, to prevent their invasive thrust, was minimal. The change, therefore, must happen between the species facing extinction.

The task was monumental; the outcome unlikely, but accepting it, was the only option.

East of Graylen Forest
The Country Travelled by Gatran

Xeltar Mountain
Dwarf Kingdom

Hills of Jerev
Troll Kingdom

The Plains of Krahor
Home to small Settlements of a Variety of Species Living Solitary Lives

Mandrade Mountains
The Last Auk Outpost

Karvil Marshlands
Inhabited by Evil Mud Dwelling Creatures

Gomar Desert
Arid, and inhabited by Dormant Domain Flies

Omintic Sea
Inhabited by Huge Multi-Headed Creatures

Graylen Forest
The Last Wood Elf Community

Rag Dire Pass

Dangorg Petrified Woods
Witch Stronghold

Chapter 1:

"Enter my children, take your place at my table."

Agran, King of the Wood Elves, sat at the head. His wife, and Queen, Nervita, next to him. He smiled fondly at them as they sat, but his face held a serious demeanour.

"Normally Father, matters of state are dealt with at an earlier time," Putraya smiled, hiding her curiosity.

"What makes you believe I summoned you here for a state meeting?" Agran asked.

"My sister is right father, I can't remember a formal gathering for anything except matters of state," Gatran added his opinion.

"Your intuition always impresses me Gatran, as does your sister's, but what we have to discuss stretches beyond matters of State."

"Speak what troubles your mind, father, so we might solve the issues."

Agran ignored the request, turning his head to face his youngest son, Manudan.

"As usual, you remain silent, yet I know your restless mind has questions Manudan."

"You are correct, father, many questions. One is sufficient to start with."

"Which is?"

"There are additional chairs at the table remaining unfilled. Who is joining us?"

"You'll receive your answer, but not yet."

"Notice anything else, Brother?" Gatran asked.

"Plenty, but it can wait. I sense our father's need to speak first."

"Your powers of observation are acute, as is your ability to read a situation Manudan."

"Coming from the woman who taught me these skills makes the compliment sweeter, Mother."

Nervita smiled at her children, recognising traits and skills in each, and understanding her kind's future rested in capable hands.

Agran assumed charge of the dialogue.

"I asked you here to discuss several matters of utmost importance for the future of Elven society. I'm sure it hasn't escaped your attention that our numbers are severely depleted. In reality, the population of Wood Elves is at its lowest point ever. Graylen Forrest is now the last homeland of Wood Elves. Ten sun-cycles ago, there were twenty such forest populations. Now there are less than seven-thousands of our kind existing today."

Agran paused, allowing his revelations to dwell in the minds of his children. It was time to appreciate the sheer scale of diminishing numbers and their uncertain future.

"Several factors contribute to this. The continuing war with the Dwarves depletes our population, they alone account for the decimation of at least four forest homelands.

The sickness is deadly and incurable, targeting Elves and many other species. Its spread is a mystery. There is no doubt it results from witchcraft.

"The rise of man and his destructive and insatiable quest for land, contributes too. They seem immune from the sickness and their population is exploding beyond normal proportions. Their drive to own land has reduced the numbers of many species, who they discriminate against openly."

"These issues are known, Father," Gatran interjected, "why discuss what is known?"

"You're correct Gatran, but we've gathered to discuss something far greater. It's time to introduce my guests."

Agran rang a small bell on his table. Three individuals walked into the state room. At the sight of their first guest, everybody rose. A High Elf, towered over the other two guests.

"Allow me to introduce my guests. High Elf Dravel who acts as a representative of his kind. Taymar of both Elves and Humans, and Frake, the most widely travelled Elf of our time."

Customary wrist grips of welcome ensued before they took their seats. None spoke.

"The true purpose of this meeting is to prevent the inevitable extinction of three species, The Dwarves, High Elves and Wood Elves. At our current rate of decline, our populations will cease to exist in three short sun-cycles. The Princes' and Princess stared briefly at each other, alarm on their faces as they absorbed the word extinction."

"Why concern us with Dwarves? Their demise would end the war," Gatran queried.

"End the war, yes, but their demise would leave an imbalance among other species who would vie for territory. They, as well as Elves, must survive."

"I'm assuming you have a plan, Father, recognition of the issues, and guests brought to assist, suggests so."

"You are correct Manudan, we have a three-point plan. The difficulty of each cannot be understated. First, Gatran will travel East, with what's left of our army to Xeltar Mountain, the last remaining Dwarf Kingdom. Your mission is diplomatic and is simply to end the war. Dwarf numbers are as low as ours, any lower, and they will suffer the same fate as us. It's a difficult task, Gatran, for the Dwarves are notably devious and self-serving. Not to be trusted easily. To help you with this High Elf, Dravel will travel with you and lead the negotiations."

"I'm honoured to travel with you Dravel."

"As I am with you Gatran. Our mission is fraught with danger, the route alone could see the loss of many Elves."

"I'm confident the travel will be safer for your presence."

Dravel bowed his head slightly, acknowledging of the compliment.

"Manudan, while your brother seeks peace with the Dwarves, you will travel West, seeking a new homeland for Wood and High Elves far from the reach of man. We seek a place with mountains and woodlands; once discovering it, the High Elves will shroud it in an invisibility shield and Elven Folk will retire from the world."

"Father, one place for High and Wood Elves, this is unheard of throughout our history."

"There is reason. The High Elf population has declined to a hundred, even with natural birthing the number verges on unsustainability."

The sickness has decimated my kind. It appears we are more vulnerable than most species," Dravel responded.

"It saddens me to hear this."

"I appreciate your sentiment, Manudan."

Agran continued. "You will have the help of Frake. He is widely travelled and has contacts among most species who could help secure safe passage in problematic regions.

"It pleasures me to travel with you Frake."

"The pleasure is mine also Manudan."

"Putraya, you have possibly the most difficult of tasks. You'll travel north in search of the cure. It is rumoured a Dark Elf has the cure but for reasons unknown has not offered it."

"Dark Elves always have their own agenda, Father."

"While true, the land to the North is unchartered to us. Taymar has travelled beyond our regions and will pass as human.

"After securing the cure, you must travel to the Dwarf Kingdom and share it with them.

"Could I be forward and ask Taymar if his allegiance is to Humans or Elves?"

"If you hadn't asked, I'd be disappointed. I'm loyal to both. I mostly lived with Elves until a few sun-cycles ago, I prefer the peaceful ways of Elves, but I cannot ignore my human connection."

"I appreciate for your honesty, Taymar."

Taymar dipped his head.

"To conclude this meeting, the tasks I've assigned you all are daunting. Problematic, fraught with danger and with uncertain outcomes. The future of our kind and the Dwarves are in your hands. Failure is not an option."

"When do we leave, father?"

"Dawn tomorrow, Gatran."

Chapter 2:

The King, Queen and their three guests rose and left the stateroom.

The siblings sat silent for moments longer. The resemblance between them clear. Flawless dark coppery skin, lacking body hair except for eyebrows, lashes and head hair. Each of them wore their jet-black hair long, tied in a simple ponytail, hanging to the middle of their backs. Their eyes were green, highlighting intelligence and alertness. Like all Wood Elves, they were simply beautiful.

Gatran broke the silence. "Well, I'm surprised at their choices for each mission. I'm a warrior, not a peacemaker. My temperament is not suited to the mission I've been set."

"Father is no fool, Gatran, he would have considered every outcome. That he chose you for this task, above me and Putraya, suggests he has confidence in an area you believe a weakness."

"Manudan, you understand my concerns and appreciate a weakness in me. You've grown up alongside me and know what I say is true."

"Perhaps it is time to address this weakness, Brother. You'll be the next King. Perhaps Father's choice leads towards this." Putraya suggested.

"Possibly, but have no concern, I'll endeavour to achieve my goal."

"You're travelling with a High Elf, no higher honour for a travelling companion, I'm sure you'll learn from him."

"We learn from everyone around us, but I'll ask him to share diplomacy tactics."

"Wise words Brother."

"Why do you think he chose me to find the cure?" Putraya asked.

"I believe Father is exploiting your intuitive nature. You are second to nobody in wheedling out the truth of a situation."

"I appreciate your words, Manudan.

"You'll be dealing with a Dark Elf, possibly more. Their underhand tactics and self-serving natures will be in full flow; you realise truth in a situation quicker than most."

"I only hope your confidence in me is not unfounded."

"It's not, and you possess the drive and determination to continue until succeeding."

"Why did father ask you to seek a new home world Manudan?"

"At first, I believed it was a mistake. You'd have excelled in this task."

"And now, Brother?"

"I believe I've been chosen for my patience and ability to form relationships with members of different species, and I never accept second best."

"That sounds an accurate assessment to me."

They fell silent, enjoying each other's proximity and the connection between them. They had always been competitive. Gatran was the most aggressive, Putraya the most determined and Manudan the most patient. Each were capable, their individual skills balancing the bonds between them.

"It could be ages before we meet again," Putraya stated unnecessarily.

"If the tasks become too dangerous, possibly the last time we're together. One of us might not return."

Manudan raised his eyebrows. "That's negative, Brother."

"I prefer realistic. Each of us risk our lives in these undertakings, Father knows this."

"The rewards for our successes are amazing Gatran. Consider it, peace with the Dwarves, a cure for the sickness and a new home for our future," Putraya added.

"The rewards certainly outweigh the risk and, if successful, the travelling will begin again to our new home on our return. I can't imagine leaving these woods after so long. I'm kin to every tree."

"What about sharing our home with the High Elves?" Manudan asked.

"The benefits outweigh any problems. Finding a home containing both woodland and mountains suggests we won't be under each other's feet."

"You're right Putraya, and there's the advantage of living in a fully cloaked land. Invisible to the world, travellers will see a natural physical barrier instead of mountains and forest," Manudan stated.

"It also means half our population won't be needed to guard our territory."

"What will you do with the guard instead, Gatran?"

"I'm hoping they won't need deploying elsewhere. Perhaps in the future, all Elves will require training as soldiers without maintaining an army. We can call on them if needed."

"That's an amazing idea, I hope you have time to implement that brother."

"I believe if we think and act positive, our chances of success automatically improve. Thinking beyond our tasks enhances determination."

"You sound like Manudan, Gatran."

"To be honest, Sister, I thought he might have said it before me. He has his mind elsewhere," Gatran teased.

"You don't expect me to rise to that, Brother, surely."

"Of course not, but I'll miss the opportunity to try for the foreseeable future."

"As I will, laughing at your usual failed attempts," Manudan raised his eyebrows.

"I'll miss this the most, being together, talking, teasing and laughing. We've never been apart for anywhere near the time period this will take."

"Think of the stories we'll have to share on our return, Sister. Don't doubt we'll miss you too." Manudan added.

A sadness flashed across Putraya's eyes.

"I'm going to prepare for tomorrow's journey, but I suggest we meet in the morning before dawn and share the awakening of the sun together. Toman Hill is close by, taking only moments to reach and return from. I'll tell father we might be slightly later than dawn."

"You're risking his wrath, especially as we have guests," Manudan warned.

"Sometimes it pays to be a daughter."

Manudan smiled, knowing she could bend him towards her desires effortlessly.

Chapter 3:

The predawn sky lightened, watched by the two princes and their sister. They stood side by side, observing the darkness fade into light, brightening by the second. From their position above the majority of forest canopy, they watched the shades of green lighten within the trees. They each experienced melancholy at thoughts of leaving their home. An ethereal glow between the trees, below the canopy, held the promise of surprise at every turn. The forest never disappointed them.

Words weren't required, each secure with the understanding they all felt similarly. Instinct suggested it was probably the last time viewing the forest from this location.

As the sun birthed its arc above the horizon they turned and started walking back to their home within the trees. Arriving, their three guests, mother and father waited, already mounted and prepared to leave. Their own horses, prepared earlier, were tethered behind the king. He and the queen dismounted.

"The time has arrived to venture far beyond our forest and seek ends to our problems. Understand you each carry my heart, and the hopes of Elven kind for a successful conclusion," the king said forlornly.

The queen stood on no such ceremony. She hugged each of her children, holding the embrace for longer than usual, stating how proud as a mother and queen she felt. The king clasped each of their forearms, echoing her sentiments. Then they mounted while the king and queen spoke to each of their guest companions.

"I decree Manudan should leave first, since the length of his journey is unknown. Putraya you will leave after your brother is beyond our vision and Gatran after," the king stated.

"Frake, you would honour me by riding alongside," Manudan offered.

"It is I who am honoured, Prince," Frake returned.

He took his position and without glancing back, Manudan started forward.

Moments later, Putraya made the same offer to Taymar, and he gladly accepted the request and they too started forward.

Finally, Gatran addressed Dravel the High Elf. "It would be my pleasure to ride at your side Dravel," he said respectfully.

"I would receive the same pleasure Gatran."

The king interrupted. "Your army awaits at the forest edge, half a day ahead. I considered time alone would allow for a private discussion."

"Your thoughts are appreciated, Father."

Dravel nodded his agreement, and then they moved forward.

The first moments of travel were silent. Gatran focussed on the forest, his forest and home, for his entire life. He knew it intimately, every tree and glade. Paths on the forest floor, made by small creatures and invisible to the unlearned, were cemented in his knowledge. It was the same with the unmarked paths within the canopy branches. He had honed his warrior skills within them, high above the ground, moving at such speeds it appeared he teleported from one position to another.

Dravel broke their silence once out of view of the king and queen.

"Your family risk everything to secure our future Gatran."

"Which is why we cannot fail. Without them, living is with a failing heart."

"I appreciate you're unaware of my individual skills, and I believe we should discuss them privately before meeting your army. Awareness of where each benefits our task is essential."

"I like that honesty, Dravel. Are you honest enough to share your weaknesses and your strengths?"

"You believe I have weaknesses?"

"Everybody has. I have. We must discuss them too, because at different times the lead role needs to change from me to you or you to me."

"You are the prince and commander of your army. You would surrender command to me. I have no such position among my kind."

"Everybody learns from others and regarding this issue, I learned from Manudan. He is calm and thoughtful, often observing details lost on others, including me. When he and my sister ride alongside we each assume command at different moments, when it is beneficial for whatever our cause is. We have exploited this successfully many times."

"That you are prepared to use this, is beyond my expectation, Gatran. To my knowledge it is unheard of throughout Elven history."

"History is ours to make Dravel, our actions could shape future method. Our species are to live together under one shield, it is right to seek mutually beneficial ways to move forward. The stories we tell from this adventure will surprise and hopefully enlighten our kind."

"And you learned this from your younger brother? It appears the mist surrounding an uncertain future together is lifting already; we've not even travelled a mile yet."

"So Dravel, honesty and openness from the beginning and continuing throughout our time together."

"To show my agreement with this, and because you offered it with no encouragement. I will reveal first.

My diplomatic skills and experience with various species, such as Dwarves, made me a suitable choice for this mission. Most missions were successful, but each offers no guarantee. I have skills in seeing the broader picture quickly, and act with empathy toward those I deal with.

"As a warrior, I'm average. I detest killing, believing it's a waste. Every death signifies loss of opportunities to grow and learn from individuals. I would avoid physical confrontation at all costs unless loss of life was imminent to those around me.

"On a personal level, I retire from others. I ponder on important matters, preferring solitude while doing so. Because of this, I've found making friends difficult despite my diplomacy skills."

"I am grateful for your candour, Dravel. For the record, talking so openly has enhanced the possibility of friendship between us. Manudan often retreats to ponder issues, as you, and I would consider him a most trusted friend, as well as my brother. Differences should enhance relationships, not prevent them."

There was a momentary silence as Dravel absorbed Gatran's words.

"How many sun-cycles have you lived for Gatran?"

"Two-hundred and forty-three, why?"

"Your wisdom and foresight, for one so young, is inspiring and unexpected; please accept this is not meant as a derogative statement."

"Understood. How many sun-cycles have you witnessed Dravel?"

"Eight-hundred and seventy-two."

"Your experience will be invaluable on this mission."

"So where do your strengths lie, Gatran?"

"As a soldier first. I excel at tactical manoeuvres and as an individual warrior. Despite this, I do not lack compassion for my enemies. Every individual, fighting for a cause is worthy and honourable. They should be respected. Prisoners captured in battle are cared for appropriately, despite knowing if I was a prisoner to some, it would cost me my life.

"A warrior witnesses' life devoid of sense. The art of war is obscene and detracts from an individual's essence or spirit. To live with what I'm forced to do requires a strong family to return to, one that embraces everything decent in life.

"I have two areas of weakness I'm acutely aware of. First, is a short temper. I don't suffer fools easily. The other area is related to diplomacy. I find it frustrating, dealing with individuals who refuse to see reason. I have been attempting to control my anger and listen more carefully to those who raise my ire, but it's a slow process."

"Perhaps, Gatran, you are young in the life of Elves. Many personal characteristics are innate, passed through generations. Some change only through deliberate, concentrated and disciplined action

"I appreciate the concession. Difficult to accept, with a younger brother calm like the summer breeze, and a sister gentle as a falling feather."

"It is right to aspire to the skills of others, but I suspect they aspire to be as you also. No individual can master every skill, no matter their age or experience. Recognition of how you can improve, and striving to achieve it is commendable."

"I believe if we continue to discuss matters honestly, as we have started, then the friendship I mentioned between us is guaranteed. I welcome discussion on any topic at any level Dravel. Retreat to consider whenever you need, I will not judge you badly for this, but share with me your deliberations. I wish to learn. I will be King of the Wood Elves eventually, and I desire to be a wise and compassionate leader."

"It would be my pleasure to ensure this happens."

Chapter 4:

They fell silent for the next half hour, enjoying the peace of the forest. Moving ever eastwards, Gatran stated there was less than a mile of woodland remaining before reaching the outer edge of the forest.

"I sense we're no longer alone Gatran."

"You are astute Dravel."

"That you're at ease with this suggests it's Elven Folk in the surrounding trees."

"They cover our approach as a training manoeuvre. Lord Eckna is the longest serving member of the army and my commander and advisor. As an instructor and tactician, he excels, using every opportunity to hone the skills of my kind. There is no Elf better to care for my soldiers in my absence."

"Does he sit in counsel with you?"

"Every time we travel as a force. His thoughts and insights are invaluable. He has seen many sun-cycles.

"Are there more, privy to the counsel?"

"We have a Master of Swords, Master of Bows, Master of Calvary and a Master of Stealth."

"The last sounds intriguing."

"His skills have become legendary among our forces. There is a story where he infiltrated an enemy in disguise and ate at their table."

"I will enjoy listening to tales of his exploits."

"As he will enjoy the telling of them."

"Your soldiers are skilled. While I'm aware they're present, I've yet to see one."

"Your comment pleases me."

The forestland ceased abruptly and on a patch of open grassland Gatran's army awaited his presence. As he rode toward them, he suggested Dravel peer behind as the soldiers, unseen in the trees, formed behind them. Dravel turned to see fifty Elven warriors walking behind them.

"I thought ten, maybe twenty within the trees, but fifty? Impressive."

"We will council with Lord Eckna and the Masters of Skills and eat together before travelling towards the Ominic Sea."

"You are taking a detour from the direct route?"

"Your knowledge of the region is impressive Dravel."

Dravel nodded. "May I seek the reason?"

"Of course. I expect you to question me when you seek to understand, or if you doubt, the wisdom of a decision."

"And this will not offend you?"

"It is what I expect from all my advisors, guests or otherwise. The reason is simple: fish is plentiful and close to the shore. We can dry it over fires to take with us. There are places where food isn't abundant."

"Black-hearted creatures inhabit the Ominic Sea; they venture from the water and attack those taking its bounty."

"This is true, and I've encountered them before. We expect and prepare for an attack from them. Once the fish is dried, we will leave immediately for Rag Dire Pass."

Dravel smiled unexpectedly for the first time, and Gatran, noticing, immediately sought the reason.

"Am I the cause of mirth, Dravel?"

"The wrong emotion, Gatran. You cause a satisfaction in me, a realisation I'll enjoy this journey more than expected. The formality of our task mixed with intellect, artistry, wisdom, and a meeting of minds. Some say the journey is a reward greater than the achievement sought. I believe this might be true for us."

"Greater than securing the future of our kind?"

"Our collaboration could shape the future of our kind beyond achieving the task your father invoked on us."

"The diplomat in you Dravel?"

"No, the hope in my heart for future peace and harmony."

"I understand."

A lone Elven rider approached, sitting tall and proud in the saddle.

"Prepare to meet Lord Eckna, Dravel. He is disciplined not to show emotion, as the rank he holds demands, but know beneath his exterior shell is an Elf with a gentle demeanour and a keen sense of humour. It will take eons before he shows this to you unless you wear him down with the same openness you shared with me."

"Your insight is my advantage; it seems I'll face more challenges during this trip than expected."

"Seems that's exactly what you enjoy."

"How is it you see me so effortlessly?"

"I see my brother in you."

"Perhaps I travel with the wrong brother."

Gatran laughed. "That's exactly the sort of comment he would make."

Lord Eckna ceased his forward momentum, stopping a horse's length shy.

"My Prince, the army is at your disposal and awaits your command. Greetings Lord High Elf."

"Gratitude, Lord Eckna, allow me to present Dravel who will speak on behalf of all Elven Folk."

"It is an honour to ride with a High Elf."

"The honour is also mine, Lord Eckna, please address me as Dravel, I have no position among my kind as worthy as the one you command. I'm merely a diplomat."

"Your concession is appreciated, but I cannot display such familiarity in front of my soldiers. However, in more private situations, I can respect your wishes."

"I understand and respect your situation and know your decision derives from the experience of seeing many sun-cycles."

"You are correct Dravel."

"Lord Eckna. Would you ride ahead, tell our soldiers to feast well before we leave, and ask for the Masters of Skills to join us in council? We will feast together before starting our journey."

"It will be as you say, my Prince."

Lord Eckna nodded to Dravel turned and rode swiftly away.

"I think you surprised him Dravel. That's difficult to accomplish."

"I'm merely being myself and listening to the advice of a new companion."

Gatran grinned. "You are so like my brother."

Chapter 5:

They reached the main body of soldiers and dismounted. Dravel watched with interest as two unfolded a leaf blanket, and a third earthed four wooden stakes at angles towards the centre. The blanket was then wrapped around the frame and a private shelter formed. Another soldier unpacked woven stools and a woven table. Each stool was packed like a scroll around its wooden legs. When unrolled the legs were inserted into the woven fabric and formed the most simplistic and lightweight stool. The table was packed similarly.

"Keep the Masters waiting for a few moments, while we settle, and ask a cook to bring food sufficient to fill our table," Gatran asked Lord Eckna.

"As you desire my Prince."

Gatran led Dravel into the shelter. Seats were positioned on either side.

"You will take your place to my left Dravel; as the seat to my right is secured by Lord Eckna."

"Whose seat am I filling?"

"Nobody's, usually I head only with Lord Eckna. The position will always be yours.

"The consideration is pleasing but unnecessary, I wish for no position above those who have earned it."

"You must have earned it to be here, Dravel."

Lord Eckna entered, snapping orders to the soldiers following behind with food and wine. They placed it and retreated from the shelter.

Eckna sat down alongside his Prince. "The Masters will follow shortly."

"Excellent Eckna, travelling burns holes in my stomach."

"Your intake of food while travelling is legendary."

"Do I detect a little humour in that tone, Eckna."

"I always attempt to follow your instructions."

"And as usual, you achieve the targets I set. This is good in you."

Eckna bowed his acceptance of the comment.

"Dravel, Lord Eckna is the most serious among Elven Folk, I've instructed him to engage with humour."

"I respect your serious nature, Lord Eckna; the majority of High Elves also share your ways."

"That is no surprise to me Dravel, I admire their attention in portraying their individuality. Has my Prince instructed you to engage in this humorous manner?"

"No, but I felt inclined to partake."

"This is typical, he rarely has to say what he wants to achieve it."

"Are you becoming accustomed to this demand?"

"Indeed, I practise on whoever I converse with, the battle of wit that follows can be... rewarding."

"I will attempt to follow this way of yours and enjoy the battle you foretell."

"As will I Dravel. Perhaps we could attempt this with our Prince, so he feels the force of humour at his expense."

"That could be arranged."

Gatran burst out laughing, "seems great age has challenged the beauty of the young, I'm not sure of your wisdom, but I'll enjoy instructing you both further."

"It will require leaving the mirror behind, my Prince, Dravel commented, and the three laughed. A new bond at the early stages of cementing happening each recognised and found comfort with it. The Masters entered.

Lord Eckna introduced them to Dravel, and he shared pleasantries with each. He stated he hoped there would be opportunities to share stories around the camp fires. Each appeared pleased at the invitation; more after realising his awareness of their story-telling customs was viewed as a pastime pleasure.

Gatran started the formalities.

"Members of the King's council, I welcome you all to my table for the first of many such meetings. I will dispense with the formality of detailed introductions momentarily. After business is finished, we'll share wine and brotherhood. I hope such meetings will occur regularly at noon for the period of an hour. The men will rest and eat while we discuss anything of issue. Even without issues, the meetings will allow adequate time to explore options and varying points of view. The stakes could not be higher, no one Elf should decide a course of action alone. There are seven seated here and if necessary, a vote can be utilised to decide split-decision issues."

"My Prince, never before has a member of royalty conceded decision making to lower-ranked Elves."

"I appreciate your comment Lord Eckna, but as I look around the table, I see you and Dravel who have lived three of my lifetimes. My Masters have lived two of my lifetimes. Having schooled in every area of battle and command by the most experienced Elves alive, the importance of our mission exceeds all from history. Should I fall in battle, then Dravel and Lord Eckna will complete the mission in the manner we start it today."

"But you're still our leader, my Prince?"

"Of course, that isn't changing, just the way we perform this mission. Its importance is greater than the ego of a Prince."

"If I may, Gatran, this decision defies the age difference between us. The maturity, foresight and courage to make it, suggests you have lived longer than us."

Those at the table buzzed with agreement.

"Your words are appreciated, Dravel. We cannot fail in our mission and I want to achieve every advantage at every stage, hence meetings for counsel. Once present, each Elf is instructed to speak as my equal, are we understood?"

Each of the council snapped a fist against their heart, accepting the command.

"Lord Eckna, my Masters, at these meetings you are to address me as Gatran. In this way, I'll know you're thinking as my equals. Dravel has already mastered this, so please follow his example."

Again, the snapping of fists against hearts.

"Excellent, now for today's travel arrangements. We will head directly to the Ominic Sea. There are many regions to cross offering no food source. We will fish for an hour, dry the fish and leave. We will not stay by the shores overnight unless the fishing is poor."

"The Sea Serpents will attack, they always do," Master of the Swords warned.

"You are right Dorna, and we'll be prepared for them. The army will position a mile from the shore while we use a fishing force of a hundred. Dorna, as Master of Swords you will hold a fighting force close to them. Swords are the most effective weapon against the Sea Serpents. Feren, as Master of the Cavalry, you protect the smokers and support your brother if required.

"Dravel, I could use you here also, an unusual request perhaps, but I want a third force in place to protect our Elven brothers. Could you hold a force of a hundred under a veil of invisibility? Is your magic capable of this?"

"I would be honoured to perform such a role, Gatran. It is well within my capabilities."

"Excellent, Master of Stealth. I want you positioned before our fishers commence hunting. With Dravel, make it so that your existence is completely unknown. Do not reveal your presence in defence unless absolutely forced to. Can you do this Omati?"

"Your command is all I need, my Prince... Gatran,"

Gatran smiled at the Master's correction.

"Cagen, the bow is not effective against the sea-Serpents so would you assist Lord Eckna in supervising the security of our main army?

"I would Gatran," the Master of Bows stated.

"Attention to detail at every stage of this mission is of paramount importance. Every Elven life must be protected. Our army is five-thousand strong, but only two thousand remain behind. Every life rates equal value, protecting it remains the highest priority during the mission."

"Where will you position yourself, Gatran?"

"I will stand with our fishers. Every time life is risked, Lord Eckna, or I, lead from the front. All Elves will understand their importance for the future. Currently, they are unaware of what our mission is. I will address the issue with them when we're camped securely."

"You are of importance to the success of the mission, surely it is unwise to risk harm to yourself."

"I appreciate your concern Lord Eckna, but I'm not so conceited to appreciate I must concede level of importance to Dravel. He is the diplomat; he will seek peace with the Dwarves, speaking on behalf of all Elves. Every Elf present has a role to play, each commands different skills and will play a prominent part at different times. I'm not exempt from this. I'm a leader of men, an army commander like Lord Eckna, I'm no diplomat.

"Dravel is the one Elf at this table who is indispensable. If you didn't realise this before, understand it now. Little time remains before we leave, eat and drink your fill and enjoy the comradery of those carrying the burden of our mission.

"Lord Eckna, from respect, I have never called you by name alone. I owe the skills I have today to my instructor, advisor, and friend. Could I call you Eckna without the formality of rank?"

"I would be honoured Gatran, and for those present to use my name similarly."

Chapter 6:

The army moved forward, a steady, synchronised swarm of Elven Folk, sitting erect on their mounts, and pride exuding from their faces. Any living being witnessing their passing would notice the intensity and comfortability of the army moving as one.

Gatran led, with Lord Eckna and Dravel riding alongside. At other positions, the four Masters led their individual forces. The journey to the Ominic Sea was short, the shimmer of silver-green in the distance announcing its proximity.

A mile short of the shoreline, Gatran halted his army. A force of fifty Elven Fishers moved to the front on foot, their horses already weighted with nets, retrieved from litters dragged behind. They started their journey towards the sea while a further group, the Smokers, walked behind, carrying oak logs and racks ready to dry the catch. Dorna, the Master of Swords and his attachment of a hundred followed behind, alongside Feren, the Master of Cavalry. Finally, Dravel and Omati, the Master of Stealth moved a group of a hundred Elves at the rear. Three-hundred soldiers guarding a hundred fishermen.

Gatran signalled to Lord Eckna, stating his immediate departure, and Eckna thumped his heart in acknowledgement. Riding at a canter, Gatran assumed position at the front. He walked alongside the fishers, instructing them to relax in his presence and relating warnings about the potential dangers ahead.

Omati moved the Elven Stealth Warriors into position close to the water's edge. They dragged branches across the sand to conceal their tracks and break any scent markings they left. They formed into five separate rows, three facing the fishers and two facing the smokers. Once positioned, Dravel made a sweeping movement with his arm and they became lost to vision. Gatran smiled at his efficiency.

Feren and Dorna positioned themselves according to plan. One unit guarding the fishers, the other the smokers, and Gatran stood directly behind the fishers as they cast their nets. Every member of the guarding forces concentrated on watching the water surrounding them. The sea was calm and translucent, no Sea Serpent could come close without forming a dark shadow in the water.

The nets were dragged up and down the surf line until their catch weighed the net to a point when it became difficult to move. Load upon load, piled the beach, awaiting smokers to clear the nets and gut the fish; fresh nets were continually dragged through the surf, being returned to the fishers after clearing. It was a synchronised operation; a strategy utilised many times before, successfully.

The smokers gutted each fish with a flare of knife skills, flashing an almost musical display of rhythm. Others threaded them on sticks to place above the fires created for drying. Gatran watched their efficiencies, appreciating their combined skills.

So far, the task had run smoothly without interruption, but it wouldn't last. Elven body odours, while minimal, would be registered by the Sea Serpents leagues away, their presence was imminent. As the final nets dredged the water, shadows emerged half a league from shore.

Many of those watching saw them at the same instant, Gatran among them. He gave order for the fishers to leave the water. They withdrew quickly, dragging their nets higher up the beachhead, and the two guard units dismounted and moved in to cover their retreat. They formed triple lines along the water's edge and withdrew their swords in readiness. Gatran stood front and centre, facing the water and approaching shadows.

Reptilian bodies emerged above the depth of water, gradually revealing the full scale of their immense bodies. Snake-like heads, each with mouths capable of swallowing a warrior whole, adorned multiple, elongated necks. Each longer than several Elven warriors. The bodies were rotund and cumbersome, unsuited for carrying out of water, and yet done so by eight short, stocky legs. A long tail, capable of generating incredible propulsion doubled as an extensive weapon on land. Fully scaled, it was covered in massive spines, each capable of tearing a warrior to pieces.

Cuts to tendons at the back of their legs left them incapable of walking. However, nothing could prevent the swing of their giant tails, or their necks, except death. To despatch one permanently, severing all of their heads was necessary.

Gatran had fought these creatures before, they were formidable opponents. There was only one tactic usable to safeguard those attacking them.

Dorna cried out a readiness for action as they emerged from the water and then as the Serpents lumbered up the beach the Elven Warriors attacked. Wave after wave of individual warrior assaults continued. Each moving in acrobatic style. Somersaulting, back flipping and leaping through the air for great distances, slashing with their swords. The speed of their attack challenged the visibility of those watching; the accuracy of their swords incredible, despite their swings commencing and finishing while airborne.

Beast after beast succumbed to the onslaught and still more emerged from the water. Feren and the cavalry joined the fight, horses covering great distances through the air like the swordsmen before them. Their riders, balancing by their knees as they leant over at impossible angles to slice their victims.

Gatran noticed the number of Serpents emerging from the water reduce and then the unexpected. Serpents, already killed, started moving again. Decapitated heads lifted and glided back to the necks they were severed from. The beasts attacked again.

Dorna called a warning cry to those with their backs to the dead creatures. The battle raged for an hour and Dravel and Omati joined the affray after witnessing events.

The fishers worked on despite the surrounding battle, focussed entirely on smoking their catch. Their discipline unwavering and their confidence in their comrades, total. All fish required a minimum two-hours of smoking; the first batch almost finished. It was swiftly packed, and runners were sent to transport it to the main army. Such a bountiful catch, would require the evening to finish the process.

Dravel fought his way to a position alongside Gatran.

"I have a plan Gatran," he stuttered between slashes.

"Speak Dravel, your presence at the centre of battle is unwarranted, the risk is excessive."

"The creatures are controlled by dark magic, but despite this, they need the water to prevent their scales drying and seizing. Instead of fighting them and their magic, force them closer together. I believe I can circle a barrier, enclosing them, preventing them reaching us and the sea. They would lose movement; scales would dry and decay."

"Make it happen Dravel, we cannot kill beasts that reform after decapitation."

"Give the order to squeeze them in, Gatran and I will form the barrier behind them first and slowly hem them in. Our warriors will need to retreat at my command."

"Understood."

Gatran gave the order, and the flanks started to push in. Dravel weaved his magic and placed a barrier to block the sea. Gatran called the cavalry retreat, and they eased away from battle. The swordsmen fought on.

"The next instruction to retreat must be realised in a few seconds. Failure to withdraw in time will sentence those trapped inside to a guaranteed death."

Gatran called the warning and instructed them to listen for Dravel's call. Dravel called it, and Dorna and his swordsmen retreated at a speed, mocking the time spent fighting. Every Elf made it out successfully.

"I must stay here to prolong the period the magic holds Gatran. Leave me here to cover your retreat."

"Not happening Dravel, we wait together."

He snapped orders to Dorna who supervised the retreat and oversaw the safety of the smoking unit, now fully swollen in number by the fishers.

"This warrants discussion, Gatran."

"I agree, Dravel, but we'll wait for the council to gather once more."

Chapter 7:

The beasts inside Dravel's enclosure charged at invisible walls to retreat to the sea. But the magic stood firm. Held in position with concentrated effort from the High Elf, his focus was complete, seemingly in a meditative state. He neither blinked nor moved. For four hours he maintained his hold and still the creatures within charged the barrier. It should have been over hours ago. No individual ever witnessed Sea Serpents last so long out of water.

Gatran waited alongside Dravel with a small unit from the Cavalry guard behind, holding their leader's horses. Attentions focussing fully on the beasts in case they broke through. The wait stretched to six hours before the first beast fell. Black fluid secreted from between its dried scales. Another unnatural sign, their blood was normally green. One after another the Serpents fell, secreting the black fluid.

Gatran expected Dravel to release his hold on the barrier, but he held the barrier firm. He posed the question *why*, but Dravel maintained focus, unhearing. Gatran fell silent, knowing Dravel had reason despite his silence. He continued watching. The creatures had fallen but clung to life, despite their imminent demise. Slowly, their grip on life relinquished and, after breathing ceased another movement began.

The secreted black fluid, from one beast, started to river across the sand, joining with more from another beast. Gradually, all moved toward a central beast, and pooled to its side. Gatran noticed it rippling; there was no breeze inside the barrier, no ground tremors below, but the rippling increased. It started rising, forming an orb-like shape, higher and higher. Gatran wondered how high Dravel's barrier reached. He glanced at Dravel. He was shaking, still deep in concentration, but the effort was taking everything he had.

"Fire arrows," Dravel stammered, "Fire arrows."

Gatran turned to the cavalry soldiers behind him.

"Load, you bows with flaming arrows and fire at the black mass when instructed."

The soldiers dismounted and placed arrow tips into the still smoking fires until they caught. They took position on either side of Dravel and Gatran and drew back their bows.

"Now!" Dravel cried, collapsing to the sand.

Every soldier let fly at the black orb. It caught fire and writhed in erratic motions. Eerie screams and wails emerged from it before it exploded into a steam like gas and vanished.

Gatran knelt to Dravel. His eyes were closed, but he breathed easily. Gatran struggled to lift him. The High Elf was a head taller and wider than him, but Gatran managed it and carried him back toward the army, a mile away. Two Cavalry Elves offered help; another offered his horse, but Gatran refused.

"This High Elf barely knows us and yet he has proved beyond doubt he stands with us. He gave every ounce of his strength to maintain that barrier. Ensure his exploits are shared around the campfires tonight, so all know and understand he stands with us on our journey. As he honoured us today, so I honour him. I will carry him to our encampment."

The Calvary Elves snapped their fists across their hearts. "We will share the story of Dravel and the Sea Serpents and the demise of the black blood."

The soldiers formed an arc behind their Prince, dismounted, and walked beside their mounts. A sign of respect to Gatran and Dravel.

Two hours later, Dravel finally opened his eyes. Gatran sat by his side.

"You have woken. I feared you might not Dravel."

"Sustaining the barrier is not life-threatening but exhausting for prolonged periods."

"I could tell."

"You stayed by my side throughout, Gatran. I'm honoured by your display of loyalty."

"It was more than loyalty. My men have no knowledge of you, no reasons for your presence, no awareness of what you offer. You will be known by the example you set by the morning. The reasons for your presence, I will explain to them shortly. I plan to visit each legion during the peace of the evening."

Gatran reached for a water skin and removed the stopper. He held it gently to Dravel's lips while he drank.

Dravel nodded his gratitude.

"How long will your weakened state last?"

"I will recover by morning after a good rest."

"We will wait until the morning to discuss everything from today Dravel. You must attend and explain what you know to the council."

"And you can wait until morning?"

"The only thing I lose by waiting until morning is a period of travel. Since the council is strong and wise, we can contemplate all implications together."

"Your consistent consideration to all around you is rare in a leader Gatran."

"A wise soldier taught me that, when I was learning the art of soldiering."

"Eckna?"

"Yes, he shows the same considerations to his soldiers and enemies alike. I'm fortunate to experience the guidance of two fathers, one in life matters, one in matters of soldiering."

"Your bond with Eckna is understandable,"

"I'll leave you to rest now Dravel, sleep well knowing we are grateful for your presence and efforts today."

"Rest well yourself."

Gatran left Dravel, who closed his eyes immediately, and sought Eckna. He found him sitting by a fire, listening to stories from past battles. Like Gatran, he felt at ease with his soldiers and mixed with the lower ranks comfortably.

The soldiers stiffened as he approached, and Gatran told them to relax.

"Lord Eckna, would you accompany me on a tour around the encampment?"

"It would be my pleasure, my Prince."

Eckna rose and moved to Gatran's side.

"Is the purpose to share events from today with me?"

"All Elves must learn the purpose of our journey. Of what my brother and sister do in our absence. We must share what Dravel did today, his acceptance, by all, is important if anything happens to us."

"I've heard an account of what he did. You stood at his side until it ended. You take my lessons of the past to new levels of consideration."

"The lesson I remember most, is that we rise or fall with those alongside us. We have rank, but we are Elves, foremost. As soldiers, we're forced into actions and deeds that oppose the life-codes of Elves; those following us, break the codes also, they're worthy of the same degree of respect as us. As I walk among our soldiers, I see Elves at one with each other, as with their families at home.

"In peacetime, they extend the bond of camp with those not soldiers. The peace and unity of our kind is stronger for their ways. I respect nothing at a higher level than this."

"Gatran, you take my lessons to a new level of reasoning and understanding. I am proud of my student."

"I share that pride for the relationship we forged through your actions and teachings, Eckna. Now come, let's witness the reactions of our army to the news we share."

Chapter 8:

Dravel rose at dawn. Revitalised, he stood to stretch his legs. As he walked past, a few sentries rapped their chests with their fists, and he reciprocated the sign. A few plucked the courage to wish him well. He realised most had never engaged with a High Elf. He asked to be addressed as Dravel and gained respect for his manner and his actions from the previous day.

He was deep in conversation with a small group of Elves, sitting by fire embers warming a broth when Gatran sought him. None of the Elves held rank and were enjoying the attentions of a High Elf. Gatran hung back from joining them, allowing Dravel to forge the early bonds of kinship. When The High Elf finally stood, Gatran moved forward, greeting his soldiers and Dravel on equal terms.

"I trust you are refreshed Dravel?"

"I am, and enjoying the company of soldiers in the manner you do. I understand why you enjoy this and will partake in early morning greetings regularly. It is... pleasurable."

"We're all Elves, united on a common cause, rank during times of ease does not need enforcing."

"You're wise. I have heard tale you carried me here from the sea. I am grateful for this."

"I wanted my forces to witness the value of your efforts, and for future endeavours. I spoke with Eckna, while you rested. If we fall in battle, you will assume command. While you are not a soldier, the Elves will respect you enough to follow. The Masters would advise where tactics are required."

"I had not considered this possibility."

"It matters not, Eckna and I will teach you the basics of battle as we travel. You would not have to fight yourself, since your role is destined for negotiating peace with the Dwarves."

"I will heed the training."

"We'll eat with the council before leaving."

"I feel the need for food."

They walked together, a longer walk back to their enclosure, bidding greetings to all awake. Gatran watched the ease the High Elf displayed as he conversed with many. He was a worthy companion for the journey.

Food had already been laid at their table and the Masters and Eckna were seated. Pleasantries were shared and Gatran instructed them to eat.

After the meal had been cleared away Gatran started the formalities of the meeting.

"It is clear the Sea Serpents were supported by dark magic. Without Dravel's shield, the result of our encounter with them might have ended differently. Please, share your thoughts."

"My brother and I were in the thick of battle, we agree, they fought unlike before," Dorna stated. "They lasted longer out of water. That they were under dark magic is clear to us, the reasons are not."

"I noticed too. The real questions is why, who knew of our plan and why attempt ending our mission?"

"Was the magic purposely for our benefit? Eckna asked.

"Who else is present by the Ominic sea and attacking them? This was no random act, it seemed planned."

"How could you know this, Gatran?"

"Consider when the magic commenced. We had almost defeated the Serpents before they started returning to life."

"If you are stating what I believe you're implying, we're all at further risk."

"What is it you're saying, Gatran?

"It's my belief the magic was invoked during our fight with the Serpents, not before, Dravel."

"It makes sense, magic, even dark magic takes power to wield and hold. It was only used when needed."

"It means somebody close to us cast the spell," Eckna added.

"It could be something pretending to be one of us," Omati suggested.

"I prefer to accept that, rather than suspect a traitor amongst our ranks."

"News of our journey reached us the night before leaving Graylen Forest; we were not privy to the details. We were ordered to wait at the edge of the forest ready for a long mission," Eckna stated.

"Discounting the possibility of an infiltrator, or traitor, who gains from a failed mission? Certainly not Dwarves or Elves." Cagen reasoned.

The question can't be answered without consideration. Any gain from our failure would not realise immediately." Gatran answered.

"It's possible, magic was invoked by an individual for personal gain. Dark magic suggests a Dark Elf, Witch, Wizard or Sorceress," Cagen offered.

"If it is against us, it will happen again soon. We travel through Rag Dire Pass, the potential for ambush there is huge. We also have to pass Dangorg Woods. It's a Witch haven, and the petrified trees return to life when life passes by. They attack, choking the life from all those attempting passage through," Eckna warned.

"Dangorg Woods can be avoided. Entry is unnecessary, but Witches inhabiting, left cover in the past to attack passers-by," Gatran argued.

"It still leaves the pass. We cannot avoid this, there is no way around," Eckna summed up.

We will be alert for any devious schemes, but we cannot assume the Witches of Dangorg Woods will stay in the woods. The edge of the woods lies within two leagues of the Ominic Sea, they could have been responsible for the dark magic we encountered.

"Dravel, when you opposed the dark magic, did you get a sense of where it originated from?"

"I did not, Gatran. I have faced dark magic many times, but attributing its origin with confidence has always been impossible."

"Answers to our questions remain unknown, but the knowledge of magical power in play is a warning for discretion and keen observation. Masters, when returning to your troops warn and seek extra diligence from your forces. Assign additional flank riders, with the sole mission of watching for potential trouble. And as for the pass, we'll deal with that when we're closer. Let's ready our forces and be underway in an hour."

Gatran stood as his leaders left the enclosure, leaving him and Dravel alone.

"You were quiet during the meeting. Is this one time you wish to retreat to ponder on matters?"

"I'm thinking it is Gatran."

"Then go to it, give it your best deliberation; we need to procure answers before our ignorance is held to cost."

Chapter 9:

Travelling once more. Dravel took position as a flank rider, seeking the deliberation time he needed. He was pleased Gatran had trusted him from the offset, listening to his opinions and understanding his needs. Gatran differed from the stories of his exploits that had reached the ears of the High Elves. He had never met a leader quite like him. He operated in his own unique way and the respect and trust he received from his army was total.

Gatran sought Eckna and rode alongside his most senior confidant.

"What dwells on your mind Gatran? You may act like command doesn't affect you, but I know it does.

"You know me as my brother, Eckna. And, as usual, you're correct."

"So, speak, so the load is shared."

"I fear for the future of Elven Folk. Our journey is fraught with dangers, compounded now with dark magic. The destination, and subsequent talks, hold no guarantee of success. We cannot afford to lose significant numbers of our kind, and yet the enormity of our task suggests our losses will be huge."

"Every Elven soldier will willingly lay down his life to support the cause, and to support you, Gatran. I suspect Dravel is the key to our success, and I don't just mean discussions with the Dwarves. He has powers beyond ours, a quick understanding, and improvises accordingly. Losing Elven lives in battle at the Ominic Sea was likely, and yet we did not."

"He is but one High Elf."

"And despite having no rank he was chosen to support our cause, to help in its fruition and form a peaceful alliance. I believe Dravel has been offered rank frequently and refused it."

"But why?"

"Unknown. Maybe he blends in better like this. Most, with high rank, command fear in their subordinates, maybe this adds problems to his causes. Present company excepted my Prince."

Gatran smiled at Eckna. "Delayed Eckna, but a good save."

Eckna chuckled. "You realise I have trained hundreds during the sun-cycles, but only you never showed fear for my position and accomplishments."

"It's better to respect than fear. I've always believed that."

"It's something I've come to agree with, something my student taught me."

Age shouldn't be a barrier to learning.

"Never a truer word spoken."

"So dark magic. My belief is we should deflect it, not fight it so early during the journey."

"A wise decision."

"Rag Dire Pass is less than a hundred paces across at its widest point and twenty at its narrowest. Open to the Ominic Sea on one side, we can expect another visit from the Sea Serpents. I sense it's inevitable.

"Dangorg Woods, on the other side represents a whole different problem. First, the petrified trees may well extend their limbs into the open. Ambushes from the evil dwellers could be expected, both physical and magical."

"We should not travel the pass tonight. Dark magic is dangerous enough in daylight without risking it at night. I think we should camp several leagues short, secure a restful night, and start at dawn."

"I agree, we should increase the night watch as a precaution."

They fell silent, enjoying the comradery between those on a common cause. Eckna broke it momentarily.

"No Elf among us, does not experience the weight of responsibility on their shoulders and the expectations of their King."

Gatran nodded, knowing he was correct.

Later that day, they reached a point where the gap between the Ominic Sea and Dangorg Woods started decreasing, ultimately leading to Rag Dire Pass. Gatran ordered the halt, and a temporary, overnight encampment took shape during the next two hours. Guard units were established before darkness set in and Gatran watched the proceedings from the most forward position. Dravel joined him.

"I trust your deliberations were productive Dravel."

"I could not discover conclusions other than those we discussed before, but I lean towards an infiltrator amongst us. Possibly more than one."

"I agree."

"And your day, Gatran. I suspect your deliberations were as difficult as mine."

"Indeed, they were. I focussed more on what will pass tomorrow. The likelihood of attack and further dark magic."

"I too considered this; opportunities to attack us are many, from several sources and directions."

"It is impossible to predict, but I sense it will happen."

"There is no alternative route to follow?"

"Despite having the best army, a Prince could command, when you view them at rest, their number is small and their vulnerability high."

"Our course of action tomorrow will be guided by the type of attack; we cannot assume the manner of it with any certainty. This I know. The Elves respond to your command instantly. The Masters and Eckna are excellent at responding to immediate threats, none better. Improvisation will be the key. Reading the situation and acting accordingly. Because of the uncertainty, your services are better employed from observation. Oversee rather than engage. I appreciate this is not your preferred way, but you improvise faster than others. You could save many lives. Let Eckna lead."

"You're right Dravel, I prefer to lead from the front, but everything you say is correct. Your counsel is good my friend, and I will heed it. I'll discuss it with Eckna later. Maybe it's time to share a meal and rest our minds. The Masters will eat with their legions; they have already recognised the situation we're in. Eckna will patrol the ranks, he bolsters courage and confidence before any battle. Would you join me at my table Dravel?"

"I would welcome your company."

An hour later, the camp was illuminated by fire torches. Dravel and Gatran walked among the Elven soldiers sharing moments of humour, encouragement and comradery. The moon was full and the sky clear of clouds. The land surrounding them, easily visible to those avoiding the direct light of the fires. A wail carried on the gentle breeze from the direction of Dangorg Woods. The good-natured banter ceased as each soldier instantly became alert. Another wail followed, and many Elves stood, staring at the distant forest, seeking the origin of the sounds. During the next few moments, the wails increased in volume and amount.

"Scare tactics, Gatran, nothing more. Used to destroy a night's sleep and reduce focus during tomorrows march."

"I agree, but despite knowing it, we have to prepare for attack."

"It's the purpose of the tactic. The attack won't happen."

They expect us to think that way.

"A ploy, to lull us into a false sense of security."

"It makes sense not to just destroy our sleep but create an opportunity to reduce a few of our number."

"The attack, from the sea or woods?

"Has to be the sea. Evil creatures like these won't risk themselves, they would employ magic and use lesser creatures to realise their desires."

Eckna appeared between them. "I have doubled the guard on the seaward side."

"You read our minds Eckna, I was about to order that. You suspect an attack despite knowing the purpose of a scare tactic?"

"I do, attack at night under darkness and reduce our number."

A shout from the Seaward Guard announced Sea Serpents.

"Eckna, before engaging the enemy, double the guard on the wood side."

"Already on it, my Prince," Eckna called out, moving at speed.

"I must go to my soldier's side Dravel."

"No, Gatran. Stand back and observe and ready your Elves for the attack from the wood."

Gatran hesitated, knowing Dravel was correct; they had just discussed this very topic. He grabbed a soldier moving toward the action and told him to fetch Feren. The Elf disappeared, and Feren appeared moments later.

"Gatran?"

"Take your legion and guard the approach from the woods. On no account, get close to it. Just patrol our perimeter and watch for the unexpected."

Feren ran to implement his orders and rouse his legion.

Chapter 10:

The Sea Serpents appeared first and Dorna unleashed an Elven frenzy on them. His swordsmen slashed and slashed, severing heads from bodies. No dark magic returned the beasts to life. The attack raged for an eternity as creature after creature emerged from the depths.

Cagen, the Master of Bows, sounded the alarm on the opposite side of camp as indistinct shapes emerged from the woods. Feren held his cavalry, midway between the unidentified enemy and the camp. Cagen moved his archers closer to support Feren.

"Have you seen the threat, Feren?"

"They are many, too distant to identify with certainty."

"If you hold back your cavalry, I'll send a wind of arrows that will consume everything ahead."

"It's the correct course of action, Cagen."

Cagen snapped orders and his archers dismounted and formed rows. The front row loaded and stood prepared.

"Ready archers. Front row let loose; second row, advance."

The second row moved in front and drew their bows. Screams from the blackness emerged as the first flight of arrows found their mark.

"Second row let loose; third row move forward. As they drew their bows more screams emerged."

The fight on this flank continued as row after row of archers moved ever forward, closing the ground between them and their enemy. Feren closed up behind Cagen.

"Three more rows Cagen and I'll order the charge."

"Our turn to support you then, we'll follow behind and clear the ground after your charge."

"We'll do our best to make your task easier."

The three rows fired, and Feren let loose his Cavalry. They galloped at incredible speed over the flat and featureless ground. As they closed in their opposition became clearer. Feren had never observed creatures like this. Two headed individuals, the height of two elves swarmed ahead. Built like Ogres they would not be easy to fell. Many had six or more arrows sunk into their bodies, but no blood seeped from their wounds. They shrugged off each arrow with a scream and then indifference.

Gatran moved to Cagen's side.

"Your arrows have little effect on these beasts."

"Each arrow weakens temporarily and then is ignored, my Prince."

"The Sea Serpents were not enforced with dark magic and were merely diversionary. The intent was to allow infiltration from these beasts, definitely boosted with dark magic."

"I don't recognise these beasts, Gatran, we have fought most enemies during our time but never these."

"It's true, but we have never entered the petrified forest either. What lives in there is unknown."

"If they are from the forest, then they are formed from wood. It explains why they do not bleed. Wood is not exempt from fire."

"It is worth a try, but they are mixed with dark magic, it may not work."

Cagen ordered his archers to load fire arrows and Gatran sounded the retreat for the cavalry on his horn.

The retreat was instant, and Cagen set loose his first bank of arrows followed swiftly by four more. He watched from a position alongside Gatran. The screams of pain intensified as the flames took hold of the beasts and began consuming them. Dravel emerged from the dark, bearing the news the Sea Serpents had been defeated without loss. He explained Orcmar had tripled a patrol on the flank and the swordsmen were following him here. As they watched, the beasts began falling, no match for fire, and Gatran ordered the cavalry, and the recently arrived swordsmen, to stand down. Dorna and Feren dismissed their forces and stood together, watching the beast's demise.

"They are incredibly alike for brothers," Dravel commented.

"That's because they are twins," Gatran answered.

"I had heard a rumour there were twins among the Wood Elves but doubted the truth of it."

"Doubt no more Dravel, it is true."

"The rarity of twins among any branch of Elven society is so high it cannot be calculated."

"They're more alike in thought and deed at home relaxed. It is like their minds are joined at a higher power."

"In High Elf society, twins would be elevated to a position just below royalty."

"They earned their position like every other Wood Elf."

The temporary break from watching the beast's demise ended. Each witnessed the fall and subsequent consumption to fire, of the final beast.

"Feren, set a unit of cavalry walking in both directions from our flank. I want the forest observed for the night's duration, Two-hour watches."

The master of Cavalry disappeared and Gatran watched as the first unit started patrol almost immediately.

"I wonder if that's the end the hostilities tonight or if it's just the beginning?" Gatran mused his thought verbally.

"I have a feeling we're being tested. Our ingenuity and our forces are being examined to expose weaknesses."

"Why Dravel. Surely with dark magic at our enemies' disposal, they already realise they have superiority over our brawn."

"Maybe. Neither attack actually came close to our camp, though. Sea Serpents and Wood beasts remained at distance."

"A keen observation Dravel, but consider an alternative reason for this. Everything happening commanded our total attention. Perhaps it was diversionary. While we engaged, the enemy within our ranks could have engaged with those we fight, slipped in and out of camp without our knowledge."

"Of course. The dark magic came from the enemy lines, not our camp. If from inside our camp, the creatures would have been closer. I'm sure. The volume of magic suggests it arrived from more than one source too. It's possible the magic used to strengthen the Sea Serpents yesterday, was all our adversary could muster. Perhaps this diversion allowed him to sneak away for a power boost."

"The more we consider Dravel, the more options the enemy seems to have. I like the strategies you employ, the options it presents us with. We are stronger for having it."

"So, what now Gatran?"

"Rest; the guard will warn if anything else occurs."

Chapter 11:

The encampment disbanded shortly before dawn. Gatran had insisted on packing everything away under the cover of darkness, and his army were mounted and prepared to leave. They waited for the light of predawn. As the darkness faded, Gatran signalled the advance. They rode in columns of four, stretching for a distance behind their leader. The narrowing of the ranks was deliberate, impossible to attack a line of soldiers along its entirety. The Masters were strategically positioned to split from the main column and surround an attacking force from both flanks. Gatran called it the Bulls Horn Manoeuvre, as from above, the splitting pattern resembled the shape of bull horns.

They travelled at a pace, three-quarters their normal speed. It was Eckna's idea, allowing every member of their force additional time to observe their surroundings carefully.

Gatran reckoned, at their current pace, they would reach Rag Dire Pass by mid-afternoon. He was not expecting an attack prior to reaching it. It made no sense. Risking an attack in the open was not feasible, while woods offered perfect cover for an ambush. At least with the Sea Serpents, if they attacked again, their shapes were visible under water long before they reached shore.

The mood was sombre, everyone realising an attack was imminent, and wanting to spot it in time for preparation. Gatran had a plan to follow once entering the pass and tried to explain it to Dravel.

"It's simple, really. When a third of our troops are inside the pass, the column will split. On the sea side, our cavalry will stand guard, three horses apart, forming what looks like an honour guard. On the Wood side, our archers will form a similar guard. They will remain in defensive position until the rear of the column passes and then re-join the column. The second third of our column will form a similar guard and so on through the entire pass."

"It's an excellent strategy, Gatran, but it means all our troops will be in the pass longer than if we marched straight through."

"If we are attacked, Dravel, or rather when we're attacked, the centre column will ride at pace to form defensive positions at the attack point."

"This isn't totally defensive; an attempt to delay the attack by offering something our enemy wouldn't expect."

"Exactly. Only the Masters and Eckna are aware.

"A wise precaution."

"I suspect the attack won't happen until the entirety of troops are inside the pass. The column is several leagues long, a successful ambush is only effective if the escape routes are sealed, probably unlikely here though."

"I suspect the attack stronger at the front; attacks along our flanks will weaken any escape attempt."

"What stops us stampeding the front attack?"

"Nothing, except the possibility of an enemy we can't prepare for."

"Like the wood beasts from last night."

"Exactly."

"Where are you positioning yourself?"

"Eckna leads, and I'll join the left flanking teams. I'll have longer to learn about the beasts attacking us."

"They will be bolstered by dark magic."

"It seems probable we'll face dark magic throughout this mission."

They fell silent as the mouth of the pass beckoned.

Gatran had predicted the proceedings well. All his army were inside the pass before the attack started. The positioning of his forces proved excellent, the Sea Serpents attacked first and Dorna, The Master of Swords, led his forces into the attack. Once again, their attack was ferocious, the beasts succumbed to the force. No sign of dark magic either, once a beast's head had been severed it stayed severed.

An attack on the opposing flank started moments later. Similar creatures from the previous evening emerged from the woods, and Gatran ordered fire arrows to destroy them. Petrified tree limbs, roots, and branches slithered from cover. Feren led his cavalry into the attack. The riders leant from their horses at impossible angles, slashing at the countless limbs. No sooner had they been dismembered, they reattached and slithered again.

Gatran watched, frowning. The beasts took arrow after arrow, but the fire extinguished on contact. Clearly, his enemy learned from experience. The petrified branches and roots slithered closer by the second. Eckna ordered the central columns to speed up towards the end of the pass while the battle raged. Gatran witnessed his first casualty. An Elf was thrown from his horse, almost immediately a root wrapped around his unfortunate neck and squeezed until it severed the Elf's head.

"Dravel, what are your suggestions?" Gatran asked urgently.

"I have none, not already in place. The petrified limbs are relentless, they can extend for further distances than I expected. So many, I fear we'll lose more soldiers. It's like we're being chased by a forest."

Do you have magic that could help?

"Like a barrier again."

"It could slow their progress, even if they break through."

"I'll try, but it won't be enough. My barrier will not extend for the full length of limbs."

"We have to slow their progress."

How long before we leave the pass?

"Not until dark, Dravel."

"That's longer than I can sustain it for."

"Do what you can, I'll ensure your safety, should you lose consciousness again."

I'll maintain it until my magic fades, but you should reinforce the head of the attack.

Dravel rode forward, heading for a central spot to extend his barrier from. He opted for a slightly shorter length to maximise the height. As the petrified limbs reached the barrier, they immediately climbed it. Eckna saw it happen and hurried the central column of soldiers though before ordering them to attack at the front.

Eckna joined in the assault, slashing his sword in a frenetic frenzy. His skill as a swordsman evident as he launched his personal attack. Omati joined his commander, and they led their soldiers by example. Despite the onslaught, the severed limbs re-joined and extended further. The first limbs slithered over the barrier. Gatran lifted and placed a totally focussed Dravel on his horse and started forward. The barrier followed behind, extending further in front. Now the limbs followed, attacking the flank.

It seemed hopeless, with still the best part of the afternoon to travel, the volume of petrified limbs increased continually.

The huge beasts, beaten by fire the night before, lumbered towards the barrier and started climbing the petrified limbs already over it. Once at the top they jumped to the ground to face Gatran's forces.

Dravel called to Gatran, weakening his focus to speak briefly.

"What is it Dravel?"

"I'm thinking sea water."

"What do you mean?"

"The sea water might halt the petrified advance. Nothing drinks sea water and the open pores on the limbs will soak it up unintendedly."

"You want to make the limbs sick?"

"Effectively, yes."

"Leave it to me, I'll organise."

Gatran called for Omati, who came instantly.

"My Prince?"

"Omati, take a force of the Stealth soldiers and collect sea water. Make sure you all remain cloaked and pour the water on the roots."

Omati looked bewildered, but followed his orders immediately. Gatran watched as he rounded up twenty of his men to form a unit. He saw them suddenly disappear under the veil of their cloak and his attention turned to the huge beasts. Each occupied at least six soldiers; their slashing swords removing slices of their wooden bodies. He hoped they would absorb the seawater.

Chapter 12:

Gatran turned from the cloaked men after a warning shout from Eckna. It came none too soon as he faced a wall of wood bearing down. The beast was so large, it could have stepped on his head. Eckna, having seen the danger his Prince faced somersaulted to his side, slashing furiously and drawing the beast's attention. Gatran reacted immediately. He ran around the rear of the beast and slashed behind the beast's knees. Tendons should have been severed, rendering it incapable of walking. But this was no Elf. He slashed away at one leg. It was thicker than Gatran's waist, but he sliced it like he whittled a stick until it became so thin it snapped under its weight and the beast stumbled forward.

Eckna changed his approach as the beast fell, attacking the other leg. The beast thrashed away with the club in its hand and Gatran and Eckna danced around it to continue their attack. With both legs severed, the beast seemed to lose part of its strength; the swings of its club slowed and lost their previous impetus. But still, it didn't die.

Omati appeared with his stealth warriors, carrying water.

"Douse the tree limbs with sea water and do the same with the beast's feet," Gatran cried.

Omati obeyed, shedding the first water on the beast Gatran had felled. Instantly, a steam formed where water met wood, unlikely since the water was cold, but steam it did. The limbs started writhing, screams emitted from them. Other beasts retracted back towards the woods and the wailing and screams intensified.

"It's working, Omati, send more for water."

Omati obeyed and over a hundred warriors ran to the water's edge with whatever containers they could use. As they spread the liquid further afield, gaps in the enemy ranks formed as they retreated, isolating the large beasts. The amount of seawater required to force a retreat was minimal, and more soldiers joined in, collecting as the battle diminished.

Gatran grabbed a water carrier from a passing soldier and poured the contents over the beast he and Eckna downed. The creature screamed, began steaming, and thinned. Water was arriving thick and fast now and poured onto their enemies. The limbs had fully retreated into the woods and the beasts continued to scream and shrink, as they were doused repeatedly.

Gatran ordered Eckna and the main bulk of his army forward through the pass, holding back Omati and the stealth fighters. He ran to Dravel and shook the High Elf from his concentrated state. The barrier disappeared and Dravel took control of his thoughts.

"Your idea worked; the water forced a retreat."

"How many have we lost Gatran?"

"Unknown at the moment, but we'll discover soon."

"Omati, collect our fallen and send them along the pass to our army. I'll not leave them here to the mercy of these beasts."

Eight soldiers had lost their lives in the affray. Given selflessly for the Elven cause. Omati sent a few Elves to form an honour guard. Gatran knew it would be a moving sight. The dead would pass every soldier present. Each would touch the lifeless bodies as a sign of respect and emit an anguish wail. The wail would build, remaining constant until all the dead had passed. They would be cremated that evening and their ashes collected for spreading in the next forest they passed.

Looking around the battle site, only Omati's soldiers, Dravel and Gatran, remained. There were thirty plus of the huge beasts steaming and shrinking. Gatran ordered the drenching to continue until they shrivelled to nothing.

He watched the beast at his feet shrink. Already, it had lost almost half of its bulk and reduced in height, but still it steamed. Dravel moved closer to Gatran and watched in morbid fascination.

"Gatran, something else is happening here. Look at the head."

Gatran altered the focus of his gaze. The head was changing shape and colour. Blonde hair formed, pointed ears and an Elven face materialised before their eyes. The neck formed next, a creamy colour and texture.

"Dravel, they are turning into High Elves, they appear as you."

"I think the correct term would be returning to High Elf form."

He moved quickly away and peered at other fallen beasts before returning.

"All are changing, there are High Elves, Wood Elves and an Orc among them. The creatures of the woods transformed them to the beasts they appear, but now as the dark magic loses its grip they revert to their original state."

"Omati, place a guard of eight around each of the fallen beasts. We have no idea as to their states of mind and Orc's hate Elves."

"Dravel, a head count, see what we face."

Dravel didn't answer, but disappeared immediately. Omati returned after setting the guard.

"The dark magic might have released their bodies, but there is no telling if anything remains within their minds."

"It is true Master of Stealth. They will need guarding until we learn the truth of this. The Orcs can be released closer to their own territory, the Elves will remain with us. Any other creatures present can be dealt with individually."

"It's possible they may never regain a conscious state."

"I'm trying to be optimistic and assume they will. As soon as the transforming is complete, we'll leave here and join up with the main force."

Dravel returned.

"I have the count, Gatran."

"Speak it Dravel."

"There are twenty-three High Elves, nine Wood Elves, Three Orcs and two Dwarves."

"Are any conscious yet?"

"Not yet."

"Tell Omati to reduce the guard. Two for each Elf and four on the Orcs and Dwarves. We must leave this place before our enemies regroup and attack again. We can travel if they're placed on horses.

"If any regain a level of consciousness on route I want to know immediately."

"I'll see to it Gatran."

"Oh, and Dravel, your role today was significant, already you have saved numerous Elven lives. We are indebted."

"You owe me nothing for doing my duty Gatran."

"My gratitude cannot be dismissed, but I understand your sentiment."

It took only a short while to prepare their departure. Each unconscious body was secured to a horse and led by flanking soldiers. While they remained unconscious, Gatran moved at pace, leaving the pass before dark. Travelling at night here, was fraught with unseen danger, and risked lives. He hoped Eckna had journeyed well and fast and wasn't waiting up ahead for them to catch up. Of course, he wasn't. The most experienced Elven soldier knew exactly what decisions were required. Gatran berated himself for the moment of doubt and signalled, beginning the march forward. As soon as he sensed all was secure, he increased the pace to a slow canter, and they started to close the gap between them and the main army.

Chapter 13:

An hour later, Gatran caught up with Eckna's forces. Two hours of travel remained before exiting the pass and they were about to enter the narrowest part.

"Gatran, you've made good time, no further loss of life I hope."

"None, a story though, a telling of bodily transformation."

"That sounds interesting. I've tripled the flank watch as a precaution."

"A wise decision, my friend."

Gatran rode to a position alongside Eckna, content to be riding next to the Elf who had taught him to soldier, as a father would teach everything else. He related the story of transformation, and Eckna immediately suggested increasing the guard.

"We can't be sure if they'll ever regain consciousness, but they are breathing, and it suggests hope."

"Your thoughts on their origin, Gatran?"

"I would suggest they were caught by whatever dwells in Dangorg Woods and transformed, keeping them prisoner for battle."

"The power of the dark magic is beyond our understanding. The beasts and limbs were all controlled simultaneously by a force unknown."

"Dravel believes the power is being extended by many individuals working together."

"That makes sense, probably no one individual could command such power."

"Dravel saved us again Eckna. He is selfless in the mission, as we have all become."

"He is an excellent addition, and I like him as an individual. There is a calmness, an inner peace. The Elf knows his identity and his capabilities, a competent individual."

"Tactically, he understands what's required and helps in ways different from others. His manner of thinking is broad too, he sees the bigger picture."

"I suspect we'll need his services increasingly as this mission unfolds," Eckna finished ruefully.

They stayed silent for the next hour, riding in quiet companionship, like many times before. No further attack was attempted, and they left the pass an hour before dark. Eckna left Gatran to organise the camp and prepare for the cremation of their fallen soldiers.

The funeral pyres were lit as the last of the sun disappeared beyond the horizon. Every Elf stood to attention, watching the fire consume their lost brothers.

Both Dangorg Woods and the Ominic Sea lay behind them, and they had entered an area of barren land belonging to nobody. It was flat, offered a substantial view around them, and should allow two days of safe travel before encountering the next region fraught with danger.

Eckna moved about his soldiers, sharing words of comfort and encouragement. Death of their comrades was always experienced at a deeper level. Faces they travelled, ate, trained, and journeyed far from home with, would be missed. Eckna understood this more than most. He shared stories about each of the fallen, ensuring all focussed on happier times shared with them.

Gatran sought Dravel and found him examining the High Elves still unconscious.

"You have discovered something?" Gatran asked, hoping.

"I have not. Despite living for so long, I do not recognise any of the High Elves. It's feasible they've been held for incredibly long periods and are from a time before mine. It's possibly the same for the others too.

"I'm convinced they'll wake from their sleep, but their minds could be potentially damaged. There are fifteen females amongst the High Elves here."

"Females, I didn't expect that."

"Dark Magic does not discriminate between males and females; it controls both alike."

"I wonder how and where they were captured?"

"The reality is they could have been captured anywhere and brought here."

"Can you tell anything from their clothes?"

"No, it differs. Both colouring and material varies from mine."

"A mystery then."

"For now."

"Considering how depleted the numbers of High Elves are, It's a significant boost to your kind."

"Provided their minds are free from the magic, then you're correct."

"They appear healthy, considering the potential length of period under the influence of dark magic."

"They appear as the day they were captured."

"I hope their minds are not corrupted. Show me the Wood Elves, Dravel."

Dravel walked further along the line of the rescued, stopping at the face of the first Wood Elf. He examined it closely, pulling the covering blanket back to examine the clothing. His examination was thorough.

"Any thoughts, Gatran?"

"Similar to your conclusions. Different clothing and not of Graylen Forest."

"Once many forests were filled with Wood Elves."

"That's true, but I'm sensing, like you, they were captured eons ago."

Gatran moved slowly back along the line, studying each of the faces, stopping at one High Elf in particular.

"My goodness Dravel, this female is beautiful!"

"I agree, most of the female High Elves hold great beauty, but she is exceptional."

Gatran suddenly felt uneasy.

"We should not stare in such a manner that suggests disrespect."

"Your comment was true, not disrespectful, but I understand the reason."

At that moment, the body of the female High Elf moved slightly, catching Gatran's attention again.

"She moves Dravel."

Gatran knelt down alongside her and removed the water carrier from his side. He untied the drawstring at the top and drizzled a little onto her lips. He poured more on a small cloth and wiped her forehead gently.

The High Elf opened her eyes and stared at him. She made no effort to communicate, but just lay there as he moistened her forehead again.

"You are safe and under my protection. You can rest with this knowledge."

Dravel knelt down, and Gatran continued. "Know that High Elves and Wood Elves work together on a common cause. There is harmony among our kinds."

Her eyes blinked, and she glanced across to Dravel before returning her gaze to Gatran.

Gatran announced he would stay with her through the night so they could speak when she became ready. Dravel smiled inwardly, realising that Gatran was already smitten by the High Elf's beauty, unsurprisingly in his view. He left Gatran, checking the other individuals and asking for additional guards on the Dwarves and Orcs.

Gatran gently washed her face, trickling more water into her mouth, while she just watched him. An hour later, she spoke for the first time.

"What are you named, Wood Elf?"

"I am Gatran, Prince of Graylen Forest, and heir to the throne after my father, Agran."

"My location is where, Prince of Graylen Forest?"

"You are east of Rag Dire Pass and free from the creatures of Dangorg Woods."

"Familiar are these names; but reason for presence eludes me."

"You were prisoners, transformed into beasts of murderous capacity, and forced to battle those you should not. There were others too. Peer to your left and right and see others also freed. Some are High Elves, some Wood Elves, Orcs and Dwarves."

"You have freed all."

"Yes."

"But the war between Elves and Dwarves, you give quarter?"

"I have no quarrel with Dwarves. I'm on a mission to secure an end to the war between our species."

"The task bears weight Gatran, the Dwarves are full of treachery."

"The numbers of Dwarves and Elves have been reduced to extinction levels. From war, and from a sickness sweeping the land."

"I am saddened by this."

"As are we. You must rest now, and we will talk more when you wake."

"I'm tired. Your consideration is appreciated, Gatran. Please call me Kudra."

Gatran nodded and raised the blanket to her chin. "Rest well my Lady."

"Knowing you watch over me will aid this."

"I will not leave your side."

Dravel appeared by his side and sat.

"You are staying my friend?"

"Yes, she spoke Dravel, she seems normal but talks slightly different."

"Appearing normal and being normal are different Gatran. We can't know for certain, so we should take precautions. Her speech may differ because her origin is far from our own."

"I hear you, and will heed your words, but..."

"Female High Elves are known for stealing the hearts of males. It seems she has stolen yours."

"I can't explain it."

"There is no need, my friend. Lay back and rest. I will wake you in three hours and you can watch over me."

"You feel unsafe Dravel?"

"I'm worried for the task ahead, and the battle with Dark Magic."

"We worry together Dravel, it's the burden of command and the weight of expectation."

Dravel nodded, staring into the darkness.

Chapter 14:

Dravel woke Gatran as promised. He lay down a few feet away and was asleep instantly. Gatran sat.

"You sleep deep Gatran, I note. Not restless like some in your position might, Kudra spoke."

"Soldiers can sleep when required, despite what goes on. It's a discipline required to survive. How long have you been awake?"

"A while. Returning memories of before capture invade mind."

"Tell me what you recall."

"I travelled for relocation. A Western settlement of High Elves. My homeland had become barren. Hunting or growing food not possible. Nothing grew, and the animals left."

"What caused this?"

"Unknown. I travelled West with a large group and where the sea met woodland we were attacked."

"We passed through the same place, but in the opposite direction, yesterday."

"The creatures attacking did not reveal their presence, instead extended limbs from the forest emerged. Once they touched us, escape was impossible, and we were dragged deep into the woods. A frightening place, full of dark creatures, witches, Dark Elves, and beasts unimaginable. In a ritual, they transformed us into wooden beasts. Many Elven Kind were transformed before I fell victim. Between changing and waking, there is no recollection.

"You're free from the influence now. Our concern was that your minds were affected, but yours seems fine.

What is unknown is how long you've remained under dark magic."

"No memories, while remaining a beast, assisted gauging of time."

"Can you remember doing anything as a beast?"

"Nothing. I slept and woke.

"Dravel will work out the timings, he has knowledge of High Elf history. Are you strong enough to stand?"

"I feel capable."

"Let's try, lean on me if required."

Gatran helped her into a sitting position before steadying her as she stood. She was as tall as him, her long blonde hair as pale as his was dark. She was, as all female High Elves, elegantly poised with a body as toned as one of Gatran's own soldiers. In his opinion, her beauty was unrivalled and took the breath from his mouth before a sound could pass.

Dravel passed by earlier and suggested she had slept for longer than she had ever been awake.

"Strange to awaken, so many sun-cycles after sleeping."

"Dravel estimates you were present before his birth, that's over eight-hundred sun-cycles."

"If true, a lifetime is lost."

Gatran nodded. "We'll walk a little way and then return. It is possible others will wake. Your presence might allay any fears they have."

"The consideration shown is appreciated."

She held on to his arm, still unsteady on her feet. He formed an idea in his mind and head toward where Eckna slept. He was already awake, sitting with Omati and enjoying the companionship of a fellow soldier.

"Good morning Eckna, Omati. Looks to be a fine day ahead for travelling."

Both returned the greeting and Gatran introduced Kudra, explaining she was the first of the rescued to wake.

"I hope to rest this morning. The reasons are two-fold. First, our soldiers are weary from battle and second to give our new friends time to wake and recover before forcing them to travel. Maybe we don't travel at all today. This place appears safe, but maintain the night guard throughout the daylight."

"Our soldiers will appreciate this Gatran, battling beasts who cannot perish is tiring, and more time remembering the fallen is positive. How are the rescued?"

"It's difficult to say. Only Kudra has woken so far. She woke weary and required rest to manage walking with me. Her mind remembers, but nothing during the period as a beast. I hope all those rescued will wake in similar condition."

"And you, my Lady, it is easy to assume condition, but I'd like to hear from you."

"That is considerate Lord Eckna and appreciated. It is as Gatran said, he has neither exaggerated my condition nor understated it. It is refreshing you convey truth of situation as High Elves would."

Eckna bowed his head slightly. "It is the way of Gatran. Many old ways he dismisses in favour of open, and honest relationships. The loyalty he's gained is unlike I've witnessed before."

"Pride is evident, Lord Eckna."

"Indeed, Gatran was once my student, but he's surpassed my teaching and teaches me instead."

"Your methods, you view them how, Gatran?"

"It is simple, we're as family when away from home."

"I favour this, bonds formed are difficult to break."

"Ensure the men rest Eckna, light duties only today."

"I will see to it my Prince."

Gatran and Kudra walked away.

"Witnessing displays of openness within an army is a surprise. Eckna is fond of you and speaks as a father."

"He has always been a second father to me, and I'm as proud of my association with him, as he is of me."

"I have seen you converse with Dravel. Your relationship with him is... easy, relaxed."

"Dravel has become my friend in a very short time, he has the qualities you bestowed on me, and I find his company and counsel pleasing."

"Between High Elves and Wood Elves this exists in rarity only."

"It must become so?"

"But why?"

"I have explained the numbers of Elves and Dwarves have been reduced dramatically, because of war and sickness. Once peace with Dwarves is orchestrated, and a cure for the sickness found, Wood Elves and High Elves will leave for a new territory, with forest and mountains. Living together permanently, until our numbers increase."

"To my knowledge, collaboration amongst our kins has never moved beyond distant friendship. Achieving this is monumental."

"As we travel so my younger brother seeks a new home world and my sister seeks a cure to the disease. Their challenges are as difficult as mine and fraught with equal danger. Our journey is but a few days old and we have already battled dark forces twice. I fear for my brother and sister, for they do not have an army at their disposal."

"Smaller forces carry more effectiveness."

"This is true. Both are capable Elves with a loyal following."

"Are they as you?"

"My brother is a gentle spirit; he avoids using his rank as a Prince. He befriends everyone and is probably the friendliest Elf in the forest. His gentleness does not hide the strength of his determination, only death would prevent him from failing his mission."

"And your sister?"

"She, too, is gentle with a fierce determination. She is beautiful beyond belief, has a mischievous nature, and can't resist a challenge."

"It is obvious you're close to both."

"We are stronger together than apart. Leaving them, is leaving part of me behind. Do you have siblings?"

"No siblings, but two distant cousins are among those rescued. We will unite when they wake."

"Are they like you?"

"In most ways, yes."

"I have met male High Elves before, but never females. Are they all as beautiful as you?"

"You are forthright Gatran, yet no disrespect is apparent. I will answer. Most are as I, occasionally hair is redder but mostly as mine."

"I did not mean to offend with my question. Having little experience of your kind means ignorance of your ways. Perhaps as this journey unfolds you will teach me how to converse correctly."

"This is possible, but what if I wish you to remain true to your ways?"

"I am content to be as you wish. Dravel is as open as I, and our relationship strengthens daily."

"And do you wish our relationship to develop in this manner?"

Gatran suddenly smiled and his cheeks flushed slightly.

"It appears you have taken my directness of speech and used it on me."

"You have deflected answer."

I can reply without hesitation. I would be pleased to have your company daily, as I do with Dravel, and it would please me if we became friends."

"I agree. Perhaps now we have settled these matters we can return to check on the others."

"Let's go."

Chapter 15:

During the next two hours, those recently freed woke. The Orcs went berserk, trying to escape the guards Gatran had placed on them. He called Omati to his side.

"We cannot help these creatures; they are hostile, and their hatred of Elves innate. Perhaps it would be kinder to take them into the wild and free them."

"I could take a small guard and ride many leagues before freeing them."

"Make it happen, Omati. I'm thinking they have been prisoner to the dark forces long enough, they don't need to become ours."

Omati left immediately. It was necessary to restrain the creatures for their protection, but no harm was inflicted on an enemy who would kill them if given an option.

Gatran turned his attention to the Dwarves next. One of them spoke the Elven tongue and demanded to know what was happening. How they became prisoners and what would happen to them? The hostility they displayed was not mirrored by Gatran. Instead, he asked for patience for a brief period, while organising the construction of council shelter. Once ready, he organised seats, table and food. He asked his soldiers to escort the Dwarves in.

As they entered, it was clear anger raged inside them. Each required a little physical persuasion to sit at the table. Once there, Gatran ordered their restraints removed and asked the soldiers to leave. They looked surprised, but he waved them away, leaving him facing three of their lifelong enemies.

Their surprise was as acute as the soldiers and Gatran spoke before they had opportunity to plan an escape.

"Please eat your fill. It has been many sun-cycles since you last ate or drank. While you eat, I will explain what I know, which isn't much."

Sensing no threat seated across from them, the Dwarves started eating, but their eyes never left Gatran.

"I will start by explaining your memories will return during the day. You will remember everything leading to your capture, but nothing beyond that until your wakening.

"You are not my prisoners, after our discussion I will give each of you a horse and you are free to leave. No harm will be inflicted on you."

Gatran explained everything he had learned from Kudra. That they lived without living for many sun-cycles, afflicted and controlled by the demons commanding dark magic in Dangorg Woods. He informed them they would remember this for themselves soon. For the first time since entering, one dwarf spoke.

"Your words contain the truth. I was fighting dark forces during the battle of Oakendale. The last memory I have is of being captured by trees whose roots had purpose beyond my understanding."

Gatran breathed a sigh of surprise. "I have knowledge of this battle, Dwarves and Elven folk lost many of their kind to the dark magic. Oakendale no longer exists. The forest consumed by the desert sands to the north. I have no reason to lie, but that battle happened six-hundred sun-cycles ago. I learned of it during my military training."

"That's impossible. We cannot have survived under the influence of dark magic for so long."

"There is a High Elf present, and released as you, she was captured at least two-hundred cycles before you."

Gatran let a few moments pass, allowing the information to be absorbed at a deeper level. Then he explained the current situation, concerning the war, the sickness and the decimated numbers.

The hostility of the Dwarves had vanished. If Gatran was to be believed, they would be freed soon. If not, then certain death. He had no reason to tell them anything, but he chose to.

"Do you hold rank amongst your kind," Gatran asked.

"We are but humble soldiers."

"Humble soldiers don't exist. Soldiers fight for a cause they believe in, an honourable path to follow. That you were my enemy means nothing anymore. The hostilities between our kind must end, or Elves and Dwarves will cease to exist. This is why I grant your freedom and give you the gift of food and horses. When you reach your realm, tell this story to your kind, make them understand your future, and mine, depends on peace, not war."

Gatran stood and held out his arm. "I bid you well in your travels, but be warned, the dark evil spreading across our lands lurks everywhere."

One dwarf stood and grasped Gatran's arm.

"I am surprised to find an Elf with honour, no disrespect intended. I've battled many, but never conversed. When I leave this shelter I either walk to freedom or death. If you speak the truth, I will spread the word, so all will learn of this threat, if not already known among my kind."

The remaining two Dwarves stood and clasped forearms. Gatran led them outside. Eckna stood ready with three horses.

"There is food in the bags for several days and water in the skins. I will lead you through our camp and you will be free to travel alone."

"Gratitude, Lord Eckna. You travel with the most loyal and bravest of soldiers, live a true and noble life."

Gatran walked away towards the rest of the rescued Elves.

The now fully awake Wood Elves sat in two small groups. Dorna and Feren were speaking to each. That they were twins, naturally elevated their status among those they addressed.

Gatran called his Masters to him and listened to what they had learned. The Wood Elves had been captured during the same battle as the Dwarves. Like them, they had no knowledge of the current situation until learning the plight of their kind from Dorna and Feren. As former soldiers, they were invited to join Gatran's forces and were shared between the archers and cavalry.

The last and largest group of High Elves were seated in one circle and learning of their past from Dravel. Gatran walked to his side and asked politely if he could join the discussion.

Dravel invited him to sit in the same formal manner, using his title, and then was interrupted by a male High Elf.

"How is it a Prince asks permission from one with a lower rank?"

"Better to show courtesy and manners instead of assuming the privileges my birth grants. The ways of my kind are changing, necessary to meet the demands of a dwindling society."

"Commonplace or for benefit of guests?"

"Kudra woke some time before, you could ask her how matters are here, for she has witnessed it."

Gatran didn't wait for further comment and instead addressed Dravel.

"Dravel, share how the High Elves fell to the powers of dark magic, and disclose the period passed."

"It seems there are two separate incidents where the dark forces claimed them but close in periods of time. I have calculated the males were caught in battle nine-hundred and seventeen sun-cycles ago. The females were, as near as possible, taken eight-hundred and forty sun-cycles ago."

"You have recounted the current issues we face?"

"I have. They find it difficult to accept they were imprisoned by the dark magic for so long, as they simply have no memories of it."

"It is better, they're all used to battling their enemies. It would torment the peace in their minds.

"Are there any of rank among them?"

"The males originate from a cavalry guard unit; the females are daughters of traders and merchants."

"I hope to converse with you as a group and individually, but I have matters which require my attention. Please forgive this delay. I have an offer for the soldiers among you. I cannot escort you home, most likely your previous homes don't exist. I cannot advise you to travel through Rag Dire Pass as recapture is the most likely outcome. I can offer you an opportunity to join my cavalry unit. You would be welcome and treated with the utmost of respect. A trait used among all my soldiers. For the females among you, I can only offer a safe passage on our journey. Although I'm currently on a mission for my

King, it is my intention to return us all to our haven in Gralen Forest.

"I will leave you to discuss this further with Dravel, but if you decline my offer, understand my promise of safety remains. Dravel will inform you of my mission and those of my brother and sister so you can realise the enormity of what we've undertaken. Please enjoy whatever we can offer: food, water, discussion, companionship, and even friendship. It is on offer everywhere here."

Gatran stood and walked away.

Chapter 16:

Gatran was disappointed he couldn't meet alone with Dravel. He was desperate to decide on the next part of the route, especially knowing whatever direction he chose was fraught with danger. It was a matter of weighing the choices and opting for the one with least threat to them. Dravel's opinions and knowledge of the region might well influence the decision.

He realised he was relying on the High Elf increasingly, his trust in him total, and valued his counsel. How had he made such an impact? Despite the deeds he had performed, he was one of the quietest and self-contained individuals Gatran had ever met. He was like his brother, but the quiet assuredness about him exuded beyond even him. He wondered if their new friendship would extend past the return journey. He hoped so.

It was later in the day before the High Elf sought his company. Gatran shared a light meal with Eckna, about to discuss the matter he wanted Dravel's opinion on.

"Can I assume there are no issues requiring my attention regarding those we rescued, Dravel?"

"None, the males have already joined their new units and the females are content doing whatever females do."

"It sounds like you know little of High Elf female society."

"In the past, my ambassadorial duties consumed my attention. Most diplomatic envoys are male and despite engaging with an occasional female envoy, there was rarely time to socialise."

"Don't you ever get lonely for female company," Eckna enquired.

"Sometimes I wonder about having a life partner, maybe children. After assuming the role of diplomat, there was little opportunity to extend myself towards female company. Understand my success as an ambassador keeps me travelling constantly."

"Perhaps you should consider taking time away from your duties to seek a life partner. You would be held in high esteem for the role you play, a worthy partner."

"Your comments are wise and thoughtful, and I'm grateful for them, but the likelihood is slim."

"After our mission is completed, we journey to a new home We've already recognised the need for an army is reduced; your position will decrease in demand too," Gatran spoke insightfully.

"The road is long, before entertaining thoughts of new homes and purpose."

"Which brings me to my next subject, the route we take from here. Whatever route we decide upon, we travel at first light tomorrow."

"There are two choices I believe; do you have a map with you Gatran?"

Gatran unrolled a map extracted from a hollowed-out branch. Stripped of bark, it had been polished to a mirror shine and had two intricately carved stoppers doubling as handles. He unrolled it and placed it on the ground.

"The first option is to travel North between the Ominic sea and the Karvil Marshlands. Then turn west between the same Marshlands and the Madrake Mountains. The area between the sea and the marshland is a wide section of barren land. We can travel a sufficient distance from The Ominic Sea to ensure we do not engage the Sea Serpents, but we would close in towards the Marshlands.

"The last report I received, suggests the creatures live in the foulest of conditions, lurking everywhere, concealed by mud. A wilderness of plant life exists, also evil. Many of the creatures living there, leave their sanctuary to attack whoever, or whatever, passes their region. Dark magic is commonplace here."

"When we turn west, we pass between the most northern end of the Marshland and the last remaining Orc stronghold. While the Orcs have been quiet during recent sun-cycles, we cannot assume they'll remain so. To my knowledge they do not command dark magic so we could lean into their territory to avoid the marshland."

"It doesn't exactly sound inviting Dravel. What's the alternative?"

"The alternative, is to travel west. There are two options. The shorter route, travel across the southern tip of the marshlands, and risk the creatures living there. Paths and trails through exist, but are narrow. This route leads to the Plains of Krahor, a relatively safe area but populated by isolated individuals instead of communities. Some are decent and some require avoiding. Unfortunately, distinction is impossible without conversing."

"And the second option?"

"The second is a longer route. We travel south to bypass the marshlands before turning west again. In choosing this route, we will travel close to Fever Valley. Nothing on two legs lives there. It's inhabited by insects, some of enormous proportions. All the species carry a sickness, it is how they capture their prey. They don't have to bite or come close to us. The sickness hangs in the air. Winds are an important concession here. If the wind blows towards the valley, then we have a natural protection from the sickness. However, wind from the opposite direction can spread the sickness across the marshland borders.

"Whichever route we opt for is fraught with peril, and I appreciate the female guests travelling with us, will affect your decision."

"You're correct Dravel. Your knowledge of these territories is more extensive than mine, and I will heed what you shared and consider my decision carefully."

Dravel dipped his head slightly in acknowledgement of the compliment.

"My Prince. I know the Elf you are and how you consider the needs of everyone, but the purpose of our journey outweighs concessions towards others. You must not base your decision on protecting the females, but on which option gains us most chance of success. We all understand the risks, some of us may not return home, possibly many of us, but the mission must succeed."

"I appreciate your counsel, Eckna, it is direct and honest, as I expect from you. The safety of all is our priority. No circumstance exists where it isn't. Achieving our goals is pointless if few return home. The future of our species, depends on obtaining a peace with the Dwarves and having enough of us remaining to increase our population."

"Gatran is correct Eckna. From the High Elves perspective, we have rescued twenty-plus from dark magic, equivalent to a fifth of those known to be safe at home. Even with them, the survival of High Elves verges on the brink of extinction. Your own kind's survival will depend on those here making it home, otherwise extinction for your kind remains almost inevitable."

"The decision is mine to make, and I'll bear the responsibility for it. I'll retire alone a while, consider the issue, as you would Dravel."

"I wish we had longer for contemplation and further discussion. The decision affecting our future warrants more time than we can allow," Eckna mused his thoughts loudly.

"Whatever my decision, I'll make it based on the facts you've stated, Dravel, and balance it with the protection of my kind. Any other consideration will complicate it further. Rest with us today and prepare yourselves for a journey that will either save or destroy our kind."

Gatran rose and left Eckna and Dravel sitting there.

"The decision is impossible, and yet he will not shy from making it, Dravel."

"We cannot and should not influence him further. He has the facts and understands the risks. He needs no further conflict in his mind."

Gatran walked away feeling the burden of command weigh heavy on his shoulders. He left the encampment, riding a mile along the trail in a westerly direction, and stopped at a stream. Bubbling gently, the soothing sound quietened his mind, allowing him to slip into deeper concentration. After an hour, he had decided, but wanted to discuss it with someone else. This time, he wanted to share his dilemma with Kudra. She wasn't military minded and might offer a perspective to either bolster his choice or force a change of mind. She would examine risk unfettered by the difficulties of the mission decisions influencing him. He had a duty to explore potential issues to the fullest before announcing a decision. He mounted his horse and rode back.

Entering the camp, he rode straight to the horse enclosure, selected one for her, and rode casually to her position.

"Kudra, I would ask you to join me on a ride. I seek counsel with one not military minded."

"Willingly, I offer my services, Gatran."

She moved to the horse and mounted easily, and they walked out of the encampment. Dravel watched them go, understanding why he had sought her, and appreciating the diplomacy of his thinking. They stopped at the same spring, dismounted and sat on the bank. She moved closer than expected, relaxed in his presence. He knew she would speak honestly.

"So, the issue for discussion plays havoc in the mind, Gatran? Speak so the burden you carry lessons, and I'll strive to ease further."

"I am grateful for the consideration you show by accompanying me."

"Considering the gift bestowed towards life, it is simple contribution towards repayment."

"You're not of my kind, and trust between us requires establishing. You could easily have refused."

"A trust exists already; our presence here confirms. It exists with Dravel, who I've known only a short while."

"Your words are true, and direct, and I wish you to continue in this way."

"You view my natural self, my words echo meaning, Gatran. You carry equal manner. Trust exists already because of it."

She took his hands in her own. "Now speak of burdens, so I might offer words of truth."

Gatran explained the issues regarding travel, and Kudra listened carefully. She refrained from comment as he explained the dangers along both routes. After he explained what he and Dravel felt were the most important issues apart from the danger.

"The danger is known to your soldiers?"

"They know we face danger on every stage of this journey, a danger compounded with dark magic."

"One other question demands answer. Why seek peace with Dwarves? Leave alone and travel to new home without risking this journey."

"My father asked me to travel this road. He suggested the rise of mankind will soon consume the world as we know it. They are increasing in numbers, with an insatiable desire for land. They will stop at little to gain this land, including annihilating every other species to gain it. My father suggests all species live in regions away from mankind, to preserve all, for the future, even in a smaller capacity."

"Wise words, understanding the issue is clear. He seeks to preserve all life, including enemies."

"Exactly."

"A father and leader invoking great pride."

"With no doubts."

"Travel south, then west. The risks are less than the alternative."

"Any other reasons?"

"No, less risk, chance of completing the mission increases, without numbers of Elves decreasing."

"It is the choice I had decided on but found difficult in making."

"I made it easier?"

"You decided without considering the females here, I couldn't do that."

"I decided based on your father's desires. Few Kings consider plight of enemies, concentrate only on own kind. Ambition is huge, but tempered with consideration others would ignore. It's commendable, honourable, and foresight in securing future for all. It reaches beyond my appreciated expectations of Wood Elf achievements.

"In protecting all species, he demonstrates depth of mission, a challenge worth following. Should mission fall to failure, he has option to follow different cause, mentioned before. The path of least danger is obvious to follow."

"For the next few days, we should experience trouble free travel. I must spend time with my soldiers, it is how I am with them. I won't have opportunity to seek your company which disappoints me."

"I understand the burdens of command, know your absence disappoints also."

Gatran bowed slightly but allowed his eyes to dwell on hers a little longer than necessary. She met and held the look.

Chapter 17:

During the next two days, the army travelled at a comfortable pace, enjoying the isolation the open landscape offered. Gatran had spent most of his time shared among the different units, laughing with his comrades as if he was a humble soldier rather than their Prince. Eckna watched him work with a father's pride, admiring his young Prince, who still had plenty of time before meeting his full potential as a leader. He knew Gatran's achievements would become legendary.

Dravel travelled in the opposite manner, alone, although he sought the female High Elves company occasionally. On the third day, Gatran asked him and Kudra to travel alongside him. His desire to show to all the strengthening bond between Wood and High Elves.

During the evening before, as Gatran walked around the encampment he spotted Dravel walking alone with another female High Elf. Without meaning to spy on them, he noticed the way they held hands intermittently, when away from others. The High Elf's response had not fully considered the potential.

He felt pleased for his friend, realising it wasn't because of his friendship. More because he firmly believed the High Elf shouldn't spend so much time alone. He had earned a future of a different kind. Questioning Dravel about the status of this friendship, he would declare his support toward the evident bonding.

As he turned away, allowing them the privacy they sought, Kudra dominated his thoughts. Her beauty surpassed all others he had encountered. Her thoughtful, considerate, and gentle nature appealed to him beyond any female ever had. He could scarcely glance at her without experiencing the desire to forward their developing relationship. Something warned he should take his time, that she wouldn't be rushed. They would grow closer through conversation, revealing their true natures to each other gradually over periods of time. They could explore at the deepest levels. He welcomed the challenge and the closeness it would bring. Waking early the following morning, he instructed Eckna to lead while he sought audience with Dravel and Kudra.

The army started moving and Gatran took position on the right flank, drawing distance between him and the army, before Dravel and Kudra joined him. He experienced impatience, as the anticipation of her company gripped him. Dravel found him, urging his mount easily alongside.

"It pleases me to ride with you today Gatran. While I appreciate your Elves demand your attention, I have become used to our conversations and time together."

"I enjoy it also, Dravel. When we return home, I hope to introduce you as my friend to my family."

"I'm honoured but have no family to share with you."

"Maybe not yet, but you are developing a friendship with a High Elf female."

"Indeed, I am, I listened to the words of my friend and Eckna about the changing the world. My role may change and having a partner is agreeable."

"What is her name?"

"She is called Sitara."

"What's she like?"

"She is like Kudra in her mannerisms and vocalisation, the pair could be sisters."

"This is good my friend."

"And your relationship with Kudra, I see you remain drawn to her?"

"True, but I'm not versed in matching with a High Elf."

"It requires nothing specific. Communication and consideration, what most females desire."

"I cannot tell if she shares similar interest in me."

"Then I can allay your concerns. She asks after you each time I converse with her. She might appear distant because of her customs, but she is liking you."

"I require time to know her better; haste in pursuing a relationship is not recommended."

"That's a wise move and one I'm using myself. High Elves do not enjoy being rushed, especially females."

"That's good to know Dravel, your counsel is appreciated."

They ceased talking as Kudra rode toward them.

Gatran raised an arm in acknowledgement and asked her to ride by his side.

"You asked for my presence and I'm here. State purpose, Gatran?"

Gatran was surprised by her directness, and he was sure Dravel's lips formed the briefest of smiles. He decided to answer directness with the same.

"I seek company for no other reason than pleasure of your presence. This is agreeable?"

"It is, and I'm honoured."

"Do not feel this, I do not seek it. Please relax. I enjoy conversation with you; I hope you experience the same pleasure."

This time, Dravel definitely smiled as Gatran continued.

"During my time, before this mission, I have not acquainted with High Elves, I find the experience good.

Dravel is already as a friend, and I seek the same with you Kudra."

"Is friendship your desire, or more, Gatran?"

Dravel laughed loudly. "Never have two Elves been so direct. This flirtation is the strangest I have witnessed."

"Stranger than what you build with Sitara, Dravel?" Kudra asked innocently.

The grin on Dravel's face disappeared. "I could take amusement at your expense Dravel, but I am choosing not to."

This time, Gatran laughed.

"And why merriment, a deflection to avoid past question?"

The smile disappeared from Gatran's face as quickly as Dravel's had.

"It is clear in a battle of words, Dravel, we would stand defeated with Kudra."

"I'm thinking that statement is accurate."

"Is this a High Elf trait or a Kudra one? I mean is Sitara like this?"

"She can be."

"You've avoided my question two times now Gatran, no more deflecting, answer please."

Dravel looked away to spare Gatran's embarrassment, but Gatran did not display it as Dravel expected.

"Truthfully, Kudra, I experience a closeness when I'm in your presence. Everything about you pleases me and encourages me to return when I can. It is unknown if it's possible for a Wood and a High Elf to delve beyond friendship but, from my perspective, I would seek to explore it."

"While with army and running gauntlet of death?"

"The army are family, and life carries many opportunities for exploring."

"Mm, this is agreeable. I too wish to explore this further. And you Dravel, Sitara is my friend, do you wish to explore a similar path as Gatran?"

Dravel followed the example of his friend. "It is my intention, if Sitara is agreeable to it."

Kudra's face softened.

"It is within my knowledge she seeks this also."

"This is good."

"Right, now you both learn error of ways in attempting the betterment of me, perhaps the enjoyment of companionship is possible. Dravel fetch horse for Sitara and ask for her company?"

"Is that agreeable with you Gatran?"

"Of course, my friend, ensure she understands relaxing with us, and the purpose of riding is for pleasure."

He rode away at speed. "An excellent idea, Kudra."

"I have my moments."

"Know I wasn't laughing at you Kudra, more the direct manner in which you approach issues."

"Is it untrue you favour this approach?"

"My efforts pale compared to yours."

"Maybe I should instruct learning of this."

"I would laugh again, probably many times."

"That is pleasurable to witness."

She reached across and rested her hand on his.

Chapter 18:

The army travelled again at dawn. For three days, they navigated the straights between the two lands. The wind favoured their progress, north to south, reducing any possibility of catching the sickness from Fever Valley. Despite the winds, Gatran asked Eckna to keep closer to the Karvil Marshlands. *Better the enemy we can see, than one we can't,* he told him. The wind brought the smell of the marshland, and it washed over the army. The stench of foul decay, of rotting plant life, of death, soured the mood of the Elves. Gatran moved from unit to unit, conversing with his soldiers, attempting to raise the mood the smell imposed.

Dravel travelled with the female High Elves, enjoying their company, and probing their memories for details of a past before his time. Finding it fascinating they were around before him, but appeared and acted younger. His friendship with Sitara deepened, and Kudra kept a little distant, sensing their need to spend time alone. Being completely alone while surrounded by an army was impossible. Grabbed moments added to the excitement of their new relationship.

On the third day, Gatran sought Kudra's company again. He rode casually towards her and, as she saw him coming, a smile broke across her face. Gatran witnessed it, smiling back as he moved alongside her. He determined to be as direct as she, but avoid teasing since she'd bettered him on two separate occasions. Dravel and Sitara, who rode in front quickened the pace of their horses until a small but appreciated gap grew between them.

"My apologies for not having found the time to visit you, Kudra. The demands of leadership weigh heavy. The stench of the swamps wears on my soldiers, the longer it remains."

"The need for apology is unnecessary, Gatran, I appreciate your desire to state, but I understand your position demands attention."

Gatran dipped his head slightly. "I have missed our conversations and the proximity of our closeness."

"That is a bold declaration, Gatran. One which could be misinterpreted."

"I decided to be as direct as you, I mean no offence, nor am I assuming a familiarity beyond what we share already. I simply miss what I stated."

Kudra smiled at him. "The mood for teasing eludes me today, your company brightens my disposition. I'm grateful for your attempts to be as I, but I also appreciate your ways. It's unnecessary to adopt mine.

"That's considerate; perhaps a balance of both is preferable. Not saying I missed your company in your manner means I probably wouldn't have said it. Speaking the truth is easy, but in matters of relationships the truth is often guarded because of fear."

"Surely, I give no reason for fear?"

"No, the fear I refer to belongs to all. The fear of rejection, of making mistakes and destroying what's created."

"And you fear this?"

"Don't you?"

"I had not considered it. I speak the truth because my father instructed me how to deal with merchants. He taught honesty and a direct approach. Successful trades were made and led to further trading at future times. Now, as I contemplate your question, I believe you're right, fear exists. How do we allay that?"

"Compassion and forgiveness. A mistake is a mistake, not deliberate. Everybody makes them. If we are forgiving, our fears will decrease until they no longer exist."

"You surprise me often at the depth you examine issues. The conclusions you draw suggest wisdom beyond age."

"Perhaps age has less control over wisdom than elder's credit. The learning, and the use of learnings, are often those of teachers. If you believe, as I, that we learn from each encounter; it's wasteful not to use the teachings in how we live and conduct ourselves for the betterment of others."

"It is clear you've experienced good and wise teachers. If I detract the sun-cycles of captivity by dark magic forces, I've lived a similar number of cycles as you. Yet my claim to be as wise and considerate is exaggerated."

"That statement suggests discipline to self-examine and seek improvement in areas you consider weaker. I do not observe weakness in you. I admire your character and personality and am comfortable with it. It would not be so if I considered you less wise than me. Each time I leave after conversation with you, I am questioning and probing issues about you, about myself, and about situations. Few stimulate with such force. I enjoy challenge like this. In the future, I will rule my kingdom, the weight of responsibility is heavy. I wish to be the wisest King possible."

"I share this, Gatran. My thoughts consider many issues after discussions. I enjoy this, examining to improve. I consider your position and how you affect others I am with. Improving myself is important; perhaps in times distant, having children of my own, I'll be a teacher worthy for the responsibilities of motherhood.

They will grow to explore my words and customs deeper."

"You desire this for your children?"

"I simply wish my children to achieve more than I. No parent could ask more."

"Again, you demonstrate no weakness in the wisdom of your considerations, Kudra."

The High Elf smiled. "In our conversations we learn of each other at a deeper level, and quickly Gatran. It pleases me."

"And the silence between?"

"There is need also. Silence can suggest awkwardness or a comfortability between Elves. I have watched you with Dravel, you are comfortable with each other, and the silence endures without issue. You are silent and not silent with your soldiers. I've not witnessed this before, but they are at ease with you. And status is maintained.

"I explained this to Dravel; when my army is away from home, they are my family."

"It's a good way to be. Would you share the silence as we ride?"

"I'm agreeable if you want this."

"I wish to discover if it is comfortable between us."

Gatran moved his horse closer to hers so that their legs almost touched. She noticed his subtle movement and realised he was making a statement, suggesting even in silence they could be close.

They rode together for an hour in silence before shouts from the right flank caught his attention. He looked across and saw Feren, the Master of Cavalry, riding at pace towards him.

"What ails you Feren," Gatran called out.

"Movement in the distance between the swamps and our position. There is undulating ground between, and something moves parallel to us."

"Are they moving openly or discretely?"

"They are definitely attempting stealth. I have spotted them only twice, but some of my cavalry witnessed them too."

"They might have several reasons for their actions. First, they might be patrolling their territory and watching our progress to ensure we're not an invasion force. Second, they could be riding to a position of ambush somewhere ahead of our position. Third, they could be amassing forces to battle us and are not attempting to hide their presence. Which seems more likely from their actions, Feren?"

"I could not answer with certainty my Prince. The creatures of the Marshlands have dark magic capability. They are unlike other creatures we've battled before; I believe we should avoid contact with them. We can't ride south-east. The wind protecting us from the Fever Valley sickness could change and we're close to passing their lands without incident."

"A dilemma then, Feren. Perhaps no action is wiser. Double the flank watch. Let's observe them further and hope their actions might give clue to their intentions. Inform Eckna of this as you return."

"Yes, my Prince."

Gatran, called to Dravel asking him to ride beside. Kudra moved forward alongside Sitara without being instructed to, and Gatran appreciated her concession.

"We have company, Gatran?"

"I'm afraid so."

Chapter 19:

"The creatures of the Karvil Marshlands are mysterious. Many inhabit the filthy waters itself, but can manage periods away from it. Others inhabit what dry land exists. Most species are unknown, but can move at incredible speeds. They do not rely on horses."

"Do you have knowledge of their type?"

"It is said many are reptilian. Some with multiple limbs, heads and even bodies, a result of cross breeding."

"And dark magic?"

"Unless they have been cursed with it by another creature, I believe not."

"Finally, an enemy we could fight on equal terms."

"Not necessarily true, although your soldiers are quick, their speed does not match these creatures."

They fell silent. Gatran constantly watching the flank guard who periodically ceased travelling, peering into the distance..

Kudra and Sitara stopped their mounts, allowing Gatran and Dravel to catch up.

"These are matters concerning the commander of the army; we shall return and warn of impending trouble," Kudra stated.

"Stress vigilance, particularly after sun rests. These creatures are mostly from the swamp itself, living in the darkened waters. I suspect they may attack during nightfall when their vision is better than ours.

"Dravel, please escort them back while I seek Eckna, and then join us. It is necessary to make preparations for an attack before it happens."

"They will be safe under my guard Gatran."

The High Elf led them deeper into the mass of soldiers behind and then returned to Gatran's side. He was already in deep conversation with Eckna.

"The light will be gone in an hour Dravel, the enemy has been spotted several times, they still track a parallel course to us."

"Have you discussed tactics?"

"Not yet, you've something in mind?"

"Perhaps fire torches. They like the darkness, perhaps the fire might temporarily blind them. So, fire as a deterrent opposed to a weapon."

"A sudden bright light may halt their attack if lit precisely. The surprise sufficient to attack with our cavalry."

"An excellent idea; you're a battle strategist in the making."

"It would probably only work once, twice, so when using it, we must press full advantage."

"Perhaps use the archers before sending the cavalry. If they do not have a dark magic shield, they will surely fall victim to a cloud of arrows."

"The majority of creatures from the swamp are scaled. Their armour might prevent the penetration of arrows."

"If so, the swordsmen will engage."

"I would suggest, when making camp, The Master of Stealth dig a narrow trench and make ready the fire. The enemy would not expect this when they arrive. Perhaps letting them pass before raising the fire."

"Excellent idea, Dravel, but a second trench could trap them between. It would reduce the scale of their attack and allow one of our own," Eckna added.

"Our night vision will be lost after the initial attack. If there's a second wave, we might not see it until too late."

"It's a good point Dravel, I suggest we extinguish the fires after the first engagement. Allow time to adjust, if there's a gap between attacks," Gatran suggested.

"Could they be extinguished and relit for a second attack?"

"Yes, but the enemy would probably suspect it."

"I was thinking as an aid for us to see them better in battle."

"They would have to pass through the fire to reach us. Again, a second trench might prevent them from retreating."

The discussion continued and plans were decided upon. Between them, a defence strategy formed, capable of being turned into an attack strategy at the snap of an order.

Feren reappeared, riding towards them, pulling up sharply.

"They are massing to our right, Gatran. There are thousands of them, no longer hiding their presence."

"Intimidation by number, Feren," Gatran stated with an element of respect for the tactic his enemy used. "We have a plan, ask the Masters to join me; I'll share the strategy. No need to erect a conference shelter."

"I'll take care of it, Gatran."

"Any other thoughts, Dravel?"

"I can still form an invisible barrier if required, should we wish to slow their attack."

"We might need to. Stay close to me. If I give the order, I want you to hear it."

"Know, I am not as you in battle skills, Gatran."

"You are worried for your safety?"

"Not as it might sound, I do not fear fighting for our cause, but a dead Dravel cannot perform feats of magic."

"You will fight by my side; I'll have a group of my best warriors to protect you; and I'll be close by."

"I am embarrassed by this; I do not lack courage in battle, I'm just stating a point."

"I'm not suggesting you lack courage. I've witnessed the opposite. But you're correct. The Wood Elves lack your ability. We must protect you to benefit from it."

"I'm not alone with the power. Although I have trained to use this as required, the other High Elves could support me with this, including the females."

"I will not risk females during battle."

"I understand your protective nature towards them Gatran, but we fight for the future of our kind. This is no ordinary battle for land or riches, but one for survival."

"Dravel is right, Gatran. We've never fought for anything greater. The situation is as dire as it gets. We must use every resource at our disposal if required," Eckna added.

Gatran nodded. As a last resource only. Cease our travel forward and implement our plans Eckna. Dravel prepare the High Elves for the need of their help. I'll organise the Masters for the strategies we'll engage."

They separated, leaving Gatran waiting for the Masters alone. When they arrived, it took brief moments before dismissing them and riding to the right flank. He called to Feren, who immediately rode to his side.

"Feren, I can see the enemy at distance, but the number seems less than you spoke of."

Feren stared out, waiting for his eyes to adjust to the great distance. He took his time before turning to Gatran.

"You are correct, the number is reduced."

"Which means they are either hiding or implementing a strategy we aren't expecting."

"Perhaps an attack from both sides."

"I believe so. Inform the others and ask Dravel to organise a fire trench on both flanks. Time until dark runs short, triple the watch on the left flank and select the best eyes at our disposal."

Gatran rode to Eckna and the Masters, explaining the situation before seeking Dravel again.

"You have become as my right hand, my friend."

"A statement to make a High Elf proud."

Gatran smiled at him.

"You have organised the second trench?"

"Yes, the High Elves, all the High Elves are attending to it as we speak."

"I was hoping to spare the females from the harshness of war."

"They are as invested in our cause as we are."

"Who leads them?"

"They require no leader; they attend task as a team."

"I will address them when I pass."

"High Elves are proud, remark only on their efficiency. It will be sufficient for them."

Gatran nodded. "I'll heed your words."

"As I do yours."

"When all is prepared, seek my company. All will witness a High Elf and a Wood Elf together in battle."

"The unification of our two kinds will be cemented long before we reach Graylen Forest and beyond to our ultimate destination."

"A cause as necessary as the individual missions my brother, sister, and I embark on."

"Your ability to see beyond the immediate is refreshing. With respect, I know no other Wood Elf with greater ability."

"Look around you Dravel, each Wood Elf here has the ability, perhaps in varying degrees, but they have it. It is a strength in my family, my parents especially. My siblings and I learn this from them. Eckna and the Masters possess the skill too, selected as my seniors because of it. If High Elves have this ability, then the future of our kind is promising despite our numbers."

"We have it, all of us. Like Wood Elves, in varying degrees, but we have it."

"Attend your duties Dravel and seek my company once more."

Dravel turned and left, leaving Gatran alone with his thoughts. A temporary respite from the immediate battle, as his thoughts contemplated the future of Elves.

Chapter 20:

The attack came shortly after dark. Both flanks were attacked simultaneously, and the fire trenches were raised a fraction before the Elves were reached. Trapped between the fire, Dravel's belief it would blind the creatures was correct. They stumbled around in vast numbers and some inevitably fell victim to the fire. Gatran ordered his archers to attack and wave after wave of arrows struck their victims with maximum force, because of their proximity. The smaller creatures fell victim, but the larger one's scaly armour caused the arrows to bounce off. A third of the two attack waves fell victim to Gatran's forces without engaging in close combat.

The archers continued to fire despite their effectiveness reducing. The fires started to thin as they ran low on fuel and breaks within formed. Gatran ordered his cavalry to ready themselves, intending to use them first. The stealth warriors cloaked themselves and carried fuel to replenish the trenches. Omati had orders to light them at a signal from Gatran; the idea to prevent more creatures entering the battle but also trapping those already engaged. It was a risky move. Since they had never engaged these creatures before, their capabilities were unknown.

More and more creatures battled the Elves. Creatures of varying sizes, multiple heads and bodies. Vicious spiked tails swept mercilessly side to side, forcing the Elves to use their gymnastic skills in the extreme to avoid them. Gatran and Dravel were attacked simultaneously by a three-headed, snake-like creature.

It's long necks acting independently. Dravel was nimble and could use a sword adequately, but his defence against the creature was weaker than Gatran's. The creature avoided his sword with a similar nimbleness as his own and they were evenly matched. Gatran severed the attacking head, and immediately a third engaged. Dravel slipped and dropped his guard momentarily. Placing his hand to the ground, he steadied his balance. The creature responded instantly, opening its mouth to a gape to sever Dravel's head. Gatran saw the danger. Vaulting from the head, attacking him, he slashed at the threat, severing it with a single strike. It fell at Dravel's feet, and he looked up. He stood, raising and slashing his own sword above Gatran's head. Another head fell to the ground. They looked appreciatively at each other before the next creature engaged.

Eckna battled a different beast. A two-legged monster that lived on land rather than in the water. Its huge body, long neck threatened with a jaw filled with two rows of evil incisors. Covered in scales, despite being a land dweller, it was impervious to the arrow assault. Its weapon, a combination of its mouth and incredible speed. Eckna slashed away, but his sword made slow progress in breaking through the creature's armour. Eckna was weakening, when the beast suddenly reared upward, with brown fluid seeping from wounds Eckna had not caused. He watched in a confused fascination as more and more wounds appeared on the beast until it fell dead to the ground.

Several stealth warriors materialised alongside Eckna before moving to re-join their comrades. Eckna looked across to Omati who nodded confirmation he had sent his men to assist.

Gatran ordered the fires to be relit, trapping the beasts against his forces. The battlefield became illuminated, and Gatran could see his enemy clearly. The left flank made good progress, and the enemy was falling swifter by the second as their numbers reduced and more Elves engaged them. The opposite flank's situation hung in the balance, numbers identical on both sides.

He hadn't noticed Dravel had slipped away, returning with seven other male High Elves. Together, they stood in a line and raised a barrier, high enough to trap the creatures between it and the fire. Low enough not to consume their strength maintaining it.

While they held it in place, Gatran sent more Elves to clear the left flank. The creatures swarming over were dealt with quickly. Organising them into two lines, they formed an honour guard, central to the barrier.

Moving quickly to Dravel, he asked him to form a gap in the barrier position by the lines, wide enough to allow the creatures to break though. His plan worked. With the gap sufficient to allow only a single beast through, they surrounded and attacked them as they escaped the barrier. The creatures were swamped by flailing swords and cut down instantly. In the briefest moments of battle, all the first wave creatures succumbed to Elven swords and Gatran sent his forces to both flanks.

"Expect and prepare for a second wave Eckna," he called out. "And send someone to me with an injury report as soon as possible."

"Yes, my Prince," the answer followed, and Eckna disappeared.

Dravel and the High Elves removed the barrier, reporting they still had the strength to raise it again if necessary. Gatran did not dwell there, instead riding to the female High Elves.

Kudra and her merchant colleagues had formed a circle. Each of them were armed, swords ready for battle if the creatures reached them.

"Your readiness to battle the evil forces pleases me, Kudra. Stand down now; we await a second wave attacking when our trench fires die and weaken the protective guard."

"Prevention of a second attack is possible if the fire is maintained throughout the night, Gatran."

"We don't have enough fuel to maintain them much longer."

"And if white magic can prolong them?"

"You can do this?"

"Some present studied white magic before becoming merchants, a precaution to attack by the unscrupulous."

"We have four trenches, two on each flank, can they maintain two each?"

"No. One each is manageable. Extinguishing the inner trenches allows fuel for later; the High Elves will flame the outer trenches all night. When strength fails, relight the inner trenches to protect for nights remainder."

"Excellent idea, this could prevent battle during the dark, and we could travel immediately at first light. It could save countless lives. There's a Master on each flank, could you organise this? Instruct them to place a close quarter guard surrounding them. Capable of white magic, they're valuable to us and must be protected."

"I'll see to it Gatran."

Eckna caught up with Gatran. "We have lost twenty Elves to the battle. Ten more injured, but not seriously. I have a team preparing the dead for cremation. I also considered burning the remains of the beasts that attacked us. It might help prolong the fires."

"Yes, Eckna, see to it. Burn them on the outer trenches. I have female High Elves capable of white magic. They will maintain the inner trenches for us."

111

"We might prevent a second wave attack."

"That's the hope, reducing battle time and saving Elven lives is our major concern. We must reach the Dwarves with a sizeable army, showing we can reduce numbers to extinction through battle. It has to be the best deterrent for preventing war and establishing peace."

Gatran rode away, seeking Dravel. He found him among the High Elves who helped raise the barrier.

"Dravel, you told me your battle skills were short on finesse. If that statement was true, I saw no evidence tonight. You saved my life, a deed I will not forget."

"Your life would not have been at risk had you not saved mine."

"No creature is immune from injury or death in a battle, no matter the skill he fights with. Quick thought and actions is as valuable as sword play. Your thinking saved more than me alone tonight Dravel. Every day my respect for your skills and thoughts grows and deepens the friendship we've formed. I'm grateful for your presence. Please convey my thanks to the other High Elves who supported you."

Dravel moved across to Gatran. "Your words are received with pleasure, Gatran. Know I too sense the growth in our friendship daily."

Dravel grasped Gatran's wrists briefly. "For the benefit of those who watch our relationship carefully."

Gatran saw other High Elves noting the exchange of words, realising why Dravel extended arms for the wrist grasps.

They smiled warmly at him.

Chapter 21:

The Elves who lost their lives were prepared for cremation. The customary honour guard was impossible in the confines of the camp, but every Elf passed them by, touching their prone bodies in final respect. Gatran stood with Eckna and the Masters, as the funeral pyre was lit and soon consumed their bodies. Each stayed until the flames decreased to flickers.

Gatran ordered Eckna to supervise breaking camp, stating he wanted to leave in the predawn early light. His plan was to ride away at pace before the enemy attacked again. The flanking fires burned resolutely, fuelled by the fat from the bodies of the dead creatures, but the foul stench filled the air and clung to their clothing.

Eckna suggested splitting the cavalry into four units, one riding point, one the rear and the other two on the flanks. Should they need warning of an approaching enemy, none moved quicker than the cavalry. He tripled the flank watch, riders whose sole task was to seek movement beyond them.

They left at a canter, knowing it would take a further three days before reaching the Plains of Krahor and relative safety. One day's travel would leave Fever Valley behind, two, the southern end of the Karvil Marshlands, but only if they maintained a canter. At night they lit fires for warmth and to cook food, but otherwise resisted making a full camp.

For the three days Gatran drove his army hard. Nobody complained, but all felt the pace. When reaching the Plains, he rode into them for half a day before finally ceasing the journey and instructed them to make camp. He decided army and horses would rest for two days. Wild animals roamed the plains, offering an opportunity to hunt for a variety of fresh meat.

During the period of travel, Gatran had ridden alone at point, planning, scheming, weighing up options to keep his army as safe as possible. But now, as they camped, he decided to reconnect with those around him.

He started with his soldiers, visiting each unit for the rest of the day. He congratulated each for their actions during the previous battle and for the dogged determination and speed of travel used since. He received countless offers to join them for food and conversation, but declined with a good-natured smile. After, he sought Eckna, asking him to rest the army for two days, and remain with them, while he and a small unit scouted ahead. Eckna wondered at the purpose since the land was flat, and vision stretched for miles, but didn't ask.

During the evening, he sought the company of Dravel, reconnecting with the High Elf. Of everyone present, he had missed Dravel's counsel the most, his calm manner and gentle nature which exuded onto those around him. When searching for him, he wondered again how he had become so attached in such a short while, especially as he barely knew him. The answer eluded him; in reality, it was about understanding himself rather than Dravel.

"I'm seeking your company Dravel, now that my duties are rested for a while."

Gatran realised he had just explained his absence without need. As a Prince of the Wood Elves, his behaviour was beyond reproach.

"Your absence has been understandable, but I too have been working for our cause."

"Walk with me and tell me of your toil."

"My work was not toil, merely a series of verbal conversations with other High Elves."

"And the point behind this?"

"Making them understand how different the world is from their time before."

"That's wise. I suspect they found difficulty with this."

"Yes, less with the difference, more with our mission; seeking a lasting peace with the Dwarves was harder for them to appreciate. Their thinking is based on ending the war by out-living them. They believe the Dwarves' lust for plunder and riches will cause them to battle with other forces. Their number will dwindle without our intervention."

"They want them to become extinct?"

"Yes, while we live away from battle and build our numbers again."

"And their views concerning finding a cure for the sickness and home for all Elves."

"They agree this is necessary."

"What if Dwarves discovered the cure and decided not to share it?"

"They would battle for it."

"You pointed out we would be lesser Elves for this action, becoming like Dwarves who would never share the cure with us?"

"I did."

"Their response?"

"Sometimes in wars, it's necessary to act as our enemy to defeat them."

Gatran rolled his eyes upward. "Once my thinking was flawed with naivety."

"But no longer?"

"I'm trying to see beyond my existence, at the insistence of my father. All creatures own the right to live."

"What if they can't?

"Then the mission is to educate rather than battle. Isn't that what you were doing with the High Elves here?"

Dravel smiled. "Of all Elves, I was assigned to work alongside you. Your views for the future, the ways you want to achieve them mirror my own. Our cause unites us far beyond the mission itself, in the way we choose to live.

"When I was asked to join your father in discussions about these missions, I was hesitant. Unification was a task fraught with problems. You're destined for greatness, Gatran, but a greatness differing from your predecessors. Do your brother and sister share your views?"

"They do, and we all work to a common belief and goal. Will you require additional time with the High Elves?

"Yes, but I'm not alone in my efforts, Sitara and Kudra are thinking as us."

"This pleases me."

"As it does me."

"How are Kudra and Sitara?"

"They are well, tired from travelling at speed, but in good spirits."

"Tell me Dravel, does she still ask after me?"

"Every day, my friend."

"And you and Sitara?"

"Our relationship is developing at a deeper level, through conversation and companionship."

"I'm pleased."

"After a night's rest, I will trek ahead to view what awaits our army. I hope you'll accompany me. Perhaps you would ask Kudra and Sitara to join us."

"A mixture of good and evil lurks the plains, places exist that should not."

"I'm aware of this; we'll avoid the woodland areas and the Madang Undulations. Neither should exist on the plains. Tell me, within your magic, can you cloak the four of us in a shield if required?"

For a limited time only. Your Master of Stealth could achieve this for longer than I. Are you seeing Kudra tonight? The invitation to journey with us tomorrow would sound more inviting from you?"

"As much as I would like this, I cannot show too much favour with my time, especially if she joins us tomorrow."

"I understand and will explain it to her."

"Knowing her, she is already understanding this. She places no demands on me."

They had circled the entire encampment by the time they had finished conversing, and Gatran left Dravel close to the High Elves. He saw Kudra and experienced a longing, but then berated himself for the indulgence of need, especially as he would have her attention tomorrow. He sought Eckna again to discuss the temporary two-day absence from camp.

Chapter 22:

The following morning, four riders left the encampment and head north-west, deeper into the Plains of Krahor. Gatran set a casual pace, there was no reason to rush. The excursion was indulgent, seeking time alone with Kudra, and for developing his relationship further with Dravel. Sitara had been included as Dravel's companion; she showed strengths similar to Kudra's and Gatran wished to know her better too.

"It's good to leave behind the melee of the encampment," Dravel commented after half an hour, breaking the comfortable silence between them.

"While I'm at ease with the proximity of many at camp, as I age, I enjoy the companionship of fewer. The isolation allowing contemplation and thought at a deeper level, Gatran offered.

"High Elves seek similar indulgences, Gatran," Sitara joined in. "Dravel's influence affects your thinking."

"It's said we adopt ways of many others in becoming who we are."

"My belief also, Kudra, many through the cycles have influenced and shaped the way I view and respond."

"Who influenced you mostly?"

"The obvious answer would be to say my mother and father, but equally, my brother in particular, my sister and Eckna. Despite being a commander in the army, he is an incredibly calm and peaceful character who thinks at a consistently deep level."

"Is it difficult having a peaceful nature while being a soldier?"

"The realisation that life can be short for a soldier inspires Elves to seek the opposite."

"An interesting concept, Gatran. High Elves are all trained in the arts of combat yet veer from when opportunity presents."

"Your kind are wise, Dravel, nobody wins in war, they either survive until the next battle or die."

Kudra raised her eyebrows. "Surely, you don't consider all the battles you've fought futile, wars are justified, the Dwarves for example."

"It's easier to justify our actions with a truth suiting what others want to hear. Harder to say the war is pointless, wasting resources and life."

Sitara looked shocked. "Even the war with Dwarves?"

"Ask yourselves what we gained. The answer is nothing. Our losses however, and those of the Dwarfs have placed both kinds close to extinction."

"You have regrets, my friend?"

"Too much of my life fighting battles and taking lives. The intelligent should solve their issues around a table.

"Admirable thoughts, Gatran, but the likelihood of a permanent peace is unrealistic here."

"Dravel, when my father suggested finding a new land to become our home, away from the constant battles against evil and greed, my first thought was, finally. An opportunity to gain what I wanted. A permanent peace."

"And you believe this is possible?

"If we achieve our goals, mine, my brothers and sisters."

"The likelihood of achieving success on all three missions is remote."

"But possible."

"You are more optimistic than I."

"The opposite of success is failure, if we fail our kind will cease to exist."

Kudra closed the gap between her horse and Gatran's. "Let not the conversation darken the day. Stay current topic of conversation or remain in silence. We're at distance from the camp and should enjoy ourselves."

"Kudra is right Dravel. There's a lone tree ahead, lets rest in its shade and enjoy a meal."

The conversation changed as they explored each other's cultures and Elven societies. How their communities might labour together. The organisation and difference between those with position and those without.

"Not every Wood Elf seeks position. Some prefer the benefits of additional time with their families opposed to running the community," Gatran told them.

"That means the wealth of your kind is spread unevenly among you," Sitara suggested.

"The wealth of the community belongs to the community, not my father or me. We are custodians of it and when an Elf comes to us with a favourable idea for benefitting our lives, they can ask for the funding. Wealth has little value for much else. The land offers food, the woods, shelter. Why do we need wealth? Knowledge and peace are true wealth."

"I agree, the Dwarves don't use their vast wealth. They just collect it compulsively, drawn to gold with an insatiable lust."

Gatran smiled at Dravel, they were so similar in the manner they thought. He hoped he would have opportunity to share the High Elf with his brother and sister. They would like him, and he knew the sentiment would be reciprocated.

The conversation ceased as they ate, but after Gatran asked Kudra to walk with him. Sitara and Dravel looked pleased at gaining an opportunity to have time alone and declined to join them when Kudra offered. They walked away from the tree, an easy marker to return to, in silence until they were beyond earshot.

Kudra moved closer to him. "So, what purpose is reasoning for this walk, Gatran?" she asked directly.

Gatran grinned.

"Is my question amusing?"

"Only the manner in which you ask. You are direct in your speech as always."

"Would you prefer if I were not?"

"No. I like it but am still adjusting to it. Time apart in recent days has not allowed me to experience it."

"The question remains unanswered."

"I will answer in your manner, please take no offence."

"If your response is truthful, then offence cannot be taken."

Gatran paused before commencing. "The purpose of this walk was to seek time alone with you. I welcome your company, enjoy your company and have interest in you, unlike others."

Is your interest a problem?

"Only if that interest wasn't shared by you."

If I'm to understand this interest, you must say more.

"I think you understand it already and are attempting to discover if I'm truly comfortable with my feelings."

"I seek to discover if you are with comfort talking about it."

"It's not that I'm uncomfortable discussing it, I have little experience to draw from. Maybe I can reply with a gesture.

"What gesture is this?"

"Our hands collide as we walk, if I hold yours, is it agreeable."

Gatran took her hand gently. She interlocked their fingers, and he knew instantly it was acceptable.

"I am liking this contact, and you?"

"It is as I hoped."

"Does my directness make you uncomfortable?"

"No, but it challenges me, in thoughts and in conversation."

"Is that good?"

"It's very good."

"I'm pleased.

Gatran ceased talking again, hoping to avoid further intimate questions before considering the possibilities. Several moments passed before she spoke again.

"You like silence with others."

"When I am comfortable with them."

"Like Dravel?"

"Yes, and you."

"And you like me as Dravel?"

"No, it is different, more."

"You can describe this difference."

"I could, but it will save until later. Up ahead, in that slight depression, do you see what I see?"

"A dwelling. Unusual in design and low to the ground. Perhaps belonging to a Dark Elf."

"My thoughts exactly. We have three choices here. We can watch the dwelling, hoping to spot the inhabitant, walk towards it and announce our presence, or walk away. What would you suggest?"

"My thoughts perhaps veer from safest course. I seek meeting with the inhabitant, especially if a Dark Elf. I have not encountered one before."

"I'm confident that home belongs to a Dark Elf. The height of the building suggests the occupant is half our height, and that's shorter than a Dwarf. I want to meet one too. I never have either."

"It's agreed then, we greet then."

"I learned from stories, few Dark Elves are good, this individual could be either."

"If he is good, he may share what lies ahead of our position. If he's bad I have strength to cloak us to make escape."

"I didn't realise that was a possibility."

"Most High Elves have experienced some training with white magic, usually in matters of self-preservation."

Gatran looked at her closely. She showed no fear, but there was an aura of excitement about her.

"Let's meet a Dark Elf."

They moved toward the dwelling, but Kudra stooped him. "We should return for Dravel and Sitara first."

"You're right."

Chapter 23:

Moving closer, they could see the structure of the dwelling. Thin branches forced into the ground and packed with clay between. There had to be a water course close by, but it remained unseen. The roof was woven straw, and matted with a thinner layer of clay, probably due to the weight. Gatran doubted it was water tight and probably wouldn't stand for long in strong winds unless the occupant used dark magic to protect it.

"Hello in the dwelling," Gatran called.

A door, constructed similarly to the roof opened and Dark Elf emerged. He was striking in appearance. Half the height of a Wood Elf, he had the long blonde hair of a High Elf but skin the colour of darkened pine trees. Otherwise, he appeared Elf-like but smaller.

"Who are you?"

The voice didn't suit the body, deep and emotionless.

"I am Gatran, this is Dravel, Kudra and Sitara."

"It is rare to see High Elves travelling with Wood Elves."

"A united purpose."

"What do you want?"

"Nothing more than information, I can offer food in exchange."

"Information is free, food is not required. What do you want to know?"

"We travel through The Plains of Krahor but were warned about The Madang Undulations and woodland areas that shouldn't exist."

"Wise to seek knowledge of such places, they should be avoided. Woods are inhabited by Dark Elves who follow the ways of the evil magic, the undulations by other warlike creatures."

"Dark magic is not your following?" Kudra was quick to question.

"You are quick with the tongue. I use dark magic regularly, the way of my kind, but to live. It helps me survive at distance from others who wish a less peaceful life."

We heard a Dark Elf was responsible for the sickness.

"It sounds likely, especially when I tell you that Dark Elves are not affected by it, but the sickness was caused by a witches' curse. The reason my kind are not cursed, is that a Dark Elf serves her. She lives far away, three seasons of travel, the closer to her the worse the sickness becomes."

"Are there others here to avoid?"

"Others live as I, alone, but few are not involved with evil magic."

"Since most of your kind are involved with the evil side of Dark Magic, why do you resist the temptation?" Sitara asked.

"I have no purpose for it. Everything I require can be provided for by normal Dark Magic. Besides, it changes Elves into lesser creatures."

"Physically or mentally?" Sitara pressed.

"No physical change, the mind becomes obsessed with the magic and evil gains, they become no longer capable of understanding good."

The Dark Elf suddenly looked up at Dravel. "I can feel your presence in my mind High Elf. You will not find what you expect to be there, so please leave it."

Dravel apologised. "I protect those I'm with, any way I can. I had to be sure."

"And are you?"

"I am."

"Then we shall say nothing further of the intrusion, but avoid it from now."

Dravel nodded. "I will not attempt it again."

"And what about you noble Prince?"

"I never said I was a Prince."

"And yet you are, and I know. Your mission is known to many with dark magic capabilities, so to, the missions of your brother and sister."

"And your thoughts on these missions?"

"They are of no concern to me, but your quest is noble, and I empathise with your plight."

"You don't want your own kind to find haven."

This is unlikely for Dark Elves. Distrusted by most. We prefer to live alone and follow our own destiny. Too many Dark Elves together and the quest for power becomes consuming, we're not as peaceable as you."

"I do not know you well, but you seem peaceable."

"I live in isolation, nothing required from others."

"I am Prince of the Wood Elves, but sadly our numbers decline."

"There are many knowing of your missions and seek to prevent them."

"Why? We wish to separate from the world's chaos."

"Their purposes are unclear, and unshared, but they will attempt to prevent your success."

I'll have no choice but to fight them.

"This is true, and your numbers will decrease further. The future is already written, but the will of individuals are powerful; they can affect it without using magic."

"I will die trying to make these missions count."

Sitara broke into the conversation. "Look, dark cloud to the east?"

All eyes turned to it.

"That is no cloud. It's a flock of ravens; they carry the sickness in their bodies, affecting everything they touch. There is no escaping that touch except through death."

"They are approaching our army," Gatran exclaimed, "we must go to them."

"You are already too late. The ravens will reach them before you return."

"I have to do something."

You can't, but I can.

The Dark Elf reached for a staff leaning against his dwelling, he started chanting the instant he grasped it. Finishing, he hit the ground with its end and faced the group.

"What have you done?"

"I've saved them from certain death."

"How?" Gatran implored.

"I turned them to stone, every one of them. They will remain so for a season before release from the magic. It takes that period for the sickness to disperse."

"They are all stone?"

"Yes, but they live, and will stay safe for the period of infection. Understand Prince of the Wood Elves, there was nothing else possible from this distance. Even if closer, you have no magic to counteract it."

"We must return to them."

"You cannot return for a season. If you do, you will fall victim to the sickness that was intended for you also."

Dravel sensed Gatran was experiencing a mood change, and not a positive one.

"We must leave, now Gatran, no time to waste."

"I'll be here when they wake and will share what has passed when they journey forward again."

"How do you know they will pass?"

"When I tell them you're continuing your mission they'll follow."

"Seek the one called Eckna, I will wait at the Dwarf kingdom."

Dravel took Gatran's arm and led him away, nodding to the Dark Elf as they passed.

Chapter 24:

After only a few paces, Gatran stopped.

"I must witness army turned to stone, it's unwise to accept the word of a Dark Elf?"

"I sensed no evil when entering, but understand need for surety," Dravel informed.

Sitara reached into a pack on her saddle.

"I have something to assist vision, Gatran."

She passed over a tube with an unknown crystal at either end.

"This was gift from father, when I started trading missions. It allows vision at distance, avoid danger. Peer through and everything distant becomes closer. Your army is visible through this."

Sitara passed it across to Gatran who inspected it before offering it to his eye. He aimed it at a lone bush a distance away and instantly recoiled as it appeared directly in front of him.

"Is this white magic?"

"No, the crystals were discovered in a distant mountain stream and were examined closely. Their secret power was revealed by accident."

Gatran placed the tube back to his eye and scanned the distance toward his army. He found it, discerning some individuals. Each were solid stone, exactly as the Dark Elf stated.

He lowered it and passed it across to Dravel, saying nothing, but the shock on his face registered and Dravel read it. He peered through at the army, witnessing exactly what Gatran had seen. The two female Elves took their

129

turn. Nobody commented or appeared to breathe until Gatran broke the silence.

"I'm unsure of the emotion I should experience, but many course my mind. My army, my friends! Turned to stone."

"I can understand the confusion, I'd feel the same, but I've learned to be optimistic around you Gatran. Stone they may be, but they're alive and safe until the sickness disperses."

"If we believe the words of a Dark Elf, Dravel."

"It is as I say, I sensed no evil intention towards us or the army."

"We cannot wait the duration of their stone sleep; our mission is long already, but without an army to support us the danger has intensified. Dwarves cannot be trusted. The might of my army gave us leverage, and now we have none. We're alone, the four of us, we cannot return for supplies or anything else. I'm unsure about our next moves."

Kudra reached her hand across and rested it on his. "Deciding immediately is unnecessary, travel as planned and consider options on route."

"That's good advice. Dravel, Sitara, your opinions please."

Dravel spoke first. "For me, it's simple. I have already stated your future will change the history of all Elves. I'll follow, whatever you decide to do."

"Gratitude, and you Sitara."

"I am unknown to you, yet my opinion is sought."

"That you are companion to Dravel is sufficient for me."

Sitara dipped her head in acknowledgement of his concession.

"You are indeed different from other Wood Elves I've encountered. Different in thought and action. The concessions you make to each, your open-minded approach, and especially the way you think is favourable. I suspect you share guilt, absent from your army earlier. Had we been present, we'd have fallen victim to the sickness, the Dark Elf saving them from death would not have. Each of us would be dying. Suggesting this excursion, has saved us and the mission.

"We should continue the mission, it's our purpose and, as Dravel suggested, your destiny. So, lead us, your friends, forward. Let us help you overcome whatever faces; I'll follow you alongside Dravel."

Gatran dipped his head slightly and then turned to Kudra. "And you Kudra, your thoughts?"

"They are simple, I believe in the mission and in you. I also seek the path forward."

Gatran squeezed her hand.

"Very well, we continue for the present. I am grateful for your support, but I need time alone to contemplate our options before we reach The Hills of Jerev and encounter the Trolls. There are moon-cycles of travel before leaving The Plains of Krahor. I require certainty of how to proceed safely and maintain best chances of success."

"Are you sure you wish to do this alone Gatran? With so few of us, it might be beneficial to discuss our options together?"

"Do not take issue with my decision Dravel, you have the same needs for quiet contemplation, perhaps in my absence you can explain this to Sitara and Kudra."

"No issue exists, or need for explanation. They understand and share the need occasionally. All High Elves experience this."

"I will ride ahead alone until we stop for the night. During our meal, I'll share my thoughts and each of you will support or condemn my ideas, and suggest others.

You are correct in your words, Dravel, it is beneficial to discuss options between us, but for now I think alone. I carry the burden of your safety as leader, that alone demands considerable attention."

Dravel bowed and Gatran heeled the flanks of his mount, increasing his speed and moving ahead of the others.

"He speaks and acts more like a High Elf than a Wood Elf." Sitara commented.

"I agree, and I appreciate that he does. In the short time I've known him, he offers friendship, companionship and trust and has asked little in return."

"Your faith in him exudes, Dravel."

"As does yours, Kudra. My attachment to him runs deep. Deeper than expected or hoped for. He is a worthy companion, friend and carries the weight of our kind on his shoulders. He chooses this burden willingly, duties are not ignored, and he hides concerns others would show."

"And you Dravel, you are beyond an ambassador. Ability to enter the Dark Elves minds suggests so. What else can you do? What is your real position?"

"You are astute, Kudra, and I like the directness of your speech. I am forbidden to answer your question, but I will not insult you by suggesting you're wrong. Understand this is not issues of trust. Even Gatran is unaware of my real position."

"I'm sure he suspects. He misses nothing and he would know entering minds is beyond normal behaviour."

"Gatran will not admit his suspicions. They remain locked until evidence to support them appears. For now, he will trust me, as I hope you will, too. The truth will be revealed in time. I know you to be inquisitive Kudra, can you temper this until we have completed our mission?"

"I have known Sitara for many cycles, she is astute and intelligent. She trusts you, and I have trust in her. I offer this also."

"Appreciated. For Elves, as you, trust is not given lightly; I will strive to show it is warranted."

The conversation ceased, and they rode ever forward, deeper into the plains and its hidden dangers. Each watched Gatran carefully. His demeanour seemed both strange and not strange. His chin rested on his chest as if defeated and yet it was understandable, he had just lost his army, in his words his family, his loss was unimaginable. He rode ever forward, the pace constant, the direction true. His thoughts and his concentration were deep. They continued watching the Elf who had become their friend, and leader. Whoever would consider a Wood Elf commanding High Elves? It was a first in their experience, a first throughout Elven history, but Gatran never acted like their leader. Their inclusion in all matters showed he viewed them as equals, also something never witnessed in Elven history.

Chapter 25:

Night fell before Gatran finally stopped. He had maintained a steady pace throughout the day, and the three High Elves had followed faithfully.

After the warmth of the day, the evening temperatures plummeted on the open plain. A westerly breeze, flying over the Omicron Sea, compounded it before reaching them. There was little to shelter them from it, but Gatran spotted a shallow depression, deep enough to protect them once sitting. It was all they required.

Kudra tethered his horse with hers, removing their packs and the few meagre belongings they carried. Food was sufficient for now, but they realised the need for rationing it until adding fresh meat. The absence of wild life recently was surprising, but probably plentiful deeper within the plains.

Dravel and Sitara released their horses from their burdens and allowed them to graze the abundant grass. Gatran had a fire burning by the time Kudra returned with their packs. While the animals were scarce, evidence of their presence was everywhere, the dried pats caught alight easily and burned slowly.

"Did you find peace with your thoughts, or do you remain indecisive, Gatran?"

"Allowing myself indecision would be deemed as weak and negative, and I do not allow myself that indulgence. I have a basic plan to continue our course, but nothing detailed. Our experiences were not foreseen. All that is certain are the forces waiting to prevent us achieving our mission; added difficulties can be expected."

"Will you allow me to prepare food for you?"

"That's appreciated, my hunger burns like a fire inside."

"We've made good progress for lack of stopping."

"It has also prevented consuming food. We must ration until an opportunity to find more arrives."

Kudra nodded her agreement.

"Are you familiar with willow bark tea?"

"It's been a while. How do you have some?"

"I can answer by saying I've had it for many cycles. It is pleasant, and a warm drink will offset the chill of the evening."

Dravel and Sitara returned with their belongings and sat by the fire.

"Dravel, a question burns in my mind requiring your answer. You used white magic beyond normal indulgence."

"You wish to know how?" Dravel interrupted.

"No, I seek only to understand your capabilities."

"No single answer, I have ability for many tasks. It is easier to seek my help when needed. And, if I think you need it but haven't considered it, I will offer the service."

"Good enough."

"You will share your deliberations?"

"After we've eaten. It passes time before resting the night."

Sitara assisted Kudra with the preparations, and soon they sat eating and drinking the tea.

After the meal, Gatran related his plans.

"The route is simple, and I plan to use the most direct available. Through the Krahor Plains to the Hills of Jerev. I anticipate obstacles in both regions. Nobody knows where the inhabited woodland is exactly, but if we find it, we'll detour around. It will be important to keep distance between it and us. The whereabouts of the Madang Undulations are also unknown but require detouring, if possible. The extent of the undulations remains a mystery and is thought to change regularly. How, is unknown.

"We'll almost certainly encounter Trolls in the Hills of Jerev. If our route before there remains to the east, there is a passage between them and the north-west region of the Karvil Marshlands. When entering the Hills of Jerev we'll be half-way through, and close to the Mandrade Mountains. We must avoid the Orcs; they'll attack in number, and we would not stand a chance. I'd have planned further, but there is little point. We cannot bully our way through any of these regions without an army.

"Reaching conclusion did not consume a whole day of deliberation, Gatran. I mean no disrespect with words."

"No Sitara it didn't, considering the enemies we face took longer. How to avoid or battle them if cornered. As a group of four, we must safeguard ourselves. The mission fails with our demise. Using Dravel's white magic may be the difference between success and failure. If you disagree, or can suggest something to quicken, or improve safety during our journey, please state."

Nobody spoke at first and Dravel, recognising an awkward moment, spoke up.

"I think your assessment is correct. It is difficult to plan with many potential obstacles and dangers ahead. Wiser to accept journey each day."

"How are you with knowledge of leaving army behind? Kudra asked gently.

"The answer is painful and confusing. I feel their absence and counsel. I'm relieved they're still alive. That they have become stone worries, what if an enemy chances upon them and rains destruction on them? Would they wake from stone, or become lost forever?"

"I feel I should answer Gatran and yet I cannot. My white magic differs from the dark used upon them. I'm unsure if I can break the magic, but the possibility is low; I hope their survival will not depend on me. If others find them, they would fall victim to the sickness."

"Their loss weighs heavy, but I will not deter from our mission, Dravel."

"The night is cold, we should share heat from our bodies to allay," Sitara suggested. "Let's sleep and wake early to continue our journey."

Nobody commented. The suggestion was sensible in the conditions, and they needed rest. Gatran spread his riding blanket on the grass and lay down, pulling his sleeping blanket over his body. Kudra lay next to him, close enough for him to smell her hair. Under her blanket, she reached out her hand, placing it in his. Feeling it close on hers he interlocked their fingers, making it harder to separate, should the need arise. She hoped nothing would encourage that and would have smiled in satisfaction had she realised he was thinking exactly the same.

She turned to face him, content with the gentle face she saw. After a while, when she realised sleep wasn't going to grace her, she whispered, asking if he was awake.

"I'm awake, what troubles you?"

"I'm grateful for your concern, nothing troubles accepting I'm not yet ready to sleep. I seek conversation with you."

"What would you talk about?"

"I'm considering my place here."

"How so?"

"I agree with mission, and reasons for, but my position with you is unclear."

"When we walked together your hand was in mine, as it is now. The reason is unclear?"

"From your perspective, yes."

"You wish to know if I have feelings matching yours."

"You can be as direct as I, Gatran."

"Sometimes, but for you, yes. If my thinking is flawed, you'll tell me."

"What thinking?"

"I'm thinking you enjoy being with me as much as I do you."

"That would be classed as forward among my kind."

"And yet it is how you would ask me, am I correct?"

"Yes, I would, and yes I hoped you liked me as I do you."

"Then know I do. It strengthens each day. Possibly the only issue I have certainty with."

"Issue?"

"Perhaps a poor choice of word, but my meaning is clear. Now that I've answered your question are you ready for sleep?"

"I'm feeling the chill of the night."

Gatran stretched out his arm and she raised her head and rested it on it. She edged closer so their bodies touched and closed her eyes.

"This is preferable," she whispered.

Chapter 26:

When Gatran woke the following morning, Kudra appeared to sleep on. He lay still, watching the fall and rise of her breathing, her serene facial appearance and the wisp of hair blowing gently across it.

Noises from behind alerted him and he twisted his head awkwardly to witness Dravel and Sitara attending a fire and making a hot drink.

"You will remain here for a while longer, Gatran?"

He smiled having been duped into believing she was asleep, but was unclear if her words were a request or an order. He did not dwell on it, instead turning to face her,

"It pleasures me to wake and behold your face before anything else."

"I shared this when waking eons ago."

Gatran was unsure if her response was complimentary or admonishment for sleeping longer than necessary. He declined to comment further, capturing her eyes with his own and smiling. He allowed her a moment before sitting and enquiring about the meal Sitara prepared.

"It is a fine day for travelling, Dravel. Have you been deliberating our plight?"

"I have, but I'm not prepared to share my thoughts yet."

"Fair enough."

"Many days of travel lay ahead before leaving the Plains of Krahor. That doesn't include possibilities of detours."

"We'll almost certainly have to detour the Madang Undulations."

"The certainty is almost guaranteed since they are controlled by Dark Magic, the uncertainty is how far we travel before encountering them."

"They are bound to be inhabited with strange abominations controlled by Dark Magic."

"True, and likely formidable."

"Once located, it would be preferable to detour them at distance, even if forcing us from Plains," Sitara broke into their conversation. "We must battle nobody, risking the mission is not our purpose."

"You sound totally committed to the mission, Sitara, I am pleased for and grateful for your support."

"My commitment to Dravel is matched only by this. I received the gift of a second life since being released from Dark Magic, and I plan to spend it in manner more deserving than old life."

"Do not devalue your past. A merchant's life is respectful, fraught with danger and opportunity. We learn from experiences, from individuals encountered through life's journey.

"Do not misunderstand meaning, Gatran. I was not devaluing my past, simply expressing desire to improve. And you are correct about learning from each encounter. Takes many sun-cycles to appreciate; the inexperience of our younger selves leaves requirement to outgrow youthful exuberances. It allows deeper contemplation and enlightenment."

Gatran smiled at the High Elf. "I am liking the friend this journey allows me to make. It would seem she too is wiser than her age. I'll enjoy hearing and listening at a deeper level, to the words you speak and the wisdom you share. I am pleased you are travelling with us Sitara."

Sitara bowed her head, acknowledging the compliment, before breaking into a smile and passing him a warm drink.

"Your smile, also confirms the satisfaction of your position on this mission; that pleases too."

"Perhaps Dravel's influence. He has ways of sharing knowledge, wisdom and foresight, making matters clear to those listening. I'm grateful, for rebirth, I once lacked purpose and identity. He has shown me who I am."

"He has a way about him, doesn't he? Probably due to the many sun-cycles he has lived. The weight of his accrued knowledge and wisdom must weigh heavy."

"I can hear every word of your teasing, Gatran. A childish pursuit, I might add."

"But from our position, very amusing."

Dravel suddenly smiled. It surprised Gatran. The High Elf always carried a sombre and dignified look on his face. A neutral expression, concealing signs of emotion and yet maintaining a warm and friendly disposition. The smile forced Gatran to follow his example and, for a moment, the two Elves enjoyed a careless sharing of mutual and growing affection.

Kudra and Sitara took pleasure from it. Here were two Elves, sharing the weight and responsibility for the future of their entire species. Despite this, they could relax sufficiently to share their true selves.

They were soon under way, the open grasslands stretching in every direction. The gentle breeze caused long grasses to weave intricate waving patterns, like flocks of migratory starlings in the sky. The azure sky remained clear, encompassing horizons in every direction and beckoning them forward on their quest. The wilderness beauty of the land encompassed them all and as they rode, four abreast. They slipped into quiet

141

reflection, each dealing with a multitude of issues and yet sharing none. Gatran wondered if this would become the norm while travelling. He liked the bond without intrusion, offered to each other, and was equally comfortable when their minds met and they discussed issues at depth. He hoped his brother and sister would like them as he did.

Thoughts of them consumed him, and the realisation of how large a hole their absence left in his life. Each of their missions were fraught with danger, would he see them again. They were resourceful individuals, every bit as resourceful as he, but the mountains they climbed had so many precipices to fall from.

He attempted to force them from his mind, not allowing their absence to weigh further than his purpose already did. Kudra moved closer, almost as if she understood his thoughts saddened him.

"We could stop here, Gatran. Rest the horses and eat. Dravel saw animals in the distance. They offer the food we lack."

"We can aim for that small tree and shelter from the midday sun," he suggested.

"You were thinking of home, or perhaps your brother and sister?" Kudra asked.

"How do you know this?"

"Your face adopts expression when considering those parted from. Sadness and longing, present when you spoke before of them."

"When they are close, I am complete, when they are absent..."

"I understand."

"Do you miss your past?"

"I am with Sitara, have new purpose and path to follow. I am content, but should you leave, I might experience feelings of loss as you."

"You are by my side, and it suits to keep you close Kudra."

"I am liking this direct manner of speech you use."

"I like it too Kudra, it appears Gatran is adopting the ways of the High Elves," Dravel teased.

"I can't believe you waited all morning to return the teasing I gave you Dravel."

"Patience is easy for High Elves, only time before you revealed an opening to use."

Gatran laughed. "If anyone told me the Prince of Graylen Woods would fall victim to the teasing of a High Elf, I'd have doubted the wisdom of their words, despite their accuracy. You are a diamond Dravel, each facet revealed during the passage of time. Tease away, my friend, tease away."

"There is food to be hunted after our meal, perhaps I could be persuaded to allow you to lead during it."

Gatran laughed again. "Perhaps we should wager a bet on the result."

"I cannot accept taking from those who cannot match my skill with a bow."

"I have seen your skills in battle, they are not matching mine."

"You haven't witnessed my skills with a bow yet."

"Mm, can't tell if you're teasing or bluffing."

"You will discover the truth when we hunt. I know Sitara and Kudra excel at hunting, too. Can you match the skills of three High Elves?"

"The result is already a certainty, but I'll enjoy witnessing your efforts."

Chapter 27:

Dravel surveyed the landscape through the spyglass. There were signs of movement to the west, deeper into the Plains.

"We are spoilt for choice Gatran, there are beasts everywhere."

"Choose wisely Dravel, we have to transport what meat we take. The journey is lengthy and arduous. We must not burden our horses beyond the necessary."

"Small deer, in a shallow depression, a perfect choice. Two, would last for several moon-cycles."

"Your tactics for the hunt?"

"Well, there are four of us, approach from several directions."

"Whoever approaches from the north has ground to cover before the hunt can start."

"You or I?"

"Sitara, you take the southerly point, Kudra the east; I'll take the north We avoid the west; the wind originates there. If everybody agrees."

Sitara answered positively for her and Kudra, and Dravel nodded his acceptance.

"Since positioning will take me longer, I would suggest the attack starts when I move forward. You'll all be in position to see me."

They separated, Sitara remaining where she was, already in position. Gatran gave the deer a wide berth, knowing how skittish they were. When reaching his starting point, he gazed around at the other's positions. They were ready, and he edged his mount forward. The deer spotted his movement and began to twitch nervously. They moved outwards slightly before noticing Sitara's approach and veered east. Dravel noticed their confusion as they spotted him. Then they bolted north-west between Gatran and Dravel. They rode at an angle to cut them off, while Kudra and Sitara raced toward them directly. The deer, realising they were cut off changed direction to find their route blocked again.

They ran in circles as the riders closed in. Dravel and Gatran aimed at the same beast and two arrows felled it. Kudra shot another, which didn't fall, and Sitara sent a second arrow into its flesh. The creatures were still alive when Gatran jumped from his horse. He dispatched one efficiently and compassionately. He uttered a few words of thanks to Mother Earth before turning towards the second. Kudra had beaten him to the task and the second creature lay still.

Both creatures were gutted, skinned and cleaned within an hour. Sitara and Kudra cut them into manageable sized joints before placing them into cloth bags lined with the stomachs of cows, to make them leak proof.

As they finished, Kudra glanced up, staring into the faces of Anurans. Huge creatures, seven foot-tall, with toad-like facial features. Powerful legs, capable of launching them great distances, bulged. Their arms were shorter, but the muscular definition suggested great strength.

"We have company," she stated to the others, yet to notice.

They glanced up, Dravel reaching for his sword. Gatran stopped him.

"Too many, at least thirty surrounding us. Better not to antagonise them."

"What are they Gatran? I have not seen their type before."

"They're Anurans. I've seen them at distance but never close up. Wood Elves have fought individuals in various armies across the land, but I have no knowledge of groups this large being encountered. They are distantly related to Orcs.

"Do they speak our language?"

"Unknown, but communication is my first option."

Gatran addressed the Anuran closest to him. "Who speaks for you as leader?"

The creature stared at him with passive indifference. Gatran decided it was better than an aggressive posture.

He tried again. "I am Gatran of the Wood Elves from Graylen Forest; I wish to communicate with your leader."

Movement behind him invited him to turn and face an Anuran moving toward him.

"Save your words for me, Elf."

"And you are?"

"I'm responsible for keeping you alive."

"We have food if you wish to share."

"If we desire food, we'll take it from you."

"Then why are you and your kind surrounding a peaceable group who pose no threat to anyone?"

"We too, are on a peaceable mission. We collect those who travel alone and train them to fight in our army."

"And who do you fight?"

"Anyone with something we need."

"That's not exactly friendly."

"It is the way of our kind."

"Where are you from?"

"I'm keeping you alive. You have no need of answers concerning us."

"Do you intend to take us captive, then?"

"That has already happened, and since you have intellect, I suggest you know this already."

Gatran looked at Dravel for help. The dialogue was not proving helpful. Before he could intervene, the Anuran moved closer, towards the women. He reached out and lifted Kudra's chin so that he could inspect her face easily. For reasons unknown, she had lowered it and not made eye-contact with creatures.

"I am knowing this face," the Anuran stated. "I have encountered you before many sun-cycles ago. Our recognition skills are excellent, so don't deny it. I am right, yes?"

"You are correct. While you had no direct contact with me, you encountered a group I belonged to."

"I remember, close to Rag Dire Pass. It was unfortunate for you. You were taken by the limbs of the forest and failed to return."

"You speak the truth; your memory is accurate."

"Your name eludes me momentarily, but your importance does not. You are a High Elf Princess, yes? And this one attended your needs. I am correct, yes?"

"Correct with your first statement, but she is my friend and travelling companion, not a servant."

That you speak the truth has saved your lives. Had you lied, your fate, Kudra, Princess of the High Elves of the Ydran Mountains would have been a savage death."

Gatran and Dravel were stunned at the revelations Kudra admitted. They looked at her and Sitara in disbelief, but they could not meet their stare.

"So, what are your plans for us?"

"You and your friend will come with us. Your value, especially having returned from the limbs of the forest is unimaginable. Your two male companions will be taken into my army. You will be separated eventually, most probably never encountering them again."

"Let me introduce you to them formally, they may be of value to you."

"No need Kudra, I have no importance for Anurans and neither does Dravel.

"I have no desire for Wood Elves, accepting to add to my army's number."

"Do you at least have a name so that we can communicate formally."

"We communicate only when I decide it's necessary, but for the sake of simple pleasantries you may address me as Commander Gorga."

"As you desire, Commander."

He turned away from them and snapped an order. Several Anurans moved forward and separated the male and female Elves. Kudra and Sitara were swept away in one direction while Gatran and Dravel were handled roughly and forced in another direction.

Without the attention of Gorga on him, Gatran could assess the forces surrounding them. There were far more than first considered. Several hundred creatures stood waiting at distance, separate from the group surrounding them.

"No resistance Dravel. At least not yet. They are not guarding us at close quarter so we can at least talk until we reach the main body of their forces.

"There would be little point in resistance."

"I didn't believe large groups of beings lived on the Plains."

"I don't believe they live here; they've been hunting for food. Blood stains on their clothing and hands."

"We need to learn their origins, because their existence should be added to our maps. They should be avoided."

"Why not explain your status?"

"Valuable prisoners would have an increased guard. It would make it harder to mount a rescue and escape plan,"

"And you will attempt escape? Surely it would be better to negotiate?"

"That's your strength, Dravel. And as soon as we gather information, and before reaching their destination, we must escape from them. Waiting longer, and finding ourselves in their territory, will compound matters further."

"Changing the subject, what about Kudra and Sitara's deception?"

For another time, my friend. I'm sure whatever reason they have for not sharing the truth is valid. I do not believe they would lie unless the need is of paramount importance. They lied only by omitting the truth."

"The reason interests me, Kudra's return to our kind was straight forward until you add Princess to the story. The hierarchy in High Elf society would alter with her presence. Most in the royal position would be lowered in status with her addition."

"That would cause problems?"

"I cannot be certain of the outcome."

"She would understand this."

"I'm sure she would, it's possibly the reason for her silence on the issue."

They fell silent as they approached the army of Anurans.

Chapter 28:

Approaching the Anuran army, Gorga grouped the elves together and placed a circle of guards around his four prisoners. He kept them at a respectful distance but unfettered, allowing them to talk discretely and with some freedom of movement. Gatran was surprised he did not stamp his authority on them, demonstrate his power and position to his followers. Perhaps the Anuran had other matters on his mind.

"What are your thoughts Dravel?"

"Reserving judgement for now; I expected to be treated rougher."

"I expected the same."

"Any thoughts of escape?"

"Too soon. Wait and observe the travel arrangements first. We could not move as fast as they do."

"Did you know about Kudra?"

"I did not, though I should have. Historical stories of her disappearance were varied and unproven until now. I failed to make the connections, I'm sorry."

"No need for apology, I'm thinking our unexpected treatment results from her stature. It might improve further if I gave my identity."

"I believe your concealment was correct. Could be useful later, as a bartering point, but reveal this and we lose the opportunity."

"You could be right. I'll hold back for now."

Kudra and Sitara sat a few metres away from them. Gatran had not objected. If nothing else, it showed them displaying a level of respect towards her, as subjects of royalty would, to the eyes of their capturers. He wondered if the Anurans would treat him and Dravel differently because of their believed lower status.

He felt Kudra's eyes upon him several times, hoping to make eye-contact, perhaps conveying an unspoken message. It took all his resolve to resist glancing towards her, but appeasing her needs was not high on his agenda. She had lied, albeit by omission, why? He had been open and honest from their first moment together.

Delving into the reasons could wait, time alone with her was preferential when attempting to discover the truth. Dravel would share that thinking. Sitara and Kudra too; High Elves preferred the subtle approach.

What appeared simple and straightforward, now became complicated, issues of trust raised. The mission, his mission, was unparalleled in terms of importance. His feelings should not matter, but they did.

His thoughts were shut down abruptly by Gorga's arrival.

"I'm here to tell you I'll be leaving shortly. The guards present will guide you to our city. You'll remain unharmed, receive food and water as required, but attempt an escape and all decencies will end. You'll be fettered and force marched at an uncomfortable pace. Further problems will be met by physical punishment. It would not be pleasant."

"Your concessions to our comfort are appreciated and respected." Gatran acknowledged.

An hour later, they watched as the Anuran army moved west, leaving them and their guards isolated on the Plains. Poignant how small they seemed in the vastness of their location.

One guard moved forward and motioned to the north.

151

"It's time for us to leave." Gatran stated.

The High Elves stood, and the guard motioned forward. They walked, the rear-most Anuran leading their horses. Gatran had expected them to be freed, or worse, used as food. He felt relief knowing their chances of escape improved with the availability of horses.

For four hours, they travelled at a steady but relentless pace before stopping for rest. The guards indicated for them to sit; seemed none spoke their language. Gatran suspected one might, feigning ignorance, attempting to listen to their conversations. Kudra and Sitara prepared food.

"I'm sure you both believe Sitara and I violated trust between us. I cannot blame you; there are reasons you're unaware. Talking here is not suitable in our present situation. But I ask you not to be quick to condemn. We'll explain when appropriate."

She had spoken to them both, but her eyes remained constantly fixed on Gatran's. He held her stare impassively, showing no emotion, positive or negative, and Kudra could not read his thoughts.

Gatran had a sudden notion. Dravel could read minds, and yet he had read nothing in Kudra. Surely, he would have tried when she first woke from the dark magic. She was confused and disorientated, and yet he had somehow missed this. Was she capable of using white magic, to a higher degree than expected, and thwarted any form of mind reading Dravel tried? Kudra withdrew to Sitara's position.

After they finished their food, the lead guard indicated north, and travel started again. They used the same formation as before, the twelve guards circling them and Sitara and Kudra leaving a gap between them and the two male Elves. They travelled into the early evening before the guards stopped, indicating time to rest.

Gatran indicated the horses by pointing and then at a guard to follow. He nodded understanding, and Gatran retrieved a woven mat and a blanket from his mount. One by one, the guard led the others to collect their belongings.

Dravel lay his mat alongside Gatran's, effectively telling the females to give them space. A brief look of disappointment crossed Kudra's and Sitara's faces. They realised space between their prospective partners and them was now deemed appropriate.

For three days, they travelled at the same monotonous pace, nothing breaking the boredom or the repetitive nature of the open plains. On the fourth day, Dravel noted something strange ahead. Movement! No animals roamed the plains here, or other living entities, yet movement was occurring. He pointed ahead for Gatran to observe.

"I see it, it's not beings or animals moving Dravel, it's the plains. I believe the Madang Undulations lie ahead and we appear to be heading straight for them."

"Is it possible the Anurans live there?"

"It makes sense, nobody has ever ventured into the Undulations and returned to tell the tale. Nobody knew of the existence of the Anurans in their current numbers."

Dravel scratched his chin. "How can you live in a place constantly moving or changing?"

"I've no idea, but that might change very soon."

They slipped back into silence, observing the space between them and the Undulations gradually decrease until they stood at the edge.

They were larger than expected, troughs and peaks rose and fell majestically. They were formed from sand, loose and shifting like the dunes in a desert. The majority

153

of troughs were devoid of life, but one held a huge surprise. A city of magnitude, built of stone, and with a fortified wall surrounding it, lay ahead. Gatran whistled at the sheer scale of it. He whistled again when the trough lifted and moved several yards to their left.

"It's like being on a sea in turbulent weather," Dravel commented.

"That's exactly what it seems like."

Chapter 29:

"I am worried, Dravel; a feeling that when we enter the undulations the possibility of escape diminishes. Every instinct I have suggests avoiding this place."

"The alternative is escaping now, but the odds are stacked against success!"

"I appreciate that. The possibility of attempting is compounded by their distance from us."

"We don't have weapons."

"I have something to create a diversion, something they won't expect. It might cause enough distraction and chaos to create an opportunity to gain a weapon."

"I can protect you while you attempt this with a little white magic."

"The barrier?"

"Yes."

"We must give warning to Kudra and Sitara; they must come closer and gain protection from the same barrier."

Dravel turned. "You must see this, Kudra, Sitara."

There was a slight urgency to his voice, almost imperceptible, but they recognised it and moved forward.

"Sound amazed, excited even, but draw the guard's attention," Gatran ordered.

Kudra and Sitara played the part instantly, understanding something was about to happen. They began talking animatedly, and the guard unit immediately closed in. Gatran whistled and his stallion suddenly pulled away from the guard holding them. It ran straight to Gatran, knocking over three Anurans in its attempt to reach him. Gatran leapt on him and guided the horse to collide with more Anurans. Reaching down, he plucked the Anuran's swords and threw them towards the Elves before plucking one for himself.

"Now Dravel."

Dravel raised an invisible barrier, moving towards the Anurans closest to the leading trough of the Undulations. The barrier forced six of the guard unit to fall, instantly consumed by the sands and disappearing from sight. With only six guards remaining, Dravel moved his barrier toward the others, but as he did so, the Undulations moved simultaneously.

The four Elves were raised on a peak while the remaining guards dropped suddenly into a new trough, instantly consumed by the sand. Gatran watched in horror as the other three horses fell with the Anurans.

With the fall of the guard, they were no longer prisoners of the Anurans. Their escape route was cut off by a huge trough though, and having seen what happened to their enemy, they had no intention of falling to their fate.

"Don't move, any of you. Hold your position. The ground changed once; it could alter again."

"Remaining defies wisdom," Sitara stated the obvious.

"Do you have something in mind, Gatran?"

"More hope than plan. The trough trapping us might rise again. When it does, we jump across. We will skirt the undulations again. It will take perfect timing. Too soon, and we'll slip into the trough and be consumed; too late, and we'll slip off the peak and experience the same fate as our former guards."

"The wait time for this is uncertain."

"We wait as long as it takes, Dravel, I can't think of another option."

"Even if we follow your idea, a further trough might erupt and we'll still be trapped in the Undulations."

"I know."

"I might offer another option."

"Now's the time to speak it."

"The barrier I create could be placed beneath us so we could walk across to safety."

"Why didn't you suggest this earlier?"

"You lead this mission; it is not for me to be forward at moments of crisis. Your efforts so far have been admirable."

"I appreciate what you're saying Dravel, but have I not clarified we're a team in this. We won't succeed without each other. We have to play to our strengths. Use your magic Dravel, your way carries less risk of harm than mine."

"This was my thinking, too."

Dravel took a position and invoked his magic. The barrier formed underneath them and he raised it so they appeared to be standing on air.

"Stay close and still, the barrier is not lengthy. We will move with it."

They felt themselves move, almost floating across the trough. Peering down, each experienced a fleeting flash of fear, recognising the death waiting, should they fall.

Reaching the other side, Dravel kept the barrier below them, taking advantage of the security it offered. He extended their journey far beyond the danger area. Finally, he lowered and removed the barrier so they were once more standing on the Plains.

"Gratitude, Dravel. Once again, your command of white magic has come to our rescue."

"But what now, Gatran? We can be sure the guard unit will be missed and their prisoners. We won't have a lot of time before they seek us."

"You're right, and we only have one horse between us."

"We can use magic again, if required, it will prevent a fight, for a limited time. The question is which direction? We've been travelling north-west since becoming prisoners. We are positioned deeper into the Plains than we originally intended."

"My instinct is to travel due east. Leave the plains by the quickest route. We can walk between the Plains and the western border of the Karvil Marshlands. Hopefully, some trouble-free travel. With luck, we may come across someone to secure horses from; we'll need them to negotiate the Hills of Jerav and the Trolls."

"The plan is good, Gatran.

"Kudra, Sitara, do you agree?"

"I was unsure our opinions or thoughts were valid any further, so I did not offer," Kudra stated, a little unreasonably.

"You are with us by chance, not choice; I will offer you the same considerations as I do Dravel."

"We're here by choice; no matter what you think of us, we remain wholly committed to the cause."

"I appreciate those words and will treat them as honestly spoken."

"We still need to speak of matter, causing clouds to shroud friendship."

"We'll make time, but we'll speak as a group, not individual pairings. Now we must move. How long we have before they realise our escape is unknown."

Gatran led his horse forward, remaining on foot so Dravel could join him alongside. The two female Elves once again allowed a gap to develop between them.

"Your words displayed irritation, perhaps anger, towards Kudra."

"I'll not apologise, Dravel. I trusted beyond the realms of my normality, and they did not display the same curtesy."

"Kudra's position may well have influenced this. I remember from history she was trained in white magic by a witch. Her position was constantly threatened by those who did not trust magic beyond our normal restrictions."

"I have position too, of equal status. I trusted her with the truth."

"I know, it's necessary to discuss this soon, confine our current difficulties to the past."

"Changing the subject, Dravel. While knowledge of the Undulations is good, a question remains unanswered."

"You are thinking of the demise of the soldiers?"

"Yes. If they truly fell to their death, then how would they access the city? It wasn't positioned towards the leading undulation."

"I too wondered. Perhaps the movements are repetitive. What changes position also returns."

"That's an interesting concept. Access to the city then would only be possible at certain times. It's no wonder the Anuran existence is such a secret. Probably outsiders have never entered and returned. Their prisoners have the secrets, and they now fight for the Anuran army."

"How many days travel do you estimate before leaving the Plains?"

"Two, possibly three at most. That's assuming a similar rate of travel as the Anurans kept us marching."

"They can travel several times faster without horses. Possibly faster than horses. Whatever distance between us we achieve they can still outrun us."

"We'll encounter them again, I'm sure. We can't out run them, but we might hide from them."

"I can veil us for short periods, and we can move under that veil, but it takes more energy than a simple barrier."

"Perhaps we need to secure the help of others known to have white magic training."

"All the more reason to remove the uncomfortable situation between us, then."

"Perhaps, but if they want my trust, they will have to earn it. I will not give it so freely this time."

"And how will they earn it?"

"By trusting us completely."

"And when will this happen?"

"When secured by darkness, and opportunity to rest."

"I am liking this."

"You are missing the company of Sitara?"

"As much as you are Kudra, I'm sure."

"Trust is everything, Dravel. We no longer have an army; whatever challenges face us when we encounter the Dwarves must be faced by each of us. The fate of our kind rests with us. Four Elves present are better than two."

Dravel fell quiet, contemplating matters beyond what they discussed already.

"You have concerns, my friend?" Gatran asked after a few moments.

"I thought, despite losing our army, we've been fortunate to avoid conflict so far. It cannot last for ever, it's inevitable, and what you stated about four pairs of hands is poignant. The females have knowledge from earlier times to draw from, have experiences we lack. At least one has superior magic."

"Yet she has not used that magic except during the battle in Rag Dire Pass."

"Perhaps she did or perhaps she didn't. That she hasn't used it to support us at any other time suggests she has a problem with it. Maybe she cannot command it as she once could. A result of the dark magic held on her in Dangorg Woods."

Gatran edged forward. "Perhaps she can't use it because she can't control it."

"I had not considered this view. Perhaps when we discuss issues later this may also be resolved."

"Let us ponder more as we travel, but let me also state I will not be easy on them despite her status. The mission is, and will remain, my priority, and I don't need those I cannot trust."

Chapter 30:

They reached darkness without stopping and without further encounters with the Anurans. Gatran knew they would not travel much further without meeting them again. He considered travelling during the night, navigating by the stars and hiding through the daylight, before dismissing the idea. He felt exhausted, the others too. They needed rest, despite the consequences. Better to fight an enemy while alert than half asleep.

He called the halt in the middle of nowhere. They were completely exposed, and he knew they should continue in the morning while still dark. The Anurans are short-sighted; they were unlikely to travel during the night.

It was clear, a myriad of stars peppered the heavens, but the temperature was dropping rapidly. They had one sleeping mat and two blankets between them and Gatran released them from his horse. He passed them to Kudra and Sitara and instructed them to make themselves as comfortable as possible. He resisted the opportunity to gaze into Kudra's eyes, allowing connection for a brief second, and muttering something to Dravel.

Dravel dug a knee-deep hole and placed what little burnable material he had collected during their travel. Sufficient for a brief fire, it would allow an opportunity to heat some water.

Gatran spoke to nobody in particular. A move to break the silence, prevailing like an ominous cloud, and threatening to wash away the remnants of their friendship.

"The Anurans won't see the glow from the fire, and we are fortunate the breeze favours us. Coming from the west, it will carry the smell of burning away from them."

Kudra passed across a small drawstring bag filled with willow bark and Dravel took it.

"Enough tea for another in the morning. I realise we have no further fuel, but if you make the drinks now, they will still taste pleasant in the morning."

They only had one horn to drink from and Gatran waited until they each had shared the brew before speaking.

"It is my thinking it's time to break company."

Dravel's response carried concern. "What do you mean by this?"

"You of all Elves realise my mission is my priority. Accomplishing it, not an option and not open for debate; it weighs heavy on my shoulders, and I am forced to be ruthless in decisions leading to its achieving.

"Dravel, you have proved a worthy companion on this quest, an Elf I can trust, and you can continue with me. I know you follow the same beliefs as I in continuing the futures of our kinds and I am grateful for your counsel, friendship and company.

"However, I can no longer say the same for our two female guests. They deliberately concealed truths from us and thus have shown they cannot be trusted. Once we leave the Plains of Krahor, I decree our journey will be kept secret. Kudra and Sitara will choose their own path to follow."

Dravel's anger was clear. "You will abandon them in the middle of nowhere?"

"Not abandon them, they will simply leave and follow their own path."

"Gatran that is abandoning them, by any stretch of the imagination."

"Difficult times call for difficult choices."

"I have witnessed you make decisions laced with compassion and consideration repeatedly. It's the first time you've ignored those qualities.

"If achieving a successful conclusion to the mission demands a ruthless decision, then know I can make the difficult choices. I need those I can trust by my side. I offered trust at our first meeting and that alone should have invoked a similar response. I believed it had, but since the revelations the Anurans brought, it appears I wasn't trusted. For several moon-cycles prior, distrust was demonstrated."

"We cannot abandon them Gatran, it is not the way of decent Elves."

"I have no choice."

Sitara coughed to clear her throat and interrupted the proceedings. "How dare you discuss future as if those present are not. Kudra is a High Elf Princess and deserves greater respect from subjects."

"Perhaps you are correct Sitara, but I am not her subject." If you were to examine the relationship Dravel and I have, our status is of no importance, only our ultimate aim. The friendship we have forged is a welcome extra I believe neither of us expected, and I'm grateful for it. I hope it will prevail far beyond this mission despite the conclusion."

Sitara snapped back. "So, you have doubts about its conclusion?"

"While I and Dravel are alive the mission will not fail, should we die, it's over for both our species. Remember the complete quest has three parts to it. I have one part; my brother and sister have another each. None of us will fail if we remain alive. I am realistic, understanding the risks to each of us and I'm determined to achieve my goal, as are my brother and sister. Whether you appreciate it, you depend on us for a successful conclusion and a return to your kind."

"You lack respect for the Princess, that is unforgivable."

"No, Sitara, not unforgivable. Respect is earned; what we built, in a short while was disrespected by both you and her. You both carry the weight of responsibility for destroying that."

"How dare..."

"Enough Sitara," Kudra snapped, ending her indignant response, and breaking her lengthy silence. "Gatran is right, not trusting him from the beginning was a mistake. There were opportunities to reveal our true positions, and we decided against it. We have disrespected his trust, and for that, I hope in time he'll be able to forgive us."

"But the reasons, he does not understand the reasons?"

"It is simple, we didn't trust him after he trusted us. Our decisions were flawed. We will leave and follow own path when reaching point Gatran mentioned. I will not fight his decision. I am acutely aware how important the mission is. Not only his kind are at risk of extinction, ours also. The mission wasn't issue for discussion.

"At least we agree on those points Kudra, but they are not the only issues you've kept from us. There is more."

"To what are you referring to, Gatran?"

"I'm talking about your training of white magic."

"So, Dravel remembered the stories."

Dravel answered swiftly. "Being trained by a witch in white magic is no story. You can command it to a higher level than any other High Elf. You were so powerful those above you were concerned you might use it for reasons not beneficial to our kind. You were encouraged to become a trader to remove you from your home world."

"How could you know this? Only my father and Sitara know this."

"It is a simple conclusion to make. You posed a risk to his position. It is not fitting for the King of the High Elves to command when less powerful than his daughter. Am I wrong?"

"No Dravel. I commend you for accuracy of assessment. In all passing sun-cycles, you alone guessed the truth."

"Perhaps I alone sought the truth."

There is merit in that statement, Dravel."

"How powerful was your white magic?" Dravel continued.

"It grew to levels surpassing teachings of witch who instructed. When that happened, she withdrew her services, and we parted company. Then I led the most powerful practitioners of white magic known."

"You said, *then.* What of your magic now?" Gatran interrupted.

"The ability to wield such magic is mine to command, but controlling causes problem. I could accomplish much, but witch aided control. She left, as a precaution. She understood I wouldn't use what was uncontrollable."

"When you stood with Dravel and the other High Elves during the height of battle, did you, or did you not use your powers to assist us?"

"I did not. I couldn't risk it. My release from the dark magic is brief. I have no idea if being held by dark magic has weakened powers."

"Have you tried at all?"

"No."

"Then I suggest a test."

"Like what?"

"I have meat on my horse, which is raw. If you could cook it by magic, we could all eat."

"If you fetch it, I will try, but negative consequence to my actions would not be my fault. I would not attempt without request."

"I can shoulder the responsibility, Kudra."

Gatran fetched a bag of meat and took out the contents. He laid the bag down with the meat on it and gestured for Kudra to begin.

Kudra stretched her arm out towards it and her fingers adopted a claw shape. She uttered a few words, incomprehensible to the others, and a white shroud enveloped the meat. It raised from the ground and rotated and then lowered. The white shroud faded and vanished, and Kudra withdrew her arm.

Gatran touched the meat and instantly recoiled his fingers. "It would appear you've been successful. Have you any negative feelings or after event repercussions to what you've just accomplished?"

"There are none."

"You did well."

"I'm relieved, but a simple task. The power I wield frightens me still."

"After you finished your training with the witch, were you ever able to gain complete control of its use."

"To some extent, but not completely."

Gatran ended the conversation.

"Dravel, let's eat, would you do the honours and cut the meat. Eat well, a distance remains to travel, and at speed, so boost your energy reserves."

Chapter 31:

Sitara took it upon herself to be the group lookout, the following morning. Using the crystal eyeglass, she scanned the region behind, looking for the tell-tale sign of dust from fast moving creatures.

Gatran had already spoken to Dravel about covering them in a protective shroud, when the Anurans finally caught up. Dravel was confident using the shroud for the period his magic might be needed to leave the Plains. He had avoided seeking Kudra's help, remaining unconvinced she could control what she wielded. It was awkward; she was acutely aware his not asking was because he couldn't trust her control.

"It is time Dravel to improve relationships between us and the others."

"I agree. You have a plan?"

"No plan, drop back to Sitara and ask Kudra to join me and then…"

"I understand, it will not be easy."

"It is unfortunate that personal feelings compound the issue, had we been more distant, the task would be less fraught with…"

"Words are not needed, Gatran, I understand both your feelings and predicament. Fortune favours those with courage."

Without another word, he dropped back and slipped into position alongside Sitara. Almost immediately, Kudra quickened her pace to join Gatran.

"You summoned me?"

"I did not, I simply asked you join me to discuss our difficulties."

"This is good, they need discussing."

"I hope we can find a path to bring us both the peace and comfortability we shared before."

"This is pleasing to my ears; I too wish to return to chosen path. Our conversations, exploring the depths of our minds were pleasing, and the familiarity we share with common belief and goals."

"There remains one issue I was more forthcoming with my revelations than you."

"Changing what has passed is impossible, even with white magic, I can change the future through choice and action."

"And what do you offer for the honesty and disclosure I gave you."

"Equal honesty and disclosure in manner I have never shared with a male Elf."

"I'm willing to confine our transgressions to the past, but understand, I offer this once, I'll not forgive a second transgression. I'm a Prince and you a Princess, openness is not confined to one. To guide our subjects forward through difficult times will involve them trusting us. Being open and honest improves the trust."

"You are convinced of path, yet live less than I."

"I lived each of my sun-cycles, if you discount the period spent held by the dark magic, you have lived for a similar period as I."

"That's true, but I believe you misunderstood my point."

"Which was,"

"Your confidence in self, and capabilities are of no threat to me, it is positive. I admire this."

"I can understand why you didn't reveal your ability with white magic and your reservations about controlling it. The insecurity to your kind is not needed now, but I'm not your kind, making our time together different and unique. It should have allowed trust with me."

"I wanted to, believe me. White magic is a strength and weakness, both threatens others."

"Explain please."

"That I can use magic to great extent means my power is stronger than my Kings, a potential threat for destabilising the hierarchy. Not controlling it adequately, also threatens, not only to hierarchy but to all kinds. It is shameful that I cannot control it, my failing."

"When you have skills in doing something beyond the ability of others, it cannot be deemed a failing. That you cannot control it is evidence you have not practiced enough, also not a failing."

"You have a way of alleviating the pain I shoulder, but you understand the importance of stability between our kinds, especially if our kinds share future."

"If you listened close to the words we've shared, ask yourself if I've ever given you cause to doubt my honesty. Ask yourself if I have ever demeaned the areas you are more adept at than I. And ask yourself, have I not celebrated all of your accomplishments respectfully."

"You speak true, there is one area you are stronger than I, how you shoulder burdens. You do not fear them, at least not openly, and you treat each issue with respect and determination where I... I do fear mine; the weight inspires defensive approach. It is something I wish to change, and I have observed you to learn achievement."

"If this is so, then listen to my words with care, Kudra. I am strong, but so are you. There are times I doubt my abilities to achieve a goal, as you do. Together we can share issues and resolve a strength in one another when it weakens. We are stronger for this. Your self-described weakness could be seen as a strength since the power you wield is given respect before you use it, you consider it carefully, is this not so?"

"I am believing you have magic of your own. The ability to view negatives as positive. Changing consideration requires training of mind. I should practise magic, learn to control effectively, but confidence take time to nurture. Can you be patient with me Gatran."

"Before I answer, I have a last question to ask. Is there anything else you have not revealed that could cause issue when it becomes known?"

"Only one. I fear I cannot return to my kind. My presence alters positions of society. I would not be greeted favourably. I do not fear losing my position when returning home."

"When we return, everything will be different. You may be granted a place of position."

"There is nothing else. While I concealed part of the truth, I have never said untruths. What we have discussed and shared is real and honest. I desire this and wish to move forward with you."

"Then, this matter is confined to the past, a learning step. No uncertainty of trust exists from this day forward, and the burden of our journey is shared between us."

"There is one question I have for you also."

"Which is?"

"From this day forward can we return to comfortable nature of proximity. I have not shared this with another and experience loneliness despite companionship Sitara provides." Kudra moved subtly closer and placed her hand in his. "Have you missed this also?" she asked coyly.

Gatran looked into her eyes. "More than I can explain."

He gripped her hand.

A while later Sitara raised an alarm. She saw dust a few miles behind them.

"The Anurans come."

The group closed together.

"They're short-sighted, so there's time, but their heightened sense of smell is a problem. I'm hoping the invisible barrier will mask that, Dravel."

"It will Gatran. We need to remain as close together as possible, the smaller the barrier, the longer I can maintain it."

"How long can you offer this security, my friend?"

"Possibly to the mid-afternoon, but no longer. I do not wish to over-stretch my strength in case it is needed again."

"If the Anurans pass and then return?"

"Yes, it may not be today, but restoring my energy to its full potential takes longer than a day. The barrier is invisible, we'll be standing close by and view them as if no shield was present. I ask as soon as they are beyond our vision, we collapse the barrier."

"I will not ask you hold it for longer than necessary."

The Anurans were on a course parallel to theirs and would pass by closely, but Gatran took no chances, instructing Dravel to raise it while they were distant. He uttered the words in the same tongue as Kudra had used when cooking the meat.

"Can they hear us if we converse."

"No sound passes through the shield."

"When you formed a barrier during the battle at the Ominic Sea your concentration was total and yet here you can talk while commanding the magic."

"The power I wield is less here than before."

"Do you have control over every extent of the magic you use?"

"I have practised control for most of my life, no power I command is beyond it."

"Could you teach this control to another?"

"To my level, but beyond, the individual must learn this themselves."

"Could you help Kudra with this?"

"If Kudra is open to this I would be honoured to help."

"Kudra, what do you say to this?"

"Gatran, I must ask you not speak for me. I had asked Dravel to help. For our kind, it is viewed an honour for a Princess to ask another Elf for guidance and now I cannot bestow honour on him."

"Gatran speaks his mind always, Kudra. That you considered asking is honour enough."

"Now you're speaking for me Dravel. Our situation suggests we all speak for each of us, it is unavoidable. Us against the odds, and therefore necessary to act and speak as one. Please forgive my indiscretions, but know this way of acting is necessary."

"I wonder, Dravel, if you could instruct Gatran in the art of white magic, since he has no expertise in this area, despite knowing Wood Elves are capable?"

Dravel laughed. "We are about to be visited by Anurans and you express humour at Gatran's expense."

"Merely raising a point about speaking for others."

Gatran grinned. "Your point is noted Kudra, as I hope mine was."

They slipped into silence as the Anurans passed by. The army was several hundred strong and moved at an incredible pace. The shield was masked in dust, and they lost vison until it settled. The Anuran army faded into the horizon.

When the distant dust cloud dispersed, Gatran gave the order to lower the shield.

"Your reserves Dravel?"

"I feel no weakness, the shield was maintained for a short while only."

"Good. Now we keep moving, focus ahead, for if the army return, they'll come towards us. I would prefer travelling in manner accustomed to side by side."

They jostled into position and walked forward.

Chapter 32:

The following day they travelled uninterrupted, but the inevitable return of the Anuran army kept them vigilant. They took turns in monitoring the distant horizon and Sitara alerted them to a moving dust cloud which could only be their enemy. Dravel readied himself to form the invisible shield, waiting for as long as possible before raising it. This close to dusk, it was feasible the Anuran army would set up camp close by, even in the darkness Gatran knew they would smell their presence without the shield.

Under the shield, Gatran questioned his friend.

"I'm worried Dravel, worried they will make camp close by, can you maintain the shield through the night?"

"I'm unsure, certainly for most of it, but that will leave my powers severely depleted."

"What if we walk while shielded?"

"I can hold it for, half the dark hours possible."

"What we don't know is the true extent of their sense of smell. We know it is extraordinary, but to what degree is unknown. If they camp close, we'll be forced to leave before night has passed. Even as we speak, the skies darken."

They ceased talking as the Anuran army started to file by. Gatran watched them move away from their position, knowing there was insufficient light remaining for them to travel much further. Before the leading ranks had disappeared, the worst happened, they stopped. Gatran muttered something under his breath.

The rear guard took a while longer before stopping. Moving closer to their forward lines, they stopped closer to the Elves than was comfortable.

Gatran knew they couldn't remain for the night in their present position. Discovery at first light was imminent.

"Now is the time for ideas, everyone, Gatran whispered quietly.

"Sound will not pass through the shield, my friend," Dravel muttered. "My suggestion is to move now while the shield is at full strength."

"Kudra, Sitara, your views?"

"I'm with Dravel," Sitara offered. "I want distance between us and pig-faced monsters."

Gatran registered surprise at her depth of dislike.

"Have you encountered them before, Sitara?"

"No, Gatran, stories of how they treat enemies reached ears. They rip the limbs from the torso before decapitation."

"Sharing your knowledge is appreciated, Sitara, but not exactly an image I want to retain in my mind."

"If caught, our demise would mirror learning. We escaped, sending their number to death."

They are not aware of that. The bodies were consumed by the sand. While we are missing, for all they know we experienced the same fate."

"If sands move as suspected, bodies may yet reveal."

"It's possible, but an Anuran from the Undulations would travel to inform the army. We have seen no messenger. Your thoughts are welcome Sitara, please continue to share them at your convenience. Our current situation is perilous, quick thinking offers options that could increase our safety."

Sitara nodded her appreciation for Gatran's comments, as he turned to Kudra.

"Your thoughts, Kudra."

"Thoughts echo Sitara, stories of victims unpleasant. Captured alive is to suffer horrible death."

"Any thoughts on tactics?"

"Move immediately under security of shield until beyond sight of army."

"Two hours' travel would be sufficient, a third for extra peace of mind."

"After lowering shield, I suggest keep moving under cover of darkness. Rest during daylight and alternate watch."

"Your plan is good, Kudra. Dravel, are you in agreement?"

"It will draw less than I expected from my reserves and shorten the recovery period."

"Sitara?"

"This is the correct plan to follow."

"Right, let's go."

For three hours, they moved under the cover of the shield. Light from Anuran camp fires vanished and the night sky failed to betray a glow from them. Even after Dravel lowered their protection they continued travelling their easterly course. During the pre-dawn light, after a complete day and night of walking, Gatran finally called a halt.

The landscape remained featureless, offering nothing to disguise their presence. Grasses were long, sufficient to conceal them when laying down. Gatran assumed first watch; the others settled quickly into a well-earned sleep. As a seasoned soldier, Gatran decided to keep watch until midday. Knowing he had endured longer periods without sleep, he could rest instantly when the opportunity arrived. Most soldiers could.

His main concern was to rest Dravel. Who knew how many times he would call upon the High Elf to perform his white magic. He decided to test Kudra's abilities when the opportunity arrived. Small steps, allowed her to gain confidence. He was sure he would ask for her assistance before this mission was completed; he did not need her doubting herself.

Gatran kept watch diligently until an hour from midday, when he felt his eyes closing. Immediately he stood, shocked he had come so close to succumbing to the needs of his body. He rubbed his eyes, staring down at the serene face of Kudra and feeling the longing to lie alongside her and inhale the scent of her hair. He sat down again, close to her, pondering the ease he experienced; his desire to seek her presence and discuss issues at depth; how fleeting moments alone with her were treasured, revealing an unexpected peace. His eyes closed at the pleasure of his thoughts.

All too soon, he was woken by something manhandling him. As he forced his eyes open, he distinguished the shape and form of an Anuran. A lance poked at his throat, warning against any defensive move. A second Anuran secured his hands, tying them tight enough to stem the flow of blood and turn the tips of his fingers blue. Dravel fell victim to identical treatment before the females.

Gatran saw two Anurans, likely a forward reconnaissance pair, resting for the night. Neither made any attempt to communicate. Instead, one by one they tethered their prisoners to a single length of rope, two strides apart from each other. The Elves followed one Anuran, who led them in the opposite direction of the night. Lances prodded them forward and a second Anuran took the rear position.

"What happened, Gatran?"

"I'm in shame, Dravel. I succumbed to the weakness of my body and fell asleep."

"There is no shame, my friend. Each of us carry the risk of making errors in judgement. Of all of us, you have shouldered the responsibility for our safety and achieved it with respect and consideration. No Elf could have done more. I suspect the sleep required by your mind outweighed the rest your body needed. It is no surprise and no shame."

"Your words are kind, but shame is what I feel. There is another problem. They have tied my hands too tightly; the circulation has ceased. Already there is no feeling."

Dravel spoke to Kudra, and she whispered an instruction to Gatran.

"I have power to turn these ropes to dust if required, but risk turning something else to dust. The Anurans would cut us down before we could mount a challenge especially as you have lost feelings in your hands. Instead, I'll attempt to loosen the ropes sufficiently for the circulation to return. It's painful, Gatran, and carries the risk I might damage to you."

"Don't hesitate, losing hands is unacceptable."

Kudra started to chant in that strange tongue used before, and Gatran felt the ropes loosen.

"It worked, Kudra."

The first wave of pain gripped like a predatory cat's jaws. He gasped but refrained from crying out in pain.

"Now we have established your capability. I'll ask you again Kudra to release us all when the time is ready."

"A plan in mind?"

"Yes. We'll force a stop for water as soon as the sun starts its decline. Harming us would be a disadvantage, since we would bolster their army. When we stop Kudra can use her magic to unfetter us and we'll attack them. They will not expect it, but surprise is the key, they have weapons, and we don't. Dravel, you and Kudra have the forward positions, so you attack the point guard. Sitara and I will attack the rear. Everyone clear?"

"We are clear and ready," Dravel answered.

"The weight of responsibility weighs my magic."

"I know Kudra, but Dravel lacks this ability, you've proven yours. Loosen them so we can slip them off discretely when ready. Nobody attacks unless we're all unfettered."

"Sharing confidence in my magic is a dream, unlike your confidence in me."

"Kudra, if I doubted your, I'd not make the request."

Kudra fell silent, trying to steel her nerve while Gatran kept a squinted eye on the sun's position, waiting for it to pass its zenith.

"Prepare yourself, the time has arrived." Gatran warned.

Chapter 33:

"Follow my lead. When the ropes are loosened, release your hands, but make it appear otherwise. On my command, we'll stop moving. When the guards close in, we attack. Close quarter fighting only. They are large and fast-moving, but up close their manoeuvrability will be restricted. Their eyesight is a weakness, so attack them."

"You seek to attack their eyes?"

"Kudra, when we attack, they will attempt killing! Blinding them with fingers, shows preference against," Sitara warned.

"I never considered you blood-thirsty, Sitara."

"My life is risked, I'll fight. When threatening Kudra, I'll fight harder, Gatran."

"I'm pretty sure they won't expect us to attack, they hold all the advantages, size and weapons, but our advantage is surprise. Kudra, now is the time."

Kudra chanted her magic and each of them felt the ropes loosen. Gatran checked each of them were free before ordering the stop.

The two Anurans immediately conversed in their own tongue before pointing their lances at their prisoners and closing in. Dravel and Kudra turned to face the Anuran, closing in on them while Gatran and Sitara faced theirs. Gatran allowed them to close right in until their lances pointed to his and Dravel's chests. They said something in their own language and pointed forward. Gatran responded similarly.

"I know you can't understand a single word I'm saying, but if you think we're going another step with you, you're mistaken."

He indicated with arm movements, pointing forward and then backwards, but continued talking in a calm and unthreatening manner. The guards showed confusion for the first time, and then Gatran gave the order.

"On my command. Now."

Gatran moved fast, knocking the lance to the side before reaching out and grabbing the Anurans sword. On his first slash, he cut through the wooden shaft of the lance and the blade fell to the ground. The Anuran responded immediately, reaching for Gatran's sword arm. He gripped tightly, and Gatran could not break it free. The Anuran pulled Gatran closer, and he was powerless against the strength. A thick arm circled his neck, and he reacted instantly. He jabbed his thumb into the dark, emotionless eye and pushed against the eyeball. The Anuran screamed a protest but clung to Gatran tightly. Gatran released the pressure and jabbed the other eye, repeating the pressure. He was gasping for breath, but the Anuran still gripped.

The Anuran stiffened abruptly, and the grip on Gatran lessened. He wrenched himself free and pulled back. The broken lance had travelled through the depth of the Anurans chest. It protruded, a hand's width towards where Gatran was being held prior to his release. Sitara stood behind the Anuran, holding the broken end of the lance until the creature fell to the ground dead.

Gatran turned to check on Kudra and Dravel's progress. Kudra was lying prone a short distance away. Dravel was on the ground, with the Anuran sitting astride him. The lance was positioned across his neck, and the creature was applying an increasing amount of pressure.

Gatran could see Dravel was weakening and moved towards him, but he was slower now, weakened from almost being suffocated to death.

Sitara rushed by him and threw herself at the Anuran, knocking him off Dravel. The Anuran reacted instantly, jumping to his feet and turning on Sitara. She stared the Anuran down, daring him to attack, but Dravel and Gatran were both moving in and effectively surrounding him. The Anuran swung his lance, in full circles keeping them at bay. It prevented him from attacking; briefly, they were at impasse. But Kudra's voice broke through the swishing sound of the circling lance.

The familiar chanting Gatran associated with Dravel's magic started reaching his ears. She was focussed, almost in a trance-like situation as she increased the speed and volume of her chanting.

The Anuran cried out in sudden pain, dropping his lance he clutched his throat. He fell to the ground and then a crack and he lay still. Gatran knew the sound of a neck snapping and knew the creature was dead.

"Is everyone all right, any injuries?" Gatran asked.

Dravel spoke with a rasping voice. "Bruised throat."

"I'll suffer from the same Dravel, seems it's their favourite killing tactic."

"Kudra?"

"Bruising, nothing more."

"And you Sitara?"

"I have escaped injury."

"You saved my life Sitara; you are fearless and I'm content to fight with you at my side."

"As am I, Sitara. Your timely intervention, in relieving me from that animal, saved my life too," Dravel added.

"And you Kudra, you used your magic to end this battle. You controlled and applied it without issue."

"I did, but I'm saddened to use for violent cause."

"If you consider the mission, it remains possible because of your actions, it was justifiable."

My motives were protecting those I hold dear.

"We are grateful for this, and know we would do similarly to protect you."

"It's time to leave. When the rear guard does not return to the army, I suspect Gorga will send a group to search for them. They will certainly travel this way. We'll head north for a distance before turning east. Hopefully, this is sufficient to avoid further contact."

"I suggest travelling during darkness, but not for duration."

"I agree, Sitara."

They fell silent as they walked. Kudra slipped in alongside Gatran and reached for his hand.

"Encouraging words are appreciated. Always this, despite the circumstances, I'm pleased to travel with you Gatran, and to assist history in the making."

"I'm blessed to be travelling with each of you, Kudra. The friendships we forge on this mission can only enhance the joining of our two kinds. The three missions are equally important. Without this, we are doomed to extinction. There is a selfish note for my contentment in having you by my side; unconnected to the mission."

"I am understanding and share feelings. Rest your throat, swelling is visible already; losing your voice raises further problems. I am with comfort, hearing your breath while falling asleep."

"I will rest it as you suggest, he said, staring into the depths of her eyes.

She met the gaze and held it,

Behind them, Dravel and Sitara were deep in conversation.

"Thoughts say I was too late to save life when filthy beast tried to end your breathing. I experienced sense of loss before losing."

"Your timing was perfect, Sitara. That I'm breathing is proof of that. I was in a difficult situation. Fighting alongside Kudra meant I could not witness your plight, and I was uneasy with this. For future battles, I would prefer to fight alongside you. If my fate is to die, I desire your face to be the last image I leave earth with."

"Your fate is not connected with death, Dravel. I believe true because of role required. You will negotiate peace with Dwarves. You already saved many lives in protecting us with magic. I wish also to fight by your side, and I'll mention this to Gatran."

"You must not give him reasons of concern, especially as this could be deemed as selfish from our perspectives."

"This is not suggested issue. Kudra would prefer to fight alongside Gatran, as I you. As team we fight together, but when need for smaller teams, we split to strengths."

"You are determined to speak on this?"

"I am, tonight, at rest. I will suggest he is excused from watch. He barely sleeps. Our leader needs to be fresh and alert. There is distance to travel before leaving Plains in past and what lies ahead remains unknown."

"I will back your support for him; you're right. The Elf differs from us, he views differently, he wants to rule differently, and I agree with him. His ways offer both our kinds opportunities to merge with peace, and contentment. Each member is valued, regardless of status, his ideas are refreshing."

"If throat becomes restricted, I have herbs to reduce the swelling."

"I might have need of them."

"I will mix them in tea when we rest.

185

Chapter 34:

Sitara raised the issues with Gatran as they ate their evening meal. Her comments were accepted graciously, fully understanding her sentiments.

"You're right Sitara, when you fight alongside a person who is special to you, you fight harder. I agree with your proposal. Despite being a leader, I'm an Elf. I feel emotions, worries and concerns as you. It's difficult to raise these issues because I'm supposed to be impartial. Despite attempting to action this neutrality, I worry about Kudra as you Dravel. It's the simple truth."

"There is another issue to raise, Gatran."

"Speak your mind, Sitara. I'm comfortable with the directness of your communication."

"I and Dravel believe standing watch tonight will not assist. You have scarcely slept for two days; we understand Wood Elves require more rest than us. We believe, as leader, you should retain fullness of mind so decisions that follow thoughts are wise and purposeful."

Gatran shifted forward. "Do you doubt my ability to lead when I'm tired?"

"I carry no doubts about your ability to lead Gatran, none! However, decisions consume time when tired, delays cause further issues. Like earlier."

"Our capture this morning was my fault, it cannot be denied. I have regret for my failings."

"I'm not affording blame. An unfortunate side effect of previous days. We should prevent possibility of repeat. It could happen to any of us. We understand this."

"Dravel, you agree with this?"

"I do, you must rest tonight."

"And you Kudra?"

"I was unaware of their conversation, but thank Sitara and Dravel for speaking concerns. They are correct in matter; Dravel needs similar concessions after using magic. Each require ability to think and act quickly with forthcoming difficulties. You should rest uninterrupted. There remains three, sharing the night watch and we'll not assume the responsibilities beyond equal share."

"Like I did?"

"Yes. Motives were considerate, but an error of judgement made."

"I'm not above listening to the advice and concerns of those I fight alongside. This you understand. I'm content with your reasons and will rest as you suggest. I'm grateful for your consideration, and for forgiving my failings."

Gatran rose and walked from the group. He sat alone a short distance away. The High Elves respected his need for time alone and instead conversed in their own tongues. Although similar, their individual languages contained differences. Both kinds were taught variances, so communication between High and Wood Elves was never an issue. They always retreated to their own tongues with their own kind.

A while later Kudra walked to him and sat beside.

"If you wish to remain alone, say, otherwise I would enjoy company."

"I sought time to think only."

"About?"

"Mostly, what comes next. We should leave the Plains by dark the day after tomorrow. It is not the best time. The land between the Plains and the Karvil Marshlands is narrow. Beings from both invade it."

"If so, remaining on the plains until morning lessens risk. We could travel further north while here."

"I have considered this. There is equal risk in both. I will raise the question with Dravel and Sitara."

"You continue to involve us in decision making."

"They are wise and considerate: I'd be foolish to ignore what is offered."

"Nobody would consider you foolish if decided alone."

"The trust between you and me is as a rock; the same between Dravel and I, but I sense more is required to gain Sitara's."

"And why is the need strong?"

"Because I journey with her. My army has faith in me and I'm accustomed to this. I'm a better Elf for not taking this trust for granted."

"You are correct, she trusts you but not as Dravel and I. Time will allow adjustment towards this."

"I seek to be worthy of her trust. She saved my life today and Dravel's."

"Be patient. Don't force the issue. It will happen. Now rest. I wish to gaze upon your face before I sleep."

Gatran smiled, leant forward, and gently kissed her lips. She gasped in surprise, but did not pull away.

"I had no expectation of that."

"An impulsive, and necessary indulgence."

"Why."

"I'm telling you my feelings without words."

Kudra laughed, "and I believed it simply a kiss."

The following morning, Gatran posed the question before they moved out and it was agreed to remain on the plains and avoid the area of uncertainty.

Gatran was pleased, it was the decision he would have made without their involvement. Again, Sitara was vocal with her thoughts, displaying a confidence previously concealed.

Shortly before midday, Dravel spotted dust clouds to the south of their position. He called to Gatran, asking him to stop briefly, and he and Kudra walked back to join him.

"What is it, Dravel?"

"Dust cloud to the south."

He offered the eyeglass to Gatran who focussed on the horizon Dravel pointed to.

"I see it, they travel east to west, indicating they journey home, if Anurans."

"That was my interpretation. I'll watch them closely while they're in view, but the speed at which they travel will soon disguise their presence."

"If they've spotted us or picked up our trail, they will be forced to change direction, heading north towards us. If so, they'd remain a distance away before changing course, to ensure they were not seen, then travel at speed beyond our position and cut us off."

"You suspect a trap?"

"They cannot know we can see through a crystal eyeglass, as we cannot know if they have discovered our trail."

"A change of route avoiding possible contact?"

"Yes, it would be wise if we head east and leave the Plains sooner. There will be numerous places to conceal ourselves from them."

"We've discussed the risks associated with the land between Plains and Marshes."

"Yes, but the risk here is greater. Avoiding it is possible by using white magic."

"This is true, Dravel, but it weakens those who use it. I need your capabilities at a moment's notice. We don't know what we'll face. If we can avoid using the magic, you'll have full use of your powers if required."

"I'm not alone with the ability of white magic."

"I understand, but the same reason applies to each of you. The Trolls are formidable opponents, their senses are beyond other creatures. I'm convinced we'll not pass without encountering them."

Dravel nodded thoughtfully and Gatran waited for the females to offer their thoughts. When they did not contribute, he sought to engage them.

"Sitara, you've been forward in sharing your thoughts and ideas, I was hoping you'd continue with this."

"The discussion with Dravel has already included my considerations, I have nothing further to add."

"Except your thoughts of our intentions."

"I agree, it's why I remained silent."

Gatran nodded, "And you Kudra?"

"Sitara shared my thoughts and her own."

"It is agreed then."

The dust cloud disappeared beyond visible range and Gatran changed direction and head east.

Chapter 35:

As darkness fell, there were no further signs of the Anurans. Gatran called a temporary halt.

"What are your thoughts on travelling further under darkness, Dravel?"

"It will put greater distance between us and the Anurans, if they are on our trail. They will not travel at night, I'm sure."

Kudra and Sitara voiced their agreement, and they continued eastward until midnight. With only six hours of darkness remaining, the three High Elves took a two-hour watch each allowing Gatran to finally get the rest he needed.

Kudra woke him just before dawn and he sat with her as the sun blessed the world with a crimson arc, promising a fine day ahead.

With the light increasing every second, he scoured the landscape with the crystal eyeglass, searching for the tell-tale signs of the Anurans. He noticed a change of scenery to the east; they had travelled further than expected. He passed the eyeglass to Kudra.

"We leave the Plains after midday," she stated with certainty.

"I'll not be sorry; a change of scenery will break the monotony of the journey."

"Brings a fresh set of dangers. The Anurans won't appreciate losing us and will venture beyond the plains to recapture us. Creatures from the swamps will also become a risk."

"Perhaps our enemies will encounter each other, allowing us to pass unnoticed."

Gatran smiled. "I like that sense of optimism."

Dravel woke Sitara, and they moved alongside. Gatran shared the conclusions he and Kudra had drawn.

"It's an area I have not journeyed through, Gatran. What is it like? Dravel asked.

"It has a variety of different regions: there are patches of light, deep sand which makes travel slow and ponderous. Areas of loose scree also pervade, treacherous underfoot and the risk of injury is increased. Also, there are patches of swamps, not particularly dangerous, but it slows progress through the region. The region undulates with hills and valleys."

"What distance lies between the Plains and the swamps?"

"A single day's travel only. We are at risk for the duration of our stay.

"Are you aware of safe passage through region?" Sitara asked.

"The creatures from the swamps dislike the scree areas and the higher ground. The Anurans will avoid the swamps and the sandy areas."

"It doesn't leave chance of avoiding," Kudra intoned.

"Perhaps not but opting for the higher regions gives advantages of viewing our surroundings and is easier to defend."

"Defend with what? We have only a few Anuran weapons."

"And white magic, Sitara. And speaking of the magic, I am unfamiliar with your capability using it."

"My abilities are like Dravel's, matching power, but have a wider range of use, thanks to Kudra's teachings."

"And you, Gatran, you are royalty, you have received training, are with ability?"

"It's an area I have no ability. I received training, but to little avail. I can scarcely make myself invisible, Sitara. As a result, my training was suspended when I was young, focus turned to becoming a soldier."

"Admitting a failing is difficult, Gatran. I appreciate your candid nature."

Dravel had picked up the eyeglass and was checking the horizon.

"There is a dust cloud to the south-west of us and it's heading north. It must be the Anurans."

"Time to leave, travel as far as possible before becoming visible to them."

Once more they travelled east, at a faster pace than before.

By mid-morning, it was clear the Anurans had discovered their scent. They altered direction and were closing in on the Elves. The distant hills loomed in front, but seemed tantalisingly out of reach.

"The Anurans will catch us before we reach the hills," Dravel warned.

"What if we run,"

"I fear we'll not be swift enough, Gatran."

"We still have one horse. Kudra and Sitara could ride ahead of us. They will reach the hills before the Anurans arrive, secure a hiding place, and conceal themselves with invisibility."

"We should stay together," Sitara snapped.

"They outnumber us regardless; risking all being captured is pointless. We have the same opportunity to veil ourselves with invisibility. Even if they stumbled upon one pairing, the other might avoid capture."

"The Anurans wanted Kudra badly enough to stop them hurting any of us. Although that's certainly changed, they still want her."

"For what purpose?" Kudra joined the conversation.

Dravel answered. "I suspect for ransom or bartering. Unless they're aware of your white magic capability, a possibility I never considered before."

"More reason to adopt my strategy then," Gatran said firmly. "As leader, I realise agreement on this is impossible, so the decision is mine alone. Kudra and Sitara will ride away from us and hide in the hills."

"I don't believe it is the right decision," Sitara snapped angrily. "We have decided strategies as a group since separated from the army."

"Save your anger, Sitara. Use it to defend Kudra if necessary. Make no further argument, the strategy is correct, leave now."

"But..."

Kudra stopped her abruptly. "No buts, Sitara. Gatran leads and we obey his decision. The time to act is now. Stay your objections."

Gatran caught her eyes and nodded his appreciation.

She leapt upon the horse and indicated for Sitara to follow. She didn't hesitate. Although she had learned to question Gatran's decisions her obedience to Kudra was absolute. Kudra turned away from Dravel and Gatran and rode. Dravel and Gatran watched them disappear.

"You ready to run, Dravel?"

"I do not have favourable thoughts about being captured. Our demise would be almost certain."

"Just before they're in range to see us, we'll use the white magic for invisibility."

"It's the only strategy left, my friend.

Chapter 36:

Kudra and Sitara rode swiftly, reaching the hilly area faster than expected. Kudra steered the horse up the slope of the first hill. Not particularly steep or high, it was sufficient to gain the advantage of seeing further than at ground level. Finding a shallow depression, she and Sitara dismounted.

"We should ride further into hills," Sitara intoned.

"Gatran and Dravel may need help, I want to remain close to offer if need arises."

"Dravel is capable."

"True, but everything that challenges, everything since awakening has been unexpected."

"You don't owe Gatran or Dravel anything."

"It's not about owing, it's believing in the mission, securing our future, the future of Elves."

"They won't accept you, Kudra, this you know. Your presence upsets balance, reduce those with power to lesser position. They won't accept you."

"It is possible, on return, I no longer seek to regain the position once held."

"You would give it up, for what reason?"

"Plenty of reasons justify. A life without position offers freedom never experienced."

"You forget dreams of reforming High Elf society?"

"No, Sitara, but reform is inevitable, surely you see co-existing with Wood Elves promises change and foresight. Beyond experiences, and discussions, before falling foul to black magic."

"We will lose purpose."

"Perhaps good. We have opportunity for fresh start and... freedom."

"Why is freedom inviting now, you've never sought it before?"

"We had no option."

"Has Gatran contributed to these thoughts?"

"Not as you might suspect. He has unique way of simplifying and thinking long term. Even those abilities have not swayed thoughts. His belief in a future of promise, his passion? I wondered if I could share passion."

"And do you?"

"Yes, for same future. A society where all Elven voices counts, no matter status. A society where all Elves contribute according to talents, and each deemed worthy and appreciated. Examine Gatran's way with army, his kind revere him. He does not dominate with power."

"And after choosing, what becomes of service to you I'm accustomed to give."

"This worry is irrelevant, Sitara. You have same freedom to choose, my equal, make choices to suit you. Does this not tempt?"

Sitara fell silent briefly, considering Kudra's words before answering.

"Change scares me beyond you. It is difficult."

"Everything will change, you'll have choices unknown before. Embrace and consider. Change will happen. First, many obstacles remain to pass. We'll discuss this more, together, but now watch for Gatran and Dravel."

They surveyed the Plains with consummate patience, and it was just before noon when the running figures of Dravel and Gatran reached their vision.

"They're almost here," Sitara commented.

"Yes, but Anurans are close behind. Too close, they'll cut progress before reaching."

As she spoke, Dravel and Gatran disappeared.

"They are veiled. It's a relief; they should avoid capture. Dravel's magic is strong, the shield lasts for long periods."

They continued watching, surprised when the Anurans passed Gatran's position and stopped abruptly.

"Why have they stopped," Sitara asked confused.

"They've lost scent and are disorientated."

Kudra studied the army of Anurans, noticing fewer than their previous encounter. Many fewer, possibly less than half, and she wondered why. Movement amongst them suggested something was happening; a few seconds later they split. Half stayed close to Dravel's invisible shield, while the remainder head straight for Kudra's position.

"They have picked up scent while losing Gatran's. There is confusion that explains splitting."

"Do they know your capability for magic?"

"I'm sure Gorga does. He remembers many sun-cycles ago, when magic capabilities were known and feared."

"He'll suspect our proximity."

"But will he remain or continue forward?"

"For now, we're trapped."

"Trapped but secure. It is time to veil us."

Kudra chanted the strange language and the surrounding shield was formed. From their perspective, the shield was invisible, but not to their enemies.

Half the Anuran army rode towards them, passing a short distance south. They did not travel far before stopping.

"They know proximity of presence, Kudra."

"They suspect because of disappearing scent. How long will they stay, I wonder?

"We could move under shield?"

"Perhaps, but our scent would be left behind, strong and fresh. They would notice and follow."

Both halves of the Anuran army showed no signs of moving on, remaining at their positions for the afternoon. As darkness encompassed, they relaxed for the night. Kudra suggested Sitara rested, she was not required for the shield. Kudra could not sleep and hold the shield but knew she could hold it for at least three days before requiring sleep herself.

Chapter 37:

Gatran and Dravel settled at a jogging pace, more suited to Gatran than the longer-legged Dravel. They travelled silently, reserving every ounce of energy they could. Dravel checked the Anuran position frequently until he announced they were almost close enough to see them. Gatran decided to stop and Dravel raised the shield of invisibility around them.

They both turned to watch for the imminent arrival, hoping the Anurans would travel past and disappear into the distance. Gatran guessed it would be unlikely. The Anurans knew they were close, and that Elves hid using magic. If he were Gorga, stopping and waiting was the correct strategy, knowing the shield was not permanent. The question was how desperate Gorga was to capture them.

The army passed a short distance to the south before stopping. All among them were attempting to gain the Elven scent. Each Anuran looked downward and extended their necks forward. Several spoke, an unusual clicking-dominated language. The Elves only suspected what was said. Then the army split. One half travelled further east towards Kudra and Sitara's position while the other made camp where they stood. It was only just past midday, so Gatran's fears were realised. They knew he was close and would wait it out.

He watched Gorga patrol his camp, stopping and speaking to some of his soldiers, much as Gatran would have done with his army.

"They're staying, Dravel. We should remain until midnight. Can you maintain the shield?"

"I can, but I've no idea how far I can travel with it over us. It's not something I've attempted before."

"We will learn the hard way. With luck we might reach the hills without them realising we've gone."

"I hope Sitara and Kudra are concealed."

"I'm confident they are, but expect they face a similar problem. The Anuran army are camped close, waiting for the magic to fail."

"Kudra's magic far exceeds my own. I suspect she could hold the shield for many moon cycles, longer than they would be prepared to wait."

"If they give up waiting, they'll return to the others here, compounding the danger to us."

"We'll deal with that if it happens."

They fell silent again, watching the sun gradually lower in the sky. It turned crimson and kissing the hills in the distance before disappearing behind them.

The Anuran army lit fires and Gatran wondered what fuel they burned since there was little wood on the plains. Still, they waited, the army slightly too distant to see if they rested in the darkness. Then they made their move.

Dravel chanted something and started walking. Gatran followed but constantly turned to watch for movement behind, signifying the Anurans were on to them.

They walked until the predawn light started spreading across the sky and finally Dravel stopped. The light brightened further, and they realised the plains were behind them. The ground had changed little, and they failed to notice during the night.

"How is your strength, Dravel?"

"The move has reduced the time I can hold the shield for. I estimate during darkness tonight it will fail."

"Excellent, my friend, you've given us a chance."

"We'll see what the army does soon. Will it remain or follow our path?"

"You said before they cannot smell us while veiled."

"I'm unsure if scent remains after moving."

"How far do you believe Kudra and Sitara will have travelled?"

"If I were them, I would stop at the first hill. The visibility it offers, and both halves of the army. It's an advantageous position."

"I agree, which means we have narrowed the gap between significantly."

"Gatran, you should take advantage of our situation and rest. I'll wake you if there are developments with the Anuran army."

"Rest will have to wait; the army moves."

Dravel turned to face them and watched. They head directly towards them, covering the ground several times faster than they had. The gap closed rapidly, and they passed by a short distance to the south.

"They've definitely picked up our scent, Gatran. The reason for them passing south is that the breeze distorted the origin. Without it, they would know our position."

The army continued on before stopping a similar distance away from them as before. They were forced to remain where they were.

"They're staying Dravel."

"That is bad fortune. I am weakening beyond what I expected and cannot retain the shield until darkness. We are too close to run and our capture is imminent."

"What about mind connection, Dravel? Could you connect with Kudra from here?"

"Alas, she could connect with me, but my powers are insignificant by comparison."

"In that case, I'm thinking we should lower our shield now."

"But why?"

"Kudra might see us and realise we need help."

"There is no guarantee."

"I know, but if I announce my identity, we might escape harm from the Anuran's."

"That's optimistic."

"I have an alternative, but you'd deter me from it."

"What is it."

"You'll have to wait and see. It's time to drop the shield. If we fight, you'll have some energy remaining. Leaving it for the duration, you won't mount much defence."

Dravel lowered the shield and instantly the Anurans picked up their scent. They moved in, surrounding Dravel and Gatran. Gorga moved to the front position and faced them.

"You have eluded me, commendable. Escaping the guard, also commendable. What was their fate?"

"They were consumed by sand at the Undulations. We saw your city, and the ground moved beneath us. We were raised and your guard lowered simultaneously. The sand swallowed them, leaving us on the outermost peak. We simply walked away."

"They were careless, they should know the timings of the movements. It happens occasionally and will happen again."

"So here we are again. The leader of the Anuran army and a Prince of the Wood Elves."

"You are a Prince?"

"I am. Everything we told you before is true except I withheld my position."

"A wise move. Your position dictates I offer you a choice of fates. That you escaped us once discounts the opportunity to remain alive and fight in my army. It also carries the death sentence, but how you die is a choice I'm able to grant an Elf with position. Your choices are simply to be beheaded or fight to the death."

"I have something else in mind. I could fight you for my freedom. I win, Dravel and I leave unharmed. You win, we die."

"That is not an option."

"Do I sense fear, Gorga."

The Anuran's eyes bulged at the insult.

"No fear exists in an Anuran soldier. What you sense is disgust. It is hardly a fair contest and Elf against an Anuran."

"I lead my army, you lead yours. Fighting and dying by your lance is an honour, but if you lack the courage to accept my challenge, how will that look to your soldiers?"

"Again, you insult my courage. The fight will happen as you desire. It will not last long and I shall inflict many wounds on you for the insults before I relieve you of your last breath. Know also the fate that awaits your companion when you lose will be most unpleasant."

"You are very good at talking Gorga, but can you fight," Gatran goaded further.

"The fight will happen before the sun sets. You will choose from Anurans weapons and then you'll die. Know also that if your companion attempts to use white magic, he will lose his head instantly."

"Dravel will not use magic. His reserves are depleted from keeping us shielded for long periods."

"This I know to be true; it was why we waited. We knew it would happen."

Chapter 38:

They remained alone until sunset. Gorga moved toward them and broke the otherwise peace of their afternoon.

"It is time, Gatran of the Wood Elves. It is an honourable death you choose, and word of your passing will spread to your kind. It is the only concession I can offer to a brave Elf."

Gatran nodded and asked about procedure.

"You'll have three weapons to select from, a lance, the serrated sword, and an axelon. You will choose before I, as is our custom. While we fight, your companion will have a sword to his throat. Escaping or cowardice and his head is removed."

"I would ask you do not. There will be no attempt to avoid our conflict, nor will there be cowardice. I would not dishonour myself or my friend."

"I will accept your request, but understand he will die shortly after you."

"Then I would ask that he too may die with honour."

"Again, I accept your request. As you can see the Anurans are honourable beings."

"If so, this fight is unnecessary, we would be considering ways to coexist and share trade opportunities."

If we needed either, that could happen.

"Doesn't the thought of having white magic at your disposal offer different possibilities?"

"We combat magic with strength and are successful in our challenges."

"I would say your confidence is masked by arrogance. I have seen magic you cannot defeat. My army was turned to stone by a single Dark Elf."

"That is because your army was weak."

Gatran did not respond. It was pointless. Gorga was supremely confident in his own abilities and had not experienced magic beyond simple use. He could not, or would not, give its power any credence. Instead, he moved closer to Dravel.

"Shortly, we'll either leave here together or we'll be dead. Despite the conclusion to my battle, it has been an honour to travel with you and to consider you a friend."

He clasped the wrists of the High Elf and squeezed.

"The honour has been mine too Gatran, I have learned more from you on this mission than during many recent sun-cycles. I wish you honour and success for what comes next, my Prince."

"The same for you also, Dravel."

Gatran released his grip on Dravel's wrists and turned back to Gorga.

"I am ready."

Gorga turned his back on Gatran and walked away; Gatran followed. He led to the centre of the encampment. A square arena was formed by Anuran soldiers. Six soldiers made their way to the centre, each carrying a weapon. Three halted Gatran by stopping between him and Gorga. The weapons were shown to him, and Gatran studied them carefully.

The sword was simple in design and honed to an extremely sharp edge. However, it was longer than the one he carried into battle, thicker and heavier. The lance was long, made from stout, hard wood with a razor-sharp metal point tied with sinew. The last weapon, the axelon, had multiple uses. It had the traditional axe blade, but also a bulbus head used as a club. The head contained spikes half as long as an Elf finger. Finally, the shaft had two separate places to hold. One for the traditional axe, towards the end, and the second further up the shaft allowing the axe to be used as a staff.

Gatran knew the weapon would be unbalanced and cause problems when using it. An Anuran wrist was three times the thickness of an Elf's. The sword's weight affected the balance. No choice, he opted for the lance. The soldier passed it to him, and he tested the weight. He knew he had made the wisest choice. His eyes turned to Gorga as he chose his weapon.

He had seen Gatran's choice and decided to match weapon for weapon. The soldiers retreated from the arena and Gorga addressed his army.

"Anurans take notice of my words. This is a battle to the death between your commander and this Wood Elf. When I win his companion will be offered a chance to die similarly, with honour. Should the impossible happen and I lose, they win their freedom. They may leave unharmed. This is the command of Gorga."

The soldiers stamped their feet on the ground in response and the earth shook under Gatran's feet. Gorga turned to Gatran.

"You have witnessed the honour in my word through the instructions to my soldiers. You choose an honourable death by challenge, and there is no disgrace in defeat. I wish you well in the afterlife. Once the fight starts, it does not end until one of us dies. In this situation, your death. Time for words is past, prepare yourself for battle."

He moved away before turning and facing Gatran again. He raised his free hand once and then gripped his lance with both hands. A horn blew from somewhere in the army ranks and the battle started.

Gorga circled Gatran, looking for an opening but finding none as Gatran followed his movements. The Anuran realised he would have to force one and feinted a charge. Gatran didn't flinch, but held Gorga's eyes, looking for the slightest movement to betray his intentions. It came, the tiniest indication and the tiniest fraction of time before he moved. Gorga jumped, high above Gatran's head and pointed the lance at his chest. Gatran side-stepped, unrushed, and the Anuran landed where Gatran had once stood.

"You move quickly, Wood Elf."

Begrudging respect was evident in his words. Gatran ignored the comment, knowing he could have moved several times faster if needed. His eyes returned to Gorga's, and he waited patiently for the next move. Gorga did not keep him waiting long. Again, the slight indication in his eyes betrayed the movement, but Gorga changed his approach by leaping forward. Gatran jumped, completing a somersault in mid-air, landing out of reach of Gorga's lance.

Gorga nodded, showing his respect of Gatran's defensive movements. Gatran just stared into his eyes. Gorga changed his stance, losing the aggressive lean forward and standing straighter. Gatran knew he was inviting him to attack and had no intention of exposing himself too early. He copied Gorga's stance, keeping his eyes firmly on the Anurans.

Gatran's consummate patience was irking Gorga's, he wanted a full assault to dominate with his substantial strength. Gatran knew his sole chance was if Gorga made a mistake. He planned to thwart a full-on confrontation until then. Gorga looked away, as if showing his disdain for Gatran's tactics. Gatran sensed a ploy and did not fall for it. The Anuran launched his attack. Jumping high and turning mid-air, he lunged his spear towards Gatran. This time, Gatran did not move aside. He swung his own lance, deflecting Gorga's to his side and then slashing his point towards the Anuran. The tip of his blade caught Gorga's leg and grey blood burst from it. The Anuran screamed in anger, rather than pain, stepping back before Gatran struck again.

As their eyes met again, a more focussed stare from Gorga dominated his determined expression. He had not expected to receive any real opposition from the Wood Elf, but he had wounded him. It was outrageous and unacceptable to the Anuran leader. He attacked again immediately, but Gatran suspected the response would be immediate and intercepted the lance easily. For the second time, the point of his lance severed the skin on Gorga's leg.

It enraged Gorga enough for him to lose his focus, and he charged Gatran. Gatran jumped but not quick enough to avoid the lance completely. It sliced into his side, causing a stinging sensation to his torso. The contact caused him to land unsteadily and closer to the Anuran than he wanted to. The watching soldiers cheered as they saw Elven blood on Gatran's tunic.

Gorga reacted quicker and charged Gatran instantly. This time Gatran was still steadying himself and couldn't respond quick enough. The Anuran collided with him, sending him flailing through the air. Gatran dropped his lance mid-air and fell awkwardly. Gorga approached with an air of satisfaction as Gatran tried to stand. Pushing his lance forward, the tip found the base of his throat and Gatran stilled his movements.

"I somehow expected more resistance from you Wood Elf, especially as you wounded me."

"Your size and speed always meant our fight would advantage you, but I show courage to meet your challenge."

"Will you meet your death as courageously?"

"I will, but my death is not imminent yet."

Gorga could not find a reason to support Gatran's statement and hesitated briefly before thrusting his lance. Gatran seized the opportunity, launching into a series of back flips, taking him quickly from Gorga's reach. Collecting his lance, he stood and faced Gorga once more.

"Impressive Wood Elf, but these tactics won't work a second time."

Gatran ignored him and instead dropped low and rolled forward in a somersault. He stabbed at Gorga before he had completed the roll and caught him by surprise. His blade caught the Anuran in his lance arm, and the wound was deep. He bellowed a response and immediately swapped his lance to his other hand and lunged back. Gatran expected the response, swiping it aside with his arm this time and thrusted the lance again. Gorga bellowed again as the lance buried deep into his other arm. The Anuran dropped the lance, both arms dangling to his sides, torn muscles preventing him from attacking with the lance.

"I offer you a chance to yield, save your life, Gorga."

"Anuran's never yield, and while I breathe, I fight."

"I will not offer you this again," Gatran stated.

"You are still outmatched by my strength."

"Your strength is of no use unless I'm close to you, that's unnecessary because I alone hold a lance."

Gorga charged him and ran straight on to Gatran's lance. The blade passed through his massive body and appeared the other side of him.

"You die with honour Gorga, and I salute you," Gatran said as the Anurans legs buckled under him and he breathed his last breath.

Gatran backed away from the Anuran and faced the soldiers surrounding him. A gap opened between two of them and he called Dravel to his side. They walked towards the gap and the Anuran soldiers stamped the ground three times.

"Seems you have won respect and the fight."

"As long as they honour Gorga's promise, we'll live to see another day, my friend."

"I can still offer a shield if required."

"I don't think we'll need it today, but we must find Kudra and Sitara."

An Anuran moved past them at speed.

"It looks like he's travelling to the other half of their forces, probably to recall them after losing their leader."

"That's to our advantage because they do not know of Gorga's promise to us."

"They will soon."

Chapter 39:

They walked to the nearest hill, to find the second half of the Anuran army breaking camp. Gatran made no attempt to avoid them but as they passed the soldiers stamped the ground.

"Hopefully, we'll get no more trouble from the Anurans. Your tactics in your fight with Gorga, they were not as I expected."

"What did you expect?"

"I thought you would attack at full speed, attempting to surprise him."

"I could not risk fighting him at close quarters, he would have swamped me. His strength was far superior to mine. Keeping distance and playing the waiting game frustrated him into a mistake."

"You continue to surprise me, Gatran. We must stop and attend your wound."

"Not in view of the Anurans. It would be seen as a sign of weakness, and they might disrespect Gorga's orders."

"Where do you think Kudra and Sitara are concealed?"

"They'll be at the top of the hill.

"You are confident."

"It's the best place tactically, views all around. They'll reveal themselves as we approach."

Moments later, Kudra dropped the shield of invisibility, revealing their position. She noticed Gatran's wound immediately.

"You will let me attend your wound, Gatran."

"Your consideration is a blessing. We are close to the swamps and foulness is carried on the wind. It would be unwise to risk infection."

"Remove your tunic."

More order than request, the wound was painful and larger than anyone expected. The full extent was revealed after she helped him when noticing his struggle. Sitara took his tunic.

"A stream nearby, Gatran, I will rinse blood from it."

"Gratitude."

"We watched the fight with Gorga, your courage matches your position. You risked it all for our safety."

"There was little choice, but I appreciate your comments."

Sitara moved away and Kudra started cleaning his wound.

"Deeper into muscle than first believed. It needs bonding. Without medicinal herbs, the process is painful and slow."

"How many connections are needed?"

"The wound is long, perhaps between twenty or thirty. There will be scarring."

"You have thread and needles?"

"I do; you allow this?"

"There is no choice. If it becomes infected my mission is at risk."

"You're right, but think of the mission as our mission, we are equally committed."

"I did not intend to devalue."

Kudra nodded. "Lie back."

Gatran noticed Dravel had disappeared and suspected he had joined Sitara. His thoughts soon disappeared as the pain from Kudra's work consumed him, forcing his attention to focus on controlling his response to it. Kudra witnessed his steely determination not to show his pain and admired his control. She felt consumed with pride, and her eyes moistened slightly. Gatran noticed.

"What ails your feelings, Kudra."

"Many things, mostly you."

"How is it I bring misery to you?"

"You misunderstand vision."

"Then speak to me of it so I understand the Elf Princess who dominates my thoughts and feelings."

"I still find it surprising when you speak of such matters openly. It is untrue of the males of my species."

"Dravel is open, we share many thoughts unspoken between Elves. This is a strength, my relationship with him has grown special because of this."

"It is definitely a strength."

"Do not deflect from answering."

"I do not deflect but sometimes words are not easily found."

"Then find them for me, Kudra. I reveal my thoughts to you, so we can be close in mind, as well as our physical attraction."

So, understanding is clear. My feelings for you deepen. Your wound pains me as you."

"I'm content you feel this way, Kudra. Lean forward so I can touch your lips with mine. My pain will be less if I kiss you."

"Such forward comments would be deemed insulting between many of my kind."

"Mine too, but when we're alone there is no insult."

Kudra leaned forward and kissed Gatran. Her gentle touch stimulated him to raise a hand to the side of her face, but she pushed it down. Breaking the kiss, her face was flushed, and a smile spread happily. She warned stretching could reopen some connections, and there remained more to complete. Gatran regretted moving as she resumed her work.

Sitara and Dravel returned, and she commented her approval for Kudra's medical efforts. Dravel commented too, suggesting the scarring would be minimal for her efforts. They ate an early meal before travelling again. This time north-west. They skirted the Plains by the least distance possible but remained the maximum distance from the Karvil Marshlands.

Several moon-cycles passed before they reached the northern-most reach of the Plains of Krahor. Gatran's horse had become lame, and he had been forced to set it free. They altered direction slightly, more easterly, and the Hills of Jerev appeared on the horizon, seemingly closer than reality. Dravel estimated they still had a similar distance to travel before reaching them, and the next danger they faced. The Trolls.

"Dravel, Gatran, teach me about Trolls, a species I am unfamiliar with," Sitara asked.

Dravel answered. "They are a primitive species. Mainly nocturnal and live in caves. They are fast, strong and dangerous as an opponent. In terms of size, twice my height and three times as wide. Their arms are as my waist. They dislike open spaces, especially while the sun is out, the light is too bright for their eyes, but their vision in the dark hours is incredible. Their sense of smell is equally incredible. They rarely leave the Hills unless forced to hunt away from their territory, but again they would hunt at night. Their strength is unbelievable, they make Anurans appear weak by comparison. They're better avoided."

"Gatran, have you encountered?" Sitara urged.

I fought against two of them. They killed twenty of my army before we defeated them. They have no real tactics for fighting, which makes fighting them difficult. No single strategy works. I agree with Dravel they're better avoided. It is my intention to travel south of the Jerev Hills to avoid them. They will know of our presence though by our scent."

"Will they leave the Hills of Jerev to attack us?"

"I would say it depends on their food situation. If hunting is poor for them, they'll attack us. They're not particular about what they eat."

"The obstacles, we face are endless, one after another."

"We'll face them together if needed. After passing the Troll region, we approach the Xeltar Mountains, the Dwarf Homeland and the furthest reach of our journey."

"More problems and enemies who hate our existence."

"Each moon cycle passing is one less before my army awakens. They will join us as quickly as possible. Eckna will see to that. The Dark Dwarf said they would remain stone for a season. That time is almost ended. Even if the Dark Elf reveals our route Eckna understands I'll attempt to complete my mission. He'll ride to catch us up."

"We will reach the Dwarf Kingdom before he catches us," Dravel stated.

"It will be close, but returning home after completing the mission will be easier and quicker for their company."

"The Dwarves may not agree to our plan."

"What we offer will make sense to them, they're more intelligent than other species we've encountered."

"I wish I shared your optimism regarding the Dwarves."

"One problem at a time, Dravel."

Chapter 40:

A season's passing was almost complete, and Gatran thought increasingly of his army. Not knowing they remained in stone untouched, was awful. Possibly destroyed, he might not learn their fate until the return journey. Despite the Dark Elf's words, he also worried about their condition when they returned to Elven form. Would their minds be untarnished, would they journey to find him? The questions were irrelevant because the mission continued, but he started to second guess everything. Not his normal way of processing.

Despite this, the one advantage of having constant thoughts, was shortening the travelling time. He lost moon- cycles, each blending into irrelevance. The boring nature of prolonged travel would otherwise irritate. Even the varying landscape, so different from the relentless Plains failed to impress.

The others sensed his concerns but did not broach them, allowing him time to focus on each without interruption. While Sitara and Dravel deepened their bond, Kudra felt left out. She was not yet privy to Gatran's thoughts. After several moon-cycles without interaction, she decided to raise the subject with him at the first opportunity.

The following day the opportunity arose. Dravel and Sitara had moved ahead, talking animatedly and not realising they had opened a gap between them and the others. Kudra seized the opportunity to move closer to Gatran.

"It is time for discussion, Gatran. I display patience, allow time alone with thoughts for many moon-cycles. Since leaving the Plains, there are few words between us. I appreciate difficulty of mission, the problems faced and those remaining. When we started together, we spoke each issue, as well as developing relationship. Now both have ceased. It worries and disappoints."

"I'm sorry, Kudra. I'm aware I've been distant. It's no fault of yours. Nothing about this mission is simple, or clear. Every obstacle we've faced is both expected and unexpected. I mean we expected trouble but not necessarily the trouble we received. It makes planning or strategising difficult, the outcomes in each area, and each enemy we face, have boundless possibilities. It dominates my thoughts."

"I understand, but words state frequently, one issue at a time. This strategy works.

"True, but the relentless routine of travel opens endless time to consider everything. I am content with our progress while discontent with what we've lost. I'm bored with travelling and yet excited with what might come next. I'm confident in our mission and yet doubtful of its successful conclusion."

"This is first time you doubt successful conclusion, or first time stating?"

"The Dwarfs are complex beings, driven by different desires than Elves. I've never agreed with the term greedy, often used to describe them because of their relentless desire to accumulate gold. It's not greed, it's a compulsion, a quest with no end. If we had gold, we could buy peace more easily than through discussion. Their customs and culture are different, dominated by physical strength. We have nothing in common. It makes the final part of the mission, achieving peace, the most difficult, finding a path where both species benefit."

"If your sister's quest is successful, then you could barter with the cure for the sickness."

"I don't know of her success, though I know she'll travel to meet us to assist with the peace process upon completion."

"You could bluff."

"No point. Failure to produce the cure would cause any peace treaty being broken. Every pillaging raid made by Dwarves, encountering Elves, would see their demise."

"Close tongue and listen to words, Gatran. Your focus on entire mission is not warranted, each step leading to the conclusion requires focus first. Cease long-term thoughts. Unknowns are too many to achieve results. Return thoughts to steps of journey. Rest your mind beyond before confusion creates further doubt and encourages mistakes."

"Your wisdom is boundless, Kudra."

"The burden of task is carried differently; I do not lead. It allows rational thought without doubt. Aim for this. Change thought, and while mission remains ever difficult, each stage becomes focus and leads closer to goal. Like stepping stones across stream."

Gatran stopped suddenly, reached for her hand and pulled her close to him. He kissed her with more passion and desire than any other before. She met the kiss with equal passion, and they stood locked in embrace.

Dravel and Sitara had disappeared over a ridge, but as Kudra and Gatran broke their embrace they both appeared, running towards them. Dravel shouted the word Trolls, and a fear of dread passed briefly across them. Dravel reached them before Sitara.

"Two Trolls a short distance head from us."

"Did they see you?"

"No, but they're heading towards us. They'll gain our scent shortly."

"Then we must hide our scent."

"How?"

"The stream, we will travel through the water. Follow me. Ensure you soak your entire body when we reach it. It will at least shorten the proximity of our scent."

They ran at full speed to the stream which meandered around a series of boulders and undulations, high enough to conceal them. Each entered the water and soaked their bodies before moving downstream. The water was scarcely knee deep, and they kept moving at speed. They repeatedly showered their entire bodies with water, stopping briefly to achieve it.

The Trolls failed to gain their scent and after a while Gatran halted their progress. Forced into the Hills of Jerev to avoid them, they ran further risk of encountering more. He desperately wanted to leave the region and return to the uninhabited lands between Jerev and Krahor.

"What are you thinking, Gatran," Dravel asked.

"I'm thinking we need to leave this land before darkness. The only reason Trolls use the daylight for is hunting. Hunger is the reason for their appearance and why we shouldn't be here.

Dravel glanced at the sun's position.

"We have enough time, but barely. We must leave now. Our choices are following the stream back or travel across land."

"We follow the stream, use the same tactics that concealed us, and if we make it, we'll spend the dark hours under a shield of invisibility. It will hide our location, but there will be a scent trail leading towards us and the Trolls are more than capable of following it."

"We could wake in the dawn and find Trolls outside our shield," Sitara warned.

"Both possible and probable," Dravel responded.

Chapter 41:

At first light, the following morning, there were no Trolls visible outside their shield. Visibility was reduced because of the shallow depression they occupied, so despite not seeing them, they could be close by.

"There are no Trolls beyond our shield," Dravel spoke the words they all were hoping. "I am uncertain it is safe to move, they could be waiting all around us but beyond our visibility."

"Gatran, while Dravel holds the shield, I could leave and check beyond depression."

"A sensible precaution, Sitara, but do not stray too far, and return quickly."

Sitara nodded and then walked from their shield. She cloaked herself and climbed the sides of the depression. At first, she witnessed nothing, but as she neared completion of her circuit, she saw two Trolls standing by a large boulder with their noses pointed upward. She guessed they were exploring the area by scent and backed away.

She returned to the main shield and reported her findings to Gatran. He quickly decided to increase the distance between them and the Trolls by walking under the protection of the shield. Dravel kept it in place, and they walked for several hours before Gatran suggested lowering it.

He had chosen the area carefully. Ahead was a flat region of land with a forest beyond. The Plains of Krahor lay to their side. Undulating ground, peppered with boulders and rocks lay to the right, not an area for comfortable travelling. Their current course seemed the most appropriate, with the Plains offering a potential escape route if needed. Without horses, escaping pursuing Trolls was impossible. They moved fast, only magic offered a true potential to conceal themselves.

To date, the area remained the most interesting and visibly aesthetic region they had encountered so far. Despite the beauty, the lack of animal life was noticeable, which might well explain the Trolls earlier behaviour. Bird life was plentiful, and their song broke the silence they had become accustomed to on the Plains.

"It's a different landscape to those we've travelled before, Gatran," Dravel commented.

"The constant change makes it interesting at least."

"I can tell from your tone you have reservations about being here."

"The Trolls are a formidable foe, despite their size they are swift of foot, ruthless and savage hunters. They represent a true threat. Their presence will remain unknown until a few seconds before attack; their stealth incredible considering their size, and without use of magic."

"We must be alert to possibilities and travel on flat ground where possible."

"I chose our course to meet that purpose. I'm thinking of approaching woodland to collect wood suitable for shaping weapons. We have insufficient to offer much resistance if attacked."

Dravel raised his eyebrows. "Did you not say the Trolls inhabit the woods?"

"Choice is unavoidable, my thoughts suggest the Dwarves we encounter will not receive us without attacking."

"We can't fight them, that would change how we're perceived."

"I agree, but we can defend ourselves. That would be acceptable."

"Entering the woodland would be a mistake, let us seek wood from the open ground first."

"I hear your warning and will lean towards caution for now, but if needs rise…"

"We must find food soon; we have little remaining."

"An absence of animals prevails here. However, if we can find deeper water, a lake perhaps. There is an opportunity for different prey. My brother and I used to hunt ducks by swimming underwater and catching them from underneath. There's no shortage of bird life."

"Cooking it will bring notice to position," Sitara intoned.

"I fear we must venture onto the Plains again to cook it on a fire."

"A contrast, this land with the bounty of wildlife on the Plains," Kudra stated.

Gatran nodded his agreement. "Yes, wilderness surroundings of the Plains offered food in abundance. Here is more beautiful but offers little."

"Both lands offer enemies hidden to world, who care nothing for others and live with violent intent."

"You're right Sitara. Since Journey stated, we've met one helpful individual, a Dark Elf, an unexpected encounter but welcome. If more exist, I hope they extend arms in friendship."

Life is peaceful at home. Away, the world is hostile to travellers. It makes sense to seek a new homeland away from other creatures, a place to live in the peaceable manner we've become accustomed to."

"Are the only peaceable folk remaining Elves?"

Gatran's eyes saddened. "It appears so, Kudra. There are other hostile folks more distant. Mankind offers the greatest threat because of their expanding numbers."

As they discussed this, they hadn't realised they had ceased travelling, such the threat their words carried. Sitara had taken opportunity to scan the area using the crystal eyeglass.

"There is bird activity ahead, flocks of incalculable numbers swarm in flight. A lake exists below them. Perhaps food is in the offering."

"The lake's position, on the Plains, or in Jerev?"

"Definitely on the Plains."

"Well done, Sitara, perhaps you could lead the way forward to it."

"As you request, Gatran."

"Take the shortest route onto the Plains, we'll keep away from encounters with the Trolls."

Sitara increased her pace to adopt the forward position. "Dravel, you would accompany me?"

Dravel moved forward and Gatran slowed his pace to allow a short distance to develop between them.

Kudra smiled at his concession, understanding the reasons behind it.

"Sitara is an excellent swimmer; she may be of use in the pursuit of duck."

"There is risk of abominations dwelling in the lake."

"Sitara fights like a male Elf. You have given opportunity allowing lead, showing trust, take it step further, allow her to accompany in lake. You seek her trust; this is way to earn it."

"Your thoughts demonstrate foresight and continue to impress, Kudra. I am stronger for your presence and counsel alongside."

Kudra smiled her contentment and slipped her hand in his.

Chapter 42:

They reached the lake just before noon. It was beautiful and teeming with bird and insect life. Larger than expected, they found a small sandy area, bankside, to sit and rest, placing their meagre possessions to the side.

"I would suggest indulging in pleasant conditions and remaining for the day's remainder. Hunt, cook and rest from constant travel," Kudra suggested.

"Your thoughts on this, Sitara."

"My princess speaks with words of wisdom. A rest much needed to revitalise soul."

"Dravel?"

"It would benefit weary feet and mind. A pleasant change."

"Then it is settled."

Dravel sat alongside Gatran. "You are in good spirits perhaps you could share the reason."

"It is my thinking we've been travelling for more than a season. I hope my army has been returned to Elven form and travels towards us as we speak."

"If they travel, they will take many moon cycles to catch us."

"The fact they travel is heartening, don't temper it with warnings of time before meeting them."

"Not my intention it offers a further option though."

"Speak your mind."

"If they now travel, we could wait for them before continuing."

"And if not, we wait for nothing. Their travel does not change my plans. They will catch up, when they catch up. Possibly before we encounter the Dwarves or possibly just after. Those who will negotiate are present here.

"There is nothing to sway your decision?"

"No, why do you ask this?"

"Because if the meeting with Dwarves becomes hostile, we have nothing to use as a deterrent to sway action. Our army was the deterrent."

"The Dwarves may see my army as a threat, their presence as a threat, it could halt negotiations before they start."

"You will risk our lives?"

"We've been risking them since leaving Graylen Forest."

Dravel fell silent, knowing Gatran was right. It was such a gamble. Everything they had endured on route could be for nothing. They were forced not just to believe in the mission, but trust in it. He required longer to fully trust in the mission, probably until after encountering the Dwarves.

Gatran announced it was time to hunt. "Sitara, I have been informed you are an adept swimmer, would you care to hunt with me?"

Sitara could not hide her pleasure at the consideration. I have not hunted this way.

"It's simple we swim down under the birds, swim up and grab their feet. They do not see it coming."

"Do you drown them?"

"No, it is kinder to break necks under water, they do not suffer."

Stripping off their outer garments, Gatran reached for the Anuran sword and waded out into the water. Sitara followed.

"The water is clear, visibility is good. We do not know what creatures inhabit this lake, so keep vigil all around your position. The sea monsters in the Ominic Sea smell blood from distance, do not spill duck's."

Gatran did not wait for an answer and instead ducked under water. Sitara followed, and they swam to a large gathering of ducks a distance away. Gatran checked on Sitara's position several times, but she maintained his pace effortlessly. Kudra had not exaggerated her swimming ability.

Approaching their prey, Gatran stopped and pointed upward. Sitara could see the mass of webbed bird feet propelling their motion and grinned. Gatran demonstrated, reaching up and grabbing bird's legs and she nodded her understanding. He smiled and pointed upward, and they began their ascent. They picked up speed, and Gatran extended his arms forward. Sitara copied. They selected their prey and focussed on it. Gatran seized a bird and pulled it under, swiftly twisting and pulling its neck. It broke, and he turned to Sitara. Incredibly, she held a bird in each hand but could not cull either. Gatran reached out and took one and ended its life swiftly while Sitara dealt with hers.

He signalled their return, and they swam back towards the shore. When the water was just waist deep Gatran broke through the surface and grinned at Dravel and Kudra.

"Dinner has been caught," he stated.

Sitara emerged from the water, holding up her two birds triumphantly. Her smile disappeared replaced with confusion. She peered down toward her feet, crying out in confusion and fright. Releasing her ducks, she reached down, crying out that something held them. The water turned turbulent, rising and falling and frothing at the surface. Sitara disappeared beneath it.

Dravel, having noted her distress dived into the water fully clothed. Gatran followed Sitara under the

226

surface. Kudra watched anxiously as her companions disappeared from view.

Underwater, Gatran could see Sitara ahead, being dragged by a creature he didn't recognise. It was large, powerful and with multiple limbs, two of which gripped Sitara's ankles. He drew the sword and swam toward her, intending to slice through the limbs. Dravel was alongside him, and he too held an Anuran sword. Together, they covered the distance between themselves and Sitara. Dravel reached her fist and gripped her arms tightly, pulling back as hard as he could. The creature now dragged them both, but slowed considerably. Gatran swam beyond them both and sliced through the limbs restraining her. Clouds of blue blood emerged from the and Gatran signalled for them to swim away.

They were just in time; three other creatures emerged to attack the injured one. Huge heads with smaller bodies and a melee of limbs swam around the unfortunate creature, gripping it and tearing it to shreds. Gatran turned away and followed Dravel and Sitara back to shore. The creatures did not follow them.

"That was an interesting experience," Sitara stated, attempting to hide both her fear and relief.

"You are unhurt?" Gatran asked.

"You and Dravel saved me from certain death. Gratitude to you both."

"We couldn't let anything happen to our best underwater hunter. Two birds on your first try, I think I'll have to improve my technique to match you."

Sitara grinned again, relief now dominating her emotions to where tears rose. Kudra moved across and sat next to her while Gatran and Dravel started plucking the birds.

"You swim well, Dravel. I thought otherwise when you did not offer your service for hunting."

"I sought to bolster Sitara's self-worth. She is the only one present without position."

"I can change this upon return to our kind. But this reminds me you have not yet stated your true position within High Elf society."

We have not shared time alone for many moon cycles.

"Also true, you seek an opportunity to talk alone with me?"

"Not especially, but I wish to be completely honest with you."

"A chance will happen, I'm sure. Understand I'm content with my friend and will not pressure him on this."

"Gratitude Gatran. When you learned of Kudra's position you were not pleased."

"I had no knowledge of Kudra's position, but I've always known you are beyond an ambassador. It's no secret, and your actions have repeatedly demonstrated the need to learn the truth is not required, unless you wish to share with me."

"Again, gratitude."

"The birds are prepared; I would use Kudra's magic to cook. No need for fire. The Trolls could smell it at range."

Gatran had swiftly changed conversation, and Dravel had no doubts about the honesty of his comments.

"A wise choice. I'm looking forward to this feast."

Chapter 43:

The following morning, they were travelling again, becoming ever closer to the Dwarf realm.

"How much further to Xeltar Mountain, Gatran?"

"I cannot be sure; it has been many sun cycles since I travelled this far from home. My best estimate would be somewhere between ten and twenty sun cycles."

"We have travelled long and yet it passes quickly."

"Like the passing of life, Dravel."

"That is true also."

"I can't believe we've not encountered the Trolls further."

"We have been fortunate, Gatran, but their lands stretch to the south of Xeltar Mountain. We could counter them on the day we meet Dwarves."

"I hope not, one enemy is enough. It is said that the Dwarves use the Trolls to protect their lands by presence alone."

"It makes sense, though I doubt an agreement exists between them. More likely, it is coincidental."

Sitara called them from behind. "There is movement in the hills," she stated, lowering the crystal eyeglass.

"Your diligence is commendable Sitara, and the early warning a necessity. You can see what causes the movement?" Dravel spoke with obvious pride for the Elf who roused his emotions.

"No, but dust flies, caused by sizeable creatures."

"Well, there's been few signs of animal, so almost certainly caused by Trolls. I fear we were too soon with our comments about them, Dravel."

Kudra stepped forward. "They are close enough to smell scent, it is wise to raise shield."

"Yes, we'll move while shielded, further into the plains. If the Trolls want us badly, we'll see them from a greater distance as they follow. If they don't then they will simply retreat from their course."

Dravel raised the shield, and they changed course to the East. The remainder of the morning passed, but Kudra announced the Trolls still followed. Kudra offered to take a turn at shielding the group, resting Dravel and saving his reserves. It was the first time she volunteered to help using magic apart from cooking.

"Your confidence grows in using magic?" Gatran asked her.

"Not really, I believe support will need offering before mission completion. It will be for task more demanding. A wise decision to practise as opportunities arrive."

"Your assumption is probably correct, and Dravel has shouldered the burden alone. It is right to offer help. Practice on smaller tasks when possible and I will rest assistance from Dravel. He must concentrate on verbal matters. How to gain peace with the Dwarves."

"Sitara will aid with small tasks, she has capability."

"I will ask this of her when needed, she has already proved herself worthy on this journey."

Sitara heard the comment and decided not to answer, but her pleasure at being trusted further ran deep.

During the afternoon, the Trolls increased their pace and closed in on the group. Four of them were clearly visible through the crystal eyeglass.

230

Dravel commented. "I'm guessing they're struggling to find food; it explains why they follow for such distance."

"Another possibility invades mind," Sitara offered.

"Speak your thoughts, Sitara," Gatran instructed.

"You have said Trolls are incapable of using magic; what if they're acting under its influence?"

"If so, whoever controls them is close. Close enough to see us, surely."

"Perhaps not, if instruction given long ago. To watch for, and capture, a Wood Elf and Three High Elves. I see no sign hunger affects bodies, they appear healthy and strong."

Gatran cast a respectful gaze at Sitara. "Your thoughts are not without merit, Sitara. The Trolls we saw did not appear starving. I had not considered this, but if true, surely whoever cast magic upon them would know of our ability to use white magic?"

"If it were I casting magic, then magic would focus on improving senses to see or smell through shield."

"When you encountered them in the hill region, did they look like they were searching for us or waiting?"

"The sniffed the air, suggesting they searched, but they appeared in no rush."

"So, possibly either or both."

Dravel offered his thoughts. "It seems we have two choices here, we could wait for them and discover their intentions, or fight them. Alternatively, we can travel deeper into the Plains."

"I don't want to travel deeper into the plains. Enemies we might face there are unknown. By the Hills of Jerev, we face only Trolls, or maybe Dwarf Scouts, this close to Xeltar Mountain."

"So, we stand then?"

"It's the correct decision."

"We lack weapons."

"We have two Anuran spears and two swords."

"The spears will be of no use. The Trolls will simply snap the wooden shafts."

"Leaving two swords."

Kudra who had been quiet since assuming responsibility of the shield spoke up. "There seems little choice in matter, magic maybe only defence."

"I want to learn if their intentions are to capture us or kill us."

"Why is this important?"

"We have met opposition at every stage of this journey. When leaving Graylen Forest, only a few had knowledge of the mission purpose. Nobody knew the route we would take. How is it our enemies act like they knew we were coming?"

"Our route was an obvious choice, born from sound reasoning. Anyone with a tactical brain would choose the same," Dravel commented.

"True, but nobody knew we were travelling until the evening before we left."

"If my interpretations of your thoughts are correct, an individual could leave the forest and inform another. The army was present outside the forest, waiting for us."

"No Elf within my army could slip away without being noticed within moments."

"And yet at the Ominic Sea you suspected someone controlled the sea creatures from close by."

"That would mean a traitor lurks within the ranks and yet my thoughts lead to a traitor closer to the King and Queen in Graylen Forest."

"Possibly a member of the King and Queens personal guard then?

"More likely, one of them acting on behalf of another."

232

"What did you know of the mission before travelling to us, Dravel?"

"Nothing, I was simply instructed to visit the King of the Wood Elves and embark on a mission on his behalf."

"Our Kings met to discuss this before our selection for the tasks. How many others would have known? Each would travel with a personal guard unit and maybe representatives."

"More were perhaps knowledgeable about our mission. Your father's choice for each part of the mission would be unknown. I would raise the issue, if there's a traitor, it could be a High Elf."

"I disagree, Dravel. A High Elf could not infiltrate our ranks and command magic at the Ominic Sea."

"He could if he had a high level of training in white magic."

"This gets increasingly complicated. I'm convinced someone controlled the encounters we had with other creatures. Somebody wants us dead and the mission to fail."

"And yet our withdraw from the realms of other creatures affects none, except us."

"Makes more sense that an Elf is behind this, Wood Elf or High Elf."

Sitara interrupted the conversation. "The Trolls are almost upon us."

"We'll examine further, Dravel, at a more appropriate time."

"I would seek the views of Kudra and Sitara on the matter too."

Chapter 44:

The four Trolls slowed as they reached the shield. They sniffed the air and assumed positions around it.

Dravel spoke in a surprised tone. "They should not be capable of smelling us, and yet they clearly can."

Gatran experienced the full weight of frustration.

"Their senses have been enhanced by magic, there's no doubt. Unfortunately, we cannot interrogate them. Nobody except Trolls speak their language and they're incapable of learning another."

Sitara was using the crystal eyeglass again. "No other creatures visible on the Plains. The Trolls act independently. What magic used on creature's senses was imparted in past times."

"That is a positive for us. The creatures operate under a general set of orders and must use their own intelligence to follow them. Intelligence is their weakness, we can out-think them."

"Perhaps possible, Gatran, but they would continue pursuing us. Hold of magic is strong and avoiding task impossible," Kudra offered.

"What if we gave them another mission?"

"If their task was given through dark magic, then it is stronger than task from white magic."

"Then we must either kill or restrain them somehow."

Dravel intervened. "Which means little option but to engage them physically."

The Trolls suddenly moved forward and extended their arms. They continued forward until stopping when touching the shield. They communicated with one another. A series of strange grunting and other guttural sounds, becoming increasingly agitated. One struck the shield with a clenched fist.

"That's impossible. No creature can discern a shield, touching it is impossible and yet they can. It's further confirmation they're acting under the influence of dark magic."

"Are you sure it's dark magic and not white magic, Dravel?"

"I'm as certain as knowing the sun will rise each morning."

"These creatures are not acting as normal Trolls, that's clear, and I want to test it further. We'll drop the shield and see how they react. Kudra and Sitara, you will stand behind with spears. Use them if you feel threatened. Before you speak, this is not about your protection, but ours. Dravel and I will invite a challenge with swords to see how they react."

"This is unwise action, Gatran. You could be injured; the mission fail as result."

"I am betting on my instinct here."

"What is it saying to you?" Dravel asked.

"That they've been instructed to capture us, not harm us."

"But…"

"No time for further debate, Dravel. Kudra drop the shield on my order. Stand ready, now."

Kudra lowered the shield, and the Trolls stepped back shocked at the sudden sight of Elves. They regained their composure quickly and regained the ground they temporarily left. Gatran stepped forward waving his sword, but the Trolls stood their ground and made no move toward resistance.

Gatran commented. "They hesitate, this is not normal behaviour for Trolls."

He took another step forward, still swinging his sword incredibly close to the nearest Troll and still he did not move. Gatran ceased his sword action and instructed his team to turn and walk away. They followed his instruction and Gatran turned his back on the Trolls and walked after them. After ten paces, he called a halt and turned to face the Trolls again. They had followed them, maintaining their distance.

"It appears we have that choice now. Either kill them or restrain them. Since I take no pleasure in killing a creature restricted from acting normally, restraint seems our only option."

"How, and with what?" Sitara asked.

"I hadn't thought that far ahead. I expected to fight."

Kudra stated the obvious. "We have nothing and there is nothing close by."

"Since they are not attacking us, but seem keen to follow, perhaps we can walk until finding something."

"You want us to walk with backs to them?" Sitara asked incredulously.

"A simple experiment first. I want to see if their instructions apply to everyone. Kudra, walk away from us, let's see if they follow."

Kudra followed the instruction before Gatran called her back after the Trolls remained disinterested. He tried again with Sitara and Dravel, but again the Trolls remained stationary.

"Right, my turn. If they follow, then follow behind them and I'll lead them towards Jerev."

"Why to their home land," Sitara asked.

"Simply, it offers more opportunities for restraint than the Plains."

He took a few steps away, and the Trolls followed immediately, neither increasing nor decreasing the gap between him and them.

"Seems we've discovered the focus of their attentions. Although they have me, they don't seem to know what to do next, so they just follow. Clearly, the dark magic placed on them was not enough."

Dravel dropped back to walk with Gatran. "It is enough, if they remain connected to whoever imposed the magic."

"Since the Trolls do nothing with us, it appears your statement might be right. Whoever controls them would have no idea exactly where we're located. Now they do. If they desire the mission to fail, something will happen soon, probably something threatening."

"We must lose them quickly and change course to prevent possible engagement with something more capable. I suggest running."

"I agree Dravel. Kudra, Sitara, I'll start running. A pace you can maintain for distance and follow the shortest route to the Hills of Jerev. Monitor the Trolls. Seek change in their position or mood and if it happens let me know."

Gatran turned and started running. He set the pace, and the Trolls followed, completely ignorant of the Elves running behind them. Gatran saw the hills ahead, but it consumed the afternoon reaching them.

Reaching the first hill, Gatran noticed a cave halfway up. It was almost concealed below an overhanging ledge that appeared ready to fall.

"Dravel, if we were to trap the Trolls in the cave could you cause a tremor to collapse the ledge and seal them in?"

"That is beyond my capability, but within Kudra's."

"Kudra?"

"Is there no other option?"

"I can't think of one and I'm sure the Trolls are connected by the dark magic. We're being followed at distance, but that distance is reducing quickly. We must lose the eyes upon us. We're no match for any creatures in number."

"How will you trap them inside?"

"I will lead them in and circle around to stand in the entrance. Once there, you will collapse the ledge. It calls for keen observation, I must remain there until the last instant. Dravel and Sitara, you must watch the ledge and warn me when to move. My life is in your hands."

"You ask us to gamble with life."

"I trust you both without reservation, I am safe with you."

"And if we fail?"

"I die knowing you'll do everything to complete the mission."

Gatran ceased talking and walked into the cave. The Trolls followed. He carried his plan perfectly, eventually standing with his back to the cave opening.

"Now, Kudra, do what you can."

Kudra started chanting, and they all felt a slight tremor at their feet. It grew and grew until they found it difficult to remain standing. A crack appeared on the overhang, and Dravel and Sitara noticed it immediately.

"Be ready Gatran," Sitara cried.

The crack opened wider and Dravel shouted. Immediately, Gatran ran from the entrance. A troll appeared by the entrance and was suddenly consumed by the mass of rock falling and covering the entrance. They had timed it perfectly. The Elves were safe, and the Trolls were no longer following. They moved quickly away, heading diagonally from the hills and onto the Plains once more.

Chapter 45:

They travelled silently, concentrating on gaining distance from the hills and any pursuer. Only when the sky spread crimson tendrils across the horizon did Gatran call a halt.

Their food supplies were dwindling; what remained of the ducks was probably sufficient for two meals. Kudra was concerned that the uncooked meat would turn and make them sick before long, so she cooked the remaining meat with magic and stored some away. She shared enough for a simple meal, recognising the need to hunt; the food was barely sufficient to replace the energy expunged during the day.

Finishing, Gatran asked Kudra and Sitara for their thoughts on who might be controlling the magic affecting their journey.

Sitara sat straighter. "Traitors exist in several places. Only this makes sense in affecting our progress. Your comment, regarding the meeting between our Kings, suggests loyalties in the Kings personal guards are suspect. I believe at least one within each unit. A High Elf and a Wood Elf."

"Are they truly Elves, or some other creature assuming the form of Elves?"

"There is no way to know, Gatran.

"And Kudra, your opinion on this?"

"I share same conclusion but include more."

"Within the King's guard?"

"No, within your army, explaining how dark magic was used at the Ominic sea. The King's Guard were not present there."

"Sitara?"

"I agree, probably more than one. Few individuals could control so many creatures. My thoughts lead to a Witch or Witches. They can maintain appearance of Elves while conducting magic."

"And at Rag Dire Pass?"

Sitara continued. "We already assumed the power required to orchestrate such magic surpassed individual capability. My thoughts are many worked together."

"Kudra?"

"Again, agreement with comments. The Dark Elf encountered on Plains suggested a Witch controlled the sickness, agreement with thoughts of many. He believed a Witch sent the Ravens to extinguish army."

"What about the Anurans. They didn't appear to use any form of magic. How do you explain this?"

"From the first meeting, they acted as Anurans were expected too. Perhaps our meeting was not foreseen. The outcome of the encounter should have rendered us dead, as formerly used magic would."

"Kudra's right, magic unnecessary, but perhaps likely ending was suspected. We should not ignore situation of Undulations. They move unnaturally, probably a result of magic."

"Gratitude for your candour. We already know the Trolls were acting under the influence of dark magic and the force colluding against us contains many individuals. Dark Elves, Witches, possibly Gnomes and even Dwarves. The question I cannot seem to find answers for is why. What is their purpose? Who gains from the resulting conclusion, the demise of our kind? We intend to retreat to live in peace.

Dravel looked up. "I believe whoever or whatever individual is orchestrating this believes retreating from the known world will allow us to flourish. Expand our numbers to a point representing a threat to whoever survives in the region."

"I can empathise, Dravel, but more threat exists from the expansion of Humankind; their spread and lust for land is beyond any threat perceived from us."

"I agree, but Humankind has no magic capability, therefore easier to deal with. I don't think land is an issue either. My kind live in the mountains, where few others could survive, and yours the forest, neither is sufficient for most species. Wealth is not a consideration. We have little of value. Our treasures do not carry the value like those belonging to the Dwarves. Ours are historical, significant to celebrating past events or occasion. Few have monetary value.

"I remain open to all possibilities. The elimination of all Elves suggests the mastermind holds a grudge. Perhaps an ultimate disliking for Elves, considering their demise as a personal quest."

"What individual would hold this grudge."

"I wish I knew, Dravel. Perhaps an individual who feels he, or his kind, has been wronged in the past."

"I have lived long, Gatran, and will search my memories to discover such an individual, but I'm unsure of discovery. Our long-term quest has always been to maintain a peace between all living kinds."

"In maintaining that, have we forced hardship on one particular species, were our decisions wrong in hindsight while correct at the time?"

"Again, no thoughts spring to mind."

"Kudra, Sitara. You were born in the distant past. Can you remember stories of past events explaining the current situation or identify an aggrieved individual from times past?"

Kudra and Sitara shook their heads but promised to consider their history prior to their birth. Each turned their thoughts to potential causes, but none found further possibilities.

Consumed first by conversation, then thought, none had noticed the night, shrouding them from the world's entirety. Gatran suggested a small fire and asked Sitara to conjure flames with her white magic. Surprised, she nodded, setting flame to the grass contained within a small ring of stones. The grass emitted heat and orange flames, but maintained an intriguing immunity from consumption. It retained its emerald green hues within.

Gatran smiled his pleasure at the fire and then its creator. Sitara again experienced the satisfaction of being called upon for matters beyond simple service. She knew her role in life was changing despite her loyal service to Kudra. She was becoming an individual whose thoughts were valued by others beyond Kudra. Not only her role changed, the tasks she was asked to perform were changing; she was changing. Abilities and intelligence, restricted by position, were at last blossoming. Her true capabilities were becoming obvious to those around her. She moved closer to Dravel, the High Elf who inspired the growth in her and fuelled her self-belief and rested her head against his shoulder.

Kudra whispered to Gatran, suggesting a stroll before resting for the night. He understood her real motivation, rising swiftly and leading her away from the fire.

"Time alone together is infrequent," she whispered sadly.

"When the journey is completed, we'll find time to be together, hold conversations, revealing ourselves further. We'll discover an understanding deeper and stronger than the desire holding our interest."

"The desire is good also?"

"Of course, but I seek a balance with the emotions you raise, and desire to use them appropriately."

"Sometimes reacting without thought, is preferential when moving together as a couple."

"True, and that should happen, especially when alone."

Kudra gasped. "That is forward."

"I agree, but I speak with the honesty and directness you favour. I do this alone with you."

Kudra grinned in the dark, knowing he would not witness it. "You speak the truth; the directness of manner excites beyond obvious."

Gatran laughed. "I share the excitement but speak no longer. I request your lips against mine."

Kudra didn't disappoint. She reached for him. Their lips met and tongue flickered against tongue, searching and probing, mouths opening to accept. She pulled him closer, feeling the growth of his arousal against her and experiencing the awareness of her own. When the kiss ended, she took a much-required deep breath.

"A time after this journey will afford opportunity to share beyond a kiss, Gatran; I will welcome you with open arms."

"Your words could be forward, Kudra."

"I speak the truth in the manner you like in me."

"You certainly do."

Chapter 46:

Despite the weight of the quest, Gatran felt contentment. He was happy beyond anything he could imagine, and Kudra was the cause. He wondered about sharing his feelings with Dravel, but the High Elf seldom revealed anything at that personal level. Gatran decided against it.

Kudra walked alongside Sitara and the two of them were laughing and blushing simultaneously. Gatran guessed they were discussing their relationships. He enjoyed seeing their closeness and longed to meet his brother and sister and share his feelings. Dravel increased his pace when Kudra slowed to walk with Sitara, allowing them time together. It offered opportunity to discuss events past and those to come.

"We have been fortunate since leaving the army behind. The challenges we've faced have been surmountable and not afforded injuries to slow us down."

"The amount of magic-induced conflict is a worry though, creatures difficult to stop and possessed with powers beyond belief."

"And yet we have achieved positive outcomes. Possibly more encounters with the forces of dark magic have been avoided due to your decision making, Gatran."

"Possibly, maybe just luck."

"I'm a firm believer in individuals making their own luck."

"Maybe."

"Our attention should turn to the matters ahead. Achieving peace with the Dwarves."

"Agreed, but many moon cycles require passing before dialogue, including the potential dangers in this location. I still expect to encounter more Trolls, and the likelihood is that we'll run into a Dwarf scouting party. Either could offer death, especially as we know those who command the dark magic force seek it."

"Maybe we should share the burden, then. I will assume responsibility for meeting the Dwarves and you concentrate on us reaching them alive."

"Once, perhaps, a wise decision. However, we have two female High Elves who have proved exceptional at understanding the issues we face and offering sound counsel. I decided a while ago to continue seeking their views and thoughts as I do yours; together, we are more effective as a force."

"You are wise Gatran. Forgive the forward nature of my comments. In High Elf society, males and females carry different roles that rarely cross. I do not intend to undervalue their contributions; I simply have little experience of working closely with them."

"Nothing to forgive my friend. It's similar in Wood Elf society, but I had the experience of a very independent and outspoken sister. She is gentle in nature, but a force to reckon with."

"I am grateful; you can offset my inadequacies."

"It's not an inadequacy, just a lack of experience. We all excel in some areas and are weaker in others. Your excellence is in diplomacy."

"Again, you are wise in your understanding of what is important."

"I've been fortunate with the individuals I am close to, my family, my army and Elf society."

"So, let's assume we reach Xeltar Mountain safely and seek an audience with their King. We must offer something of gain to achieve a peace treaty."

"There's the survival of two species initially, by ending the conflict between us. They might also like the fact we plan to retreat from the known world and therefore leave opportunity for Dwarves to rule across a wider region. Then there's a possibility we might secure a cure for the sickness."

"Each offers excellent possibilities to end hostilities in their individuality. Together they form a strong inducement."

"There is one consideration to muse. The Dwarves are viewed as greedy, with an insatiable appetite for gold. They are compelled to collect it by a desire surpassing greed. Of this I am convinced. Their need is so powerful it breaks reasoning and forces them into actions ill-advised."

"Gatran, I have only ever considered their need for gold as greed. Your thoughts have merit and require consideration, and I will ponder this when alone."

"Consider too this thought. Everything we offer may not seem enough because it is not matched by an offering of gold. We have none. It is not the sort of wealth or treasure that Elves seek."

"If needed, we could create some by magic, Kudra is capable."

"It's important the Dwarves never learn this, because they would imprison her for life."

"Perhaps we should create a treasure hoard somewhere safe before reaching the Dwarves. It could be a last bargaining attempt should events not follow as sought."

"The idea has merit, Dravel. I too will consider during time alone."

"I would ask a personal question you may not wish to answer."

"Speak your mind."

"Perhaps it would be more accurate, requesting answers for two questions. First, has your need for time alone decreased since your relationship with Kudra develops?"

"And second?"

"Are you capable of the same level of contemplation in Kudra's presence?"

"You are astute Dravel. Before I answer, are your questions born from observing Kudra and I, or born from your own personal development."

"More from a personal perspective. Despite the many sun cycles I've lived, relationships with females have been limited."

"Similar to me, everything I've experienced has mostly been restricted to training. My encounters with females, limited."

"In some ways, that makes the subject easier to discuss with you."

"Well, to answer your questions, Kudra has a calming effect on me, allowing thoughts to happen when she is present. She knows when to cease her tongue and when to use it, offering different perspectives, and I can discuss anything with her. I rarely need time alone anymore. Is that how it is for you?"

"Exactly the same. How do these females wield such power?"

"I've no idea, but I am liking the situation."

"As am I."

Sitara's voice broke their conversation. "There is movement ahead in tall grasses. Something waits in ambush situation."

"Your attention to the surrounding landscape is a constant comfort to me, Sitara. I rely on your observation skills. Point me to the direction."

Sitara pointed, and Gatran ceased moving to watch the area. Initially, there was nothing. Whoever was concealed there moved suddenly, and a dark colour contrasted the grassy area.

"I can see something. I don't think it's a Troll. Too small, possibly a Dwarf, though, which could mean we're closer to Xeltar Mountain than I expected."

"I can confirm it's a Dwarf, Gatran, it's standing. The alternative is a Dark Elf."

Whoever it was moved position again and Sitara had a good glimpse of it. "Definitely a Dwarf, absolutely no doubt."

"Well, they don't travel alone. Usually, they're in pairs or fours, so there are more concealed in the grass somewhere."

"This could be a deception, Gatran. One Dwarf drawing our attention while others circling to trap us."

"Anyone would believe you're a battle strategist, Kudra. Sitara scan all around us with the crystal eyeglass."

They ceased talking while she scanned the area.

"There are four, Gatran, closing in from every direction," she warned.

"Prepare to defend yourselves. If possible, capture, rather than kill them."

Chapter 47:

Gatran ordered the Elves to stand their ground while he moved forward towards the Dwarf closing in. The Dwarf drew his axe as the distance between them narrowed and Gatran drew his. The eyes of the Dwarf were fixed, a concentrated unwavering stare. Gatran sensed something unnatural about it and moved to the left slightly. The Dwarf altered position too, but the stare remained absolute. It was then that Gatran realised he was under the influence of magic. He called out, warning the others.

Gatran allowed the Dwarf to close in further until just a pace away. It stopped suddenly, maintaining the stare but not threatening otherwise. The Prince of the Wood Elves raised his sword threateningly and at last the Dwarf responding launching into a lightning-fast attack. Gatran parried the initial stroke of the battle axe easily and circled his enemy. He raised his sword and again the Dwarf attacked with identical outcome.

His actions were a response to Gatran's threat, so Gatran ceased his aggressive approach and kept his sword lowered. He circled the Dwarf repeatedly, noting how it mirrored his moves, but made no attempt to attack. The eyes maintaining their fixed stare.

The other Dwarves had reached the High Elves and attacked immediately. Dravel attempted magic to protect them within a shield, but his magic failed. As he parried a battle axe, he called to Kudra asking for the shield, but she too failed to erect one. The Dwarf attacking Dravel was fast, too fast and a glancing blow caught Dravel cleanly on the chin. He fell, unconscious before reaching the ground. The Dwarf made no move to end his life. He joined the other two, fighting Kudra and Sitara. Swift blows rendered them both unconscious, and the Dwarfs carried them away.

Gatran still faced his attacker, oblivious to what happened behind. He turned away to check the Dwarf's reaction, and it attacked suddenly. A vicious frenzy of axe swings Gatran could barely deflect. The Dwarf was only half his size but, wielded a strength beyond his own. He deflected swing after swing and soon felt himself tiring and weakening, while the Dwarf maintained his feverous attack. It continued until the axe contacted his head. It came on a back-handed swing, acting like a club rather than a severing action. Gatran fell, his world turning dark, and the Dwarf walked away, retaining the intensive stare in his eyes.

It was almost dark when Dravel regained consciousness. Unsteadily, he raised himself, taking in huge gulps of air and allowing his head to lose the fog temporarily obscuring the world around him. He stood and saw Gatran's prone body a distance away. There was no sign of the females. He moved to Gatran and shook him gently. Gatran opened his eyes and moaned as a wave of pain and nausea passed through him.

"What happened?" he stammered.

"The Dwarves fought under dark magic control. They were impossible to defeat."

"They did not desire to kill us."

"No, their intent was to abduct Kudra and Sitara."

"But why? So far, we assumed I was the favoured target."

"I suspect one of two reasons. Either they realise who Kudra is and her potential worth in terms of gold. Or, they took her as leverage against you."

"But why didn't they take me?"

"An idea's forming, an answer, but without a way to prove the validity."

"Speak it, Dravel."

"We have suggested there are many creatures using dark magic against us. But one individual must control them. What if the creatures attacking us, have no knowledge of their participation towards the greater cause; they're responding to a single order?"

"So, the Trolls were attempting to capture me and the Dwarves, Kudra and Sitara."

"Perhaps knowledge of her true position has reached those commanding dark magic, but they cannot issue commands to all of their followers at one time."

"It still suggests whoever commands them can see us, probably with the use of magic. How else did the Dwarves find us. It wasn't chance, they had purpose."

"Whatever the truth of it, doesn't change the fact that the Dwarves now have Kudra and Sitara. We have a weaker starting point than before."

"To hell with the negotiations, Dravel, we have to get them back."

"Quell your emotion, Gatran. It has no purpose in our mission and is likely to get us killed."

"I will not lose them; I have given everything for my kind and asked for nothing in return. I will not lose them."

"We will secure their freedom while serving the mission. Of this, I am sure. I am confident the Dwarves will not harm them. More likely, they'll be retained until the mastermind appears to collect them."

"You think he will come to Xeltar mountain?"

"Why not, everything for the future hinges on the meeting between the Dwarf King and us."

"I still don't understand why they didn't kill us or take us with them."

"It simply wasn't what they were instructed to do."

"There will be an easy trail to follow, four individuals flattening the grass they tread on."

"Yes, even if none, their destination is obvious."

"Let's waste no more time, Dravel."

They followed the path until darkness blanketed the world and they became insignificant in its entirety. Gatran commented how strange it appeared travelling without Kudra and Sitara's presence.

There was no food remaining, and they sat silently, occasionally sipping the last of their water. When Gatran lay back on his sleeping mat, Dravel followed his example and they rested. But sleep failed to ease minds. Dravel's thoughts were of Sitara while Gatran's dwelled on Kudra first, and then his army. Had they woken from their stone prisons, were they travelling to support him? How distant, and how long before they were reunited?"

He wished he had answers. As he closing in towards the point of his journey, the odds against a successful conclusion were decreasing. No army! No Kudra and Sitara! No gold to offer the Dwarves. Worse, an increasing awareness he was being observed and tracked. Thwarted at every opportunity by the forces of dark magic.

His thoughts murdered his sleep for the duration of the night, and he rose in the morning with an anger and frustration belying his normal disposition.

Chapter 48:

Gatran was still lost in the same thoughts. Delaying the inevitable was pointless. Confrontation with the Dwarves was imminent, and he no longer considered the potential repercussions of his actions.

Dravel understood his feelings and empathised with them, despite his own. Centuries of living forced a discipline of self-control beyond the capabilities of most Elves. He couldn't help rationalising everything.

"Gatran, I must urge you to put away thoughts of aggression and hasty action. It will not serve us well."

"You're correct in what you say, but my plan is to catch the Dwarves who captured Kudra and Sitara before they reach Xeltar Mountain."

"And, when you succeed, what plan do you have for defeating these creatures inflamed by dark magic?"

"My plan is simple. I do not expect to defeat these Dwarves and secure their release, so I have an alternative. Separate Kudra from them, long enough for her to conjure a stash of gold, concealed by an invisible cloak. Without gold to barter with, I believe an agreement with Dwarves is impossible."

"Achieving this, you realise you will watch Kudra and Sitara taken from us a second time."

"Their rescue will be easier when their immediate capturers leave them."

"You're not expecting the Dwarves at Xeltar Mountain to be under the influence of dark magic?"

"No. I suspect the overseer to use his power with restraint, ensuring he has enough left to achieve his ultimate goals."

"Which are?"

"Wealth beyond belief, perhaps. I believe Kudra's true identity is known and she'll be held indefinitely by the Dwarves. I think she will be used for bartering, achieving total Dwarf control."

"And Sitara."

"I'm aware she will be deemed as unrequired unless she too can assist in the production of gold."

"She can. So at least their lives are safe for now. What about us?"

"I reckon the Dwarves will use me to bribe my father into doing something he wouldn't normally do. What, I cannot be sure. Also, I would be useful to encourage Kudra to comply with Dwarf wishes and make gold. And you Dravel, it's possible you'd be used as an envoy, to barter for what they want to gain from my father. Also, an inducement to encourage Sitara to make gold. That aside, we are surplus to requirement."

"I wish the identity of the mastermind behind this, was known, along with the reason for annihilation of Elves. They have only to wait before we withdraw from the known world."

"I hear you Dravel. This is revenge for a past transgression, not necessarily during our time. It could originate from many sun-cycles ago."

"I agree, it's the most logical conclusion. Their discontent runs deep to wait so long to exact such a revenge."

They fell silent and Gatran started jogging.

"Time to increase the pace of our pursuit."

They ran for most of the morning before movement ahead announced they were catching up with their targets.

"We have an element of surprise Dravel, they won't be expecting us and are probably not watching their rear."

"What is your plan of attack?"

"I want to draw the Dwarves away from Kudra by attacking all of them. You must get her away and instruct her to make the cache of gold. A huge amount bigger than any reward from sacking an enemies' village and veil it under a shield."

"You forget our magic wasn't working."

"I believe it will away from these dwarves. If not, you must seek a place where it does."

"Since the females were their targets, you're gambling your life on us achieving this."

"I've always known this mission is bigger than me, Dravel, and I will gladly sacrifice our lives for a successful conclusion. Ensure when concealing it, you can find it again."

They ceased talking as they approached the Dwarves. Closing in, and within a few yards of them, Gatran raised his sword and narrowed the gap further. Dravel followed with his target.

"Remember me?" Gatran suddenly asked and the Dwarf in front of him turned in surprise.

He didn't hesitate and thrust his sword through the Dwarfs stomach. Dravel followed the example with his target and two Dwarves were removed from battle. The remaining two set upon them. Dravel threw his sword to Sitara and instructed her to keep him occupied while he and Kudra slipped away despite her immediate protestations.

Sitara fought like she was possessed and held her attacker's onslaught for as long as she could. She was weakening and Gatran noticed. He felt the intensity and the gradual weakening of his strength. He called Sitara to his side.

"Fight alongside me, Sitara. They won't harm you because of what you offer. We must gain time for the others to achieve their goal."

"Speak of this goal?" Sitara gasped, as she closed in and stood alongside Gatran.

"I cannot say while these Dwarves are present. I'm convinced those enhancing their powers cannot only see us, but hear us as well."

"I understand. Perhaps then we should give demonstration showing unwise nature of attacking Elves."

"I'll draw the sword from your attacker, and you finish him."

Gatran attacked with renewed frenzy, attacking both remaining Dwarves, forcing them to engage him. As they did Sitara ran her sword through one. He fell, leaving only one remaining.

"Same again Sitara."

The last Dwarf fell to the tactic and Sitara and Gatran fought to slow their breathing. A sudden blow to the head rendered him unconscious once more. Sitara turned to face the two Dwarves Gatran and Dravel had originally killed. She examined them visually, noticing the absence of the wounds Gatran and Dravel inflicted. The other two Dwarves also rose from the ground. She dropped her sword, and the Dwarves motioned her forward. Once again, leaving Gatran unconscious on the ground.

Chapter 49:

Kudra and Dravel ran as fast as they could across the Plains. Their initial intent was to create a gap between themselves and the Dwarves. Both knew Gatran and Sitara were incapable of defeating them, meaning only a limited amount of time before being pursued again.

Forming the gold cache, and subsequent veiling of it, was relatively simple for Kudra. It assumed her magic would return when distant from the Dwarves. No apparent reason suggested otherwise. It had worked prior to engaging them. Otherwise, as Gatran suggested, everything was for nothing.

Discovering a small depression less than waist deep, it was adequate for their purpose. Dravel nodded and suggested she started.

"A simple task but requiring substantial effort Dravel; I will create in stages. Control of magic is still issue."

"I understand Kudra, but because of the increased time required I'll keep watch for the Dwarves. Make as much as you can."

Kudra nodded and began. Between brief periods of chanting, stillness was broken by a fresh cache of gold. It built quickly, until its volume surpassed an average treasure haul from battle, and still she continued. Eventually, Dravel touched her arm to break her concentration and told her she had made enough.

"Your control was exemplary, Kudra."

"Thank you Dravel. Since Gatran first encouraged use of magic and practice control, it becomes easier, and I grow in confidence."

"We have an extraordinary amount of gold here. It would be beyond a Dwarfs expectation to gain so much in one haul. Can you veil it now, so it remains unseen until required?"

Kudra cast the spell, and the gold vanished from sight.

"What now Dravel? Surely, we should return to aid Gatran and Sitara. They cannot hold at bay enemy who defies a weakening of strength."

"We could return to assist, but you and I both realise it's pointless. We cannot defeat them. However, we could delay their progress to Xeltar Mountain and veer away from the cache here. It is the only way to help our friends."

"They are beyond friends Dravel, can you not admit this and say the words."

"Without hesitation, but in times more favourable, Kudra, we must leave."

Kudra nodded, and Dravel started jogging. She followed, realising just how much Sitara had affected the High Elf and how different he was becoming. Pangs of regret coursed through her. She had left them behind to an uncertain fate, but knowing the gold was a necessary inducement towards a lasting peace.

After a short while, Kudra stopped Dravel. "This is pointless, you delay inevitable. We must return for Gatran. I must again become prisoner to Dwarves."

Dravel glanced away, realising her words were accurate but without the desire to state it.

"You're right Kudra. I realised, time long ago, Gatran is key to the success of this mission. Without him, and despite our best efforts, we are doomed to fail."

"Dispel negative thoughts, Dravel. Gatran would not appreciate them."

"They are not negative, merely realistic. He has been at the forefront of every positive decision we've made. He alone holds responsibility for getting us this far and he alone can orchestrate a peace with the Dwarves."

"Why are you so sure of this?"

"He thinks and acts beyond expectations, it's what's required to secure the peace."

"You underestimate our contribution?"

"I do not. Most of our contributions result from his thinking and planning."

"You are accurate in thoughts, perhaps I had not examined course fully."

"It doesn't matter, not to the cause or Gatran. He simply follows his thoughts, regardless. He alone bears the weight of success of the mission."

"You have so much faith in him, Dravel, as I do."

"Your words are accurate, but the next decision is mine. You must allow yourself to be captured again and go to Xeltar mountain the Dwarves. It's time we separated. I should return to Gatran and leave you here. Recapture will not take long. Know we will not rest until we have secured your freedom, and the mission is completed. Know also, if Gatran's army survived the duration of magic, they will arrive soon, possibly before Gatran and I reach Xeltar."

"And the army's role, explain this?"

"A deterrent against battle. The Dwarf army cannot leave their underground dwellings without being picked off at point of exit. Their presence alone is problematic for the Dwarves. A siege of the mountain would mean eventual starvation or a desperate bid for freedom. Either would deplete their numbers significantly. Their species has reached the same point of uncertainty as ours."

"I hope arrival is soon. Gatran suffers as with loss of limb in their absence."

"Perhaps true, but he still makes the decisions and chooses the paths to follow as always. His ability to choose the correct path is unerring."

"Leave me Dravel, I'll wait for capture. Return to Gatran now and encourage him further. His esteem for you is unequalled. Your presence gives strength, I'm sure."

"Thank you, Kudra. You and he are worthy partners for one another. The options for you both are limited, yet in the melee you discovered each other."

Dravel dipped his head, turned and moved away without waiting for a reply, but Kudra voiced it anyway.

"You have Sitara's heart, as she has yours. Your options were as limited and yet you also found each other. Perhaps this is our reward for the sacrifice we make."

Kudra started following the trail back and was intercepted by the Dwarves almost immediately. They showed no hostility towards her and waited for her to walk alongside Sitara before indicating the direction to Xeltar Mountain.

"Gatran, he is unhurt?" Kudra whispered.

"Unconscious from a blow to the head. And Dravel?"

"Returning for him as we speak."

"And the purpose?"

"Completed without issue."

"The next stop for us will be the Dwarf Kingdom."

"Yes. And many days' absence from sun's warmth and cheer."

"They will return for us, Kudra."

"This I know."

Chapter 50:

Several moon cycles passed before Dravel and Gatran reached Xeltar Mountain. While Dravel concentrated his thoughts on the peace talks, Gatran was experiencing a wider range of emotions.

The relief at reaching Xeltar Mountain equated to a huge burden being lifted from his shoulders, despite not yet starting negotiations. Getting there safely had tested him fully. He had little care for his safety, but his companions weighed the mission considerably. He wanted to ensure their safety despite the odds faced. Even Sitara, who had taken longer to bond with, was a huge consideration in decision making.

Being closer to Kudra, despite the current lack in physical presence, was both a comfort and a worry. Her unknown situation in the Dwarf kingdom remained a concern. Hopefully, he would see her soon. No engagement with the Dwarf King would happen without her presence, and Sitara's too. He could still draw strength from her unseen presence.

There was also excitement too. His army were close, he could sense it. Eckna would have driven them hard to their destination, and Gatran could not wait for the comfort of their presence. He firmly believed they were essential for a successful conclusion of the negotiations. Their force, as a deterrent, crucial.

He and Dravel camped a moon-cycle away from the mountain, though the sheer size of it suggested closer proximity. They were in a small copse, thirty or more densely packed trees. It marked the end of the Jerev Hills and hopefully the end of possibilities for further Troll encounters.

Gatran wished to discuss the tactics for the forthcoming meeting with Dughork, King of the Dwarves. It was imperative both he and Dravel worked from the same plan in case of separation or unfortunate and unforeseen events. He also wanted to wait for his army, despite knowing the longer he waited, the longer Kudra and Sitara remained prisoners.

"It's time for you and I to plan, my friend. I could easily assume responsibility for the direction the intended meeting takes, but that would devalue your presence and skills. Your presence was requested by my father, my faith in him is total. He understands your capabilities, perhaps better than I. Your King would have convinced him of your worth.

"I believe there is no single approach we can decide upon with total confidence. Their kind are too unpredictable. Perhaps we should discuss the separate aspects of what's on offer. What we'll allow to happen and what we'll not accept."

"You assume control of the discussions will be ours. That may not be the case. "

"I will insist on what happens. We're offering gold, a lasting peace, an avoidance of extinction, land for them to claim after our withdraw. This grants them increased position of power in the region. Last, a potential cure for the sickness. What are we asking for in return? An end to hostilities."

"When you state the offers like this, it sounds an irresistible offer, gifts unimaginable to the Dwarves. In warning, I will state Dwarves, as an enemy, remain the most deceitful we've fought; there's one further issue to consider."

"You are talking about the unseen enemy who fights with dark magic."

"Yes! One who can warp the minds of individuals to fight for causes against their normal beliefs. He or they, must make an appearance soon. They cannot let our peace talks succeed because all their efforts will have been for nothing."

"Not necessarily Dravel, we suspect it's an individual holding a grudge against Elves, probably from the past. Failure would be a simple setback, they waited many sun-cycles to exact revenge, so patience is their strength. We know a Witch orchestrates the sickness and a Dark Elf is associated with her, but I feel there are more involved and possibly above them in position."

"Regardless of identity, the mission must remain the same until they reveal themselves. We could guess at their ultimate desires, but it changes nothing. An awareness of their possible presence is all we can assume."

"Three stipulations before negotiations can occur."

"They are?"

"First, we wait until my army arrives, they are close, I can sense them. Second, Kudra and Sitara are present at the talks. I know females at negotiations with Dwarves are frowned upon by their kind, but we must keep them close to us. They are to stay with us for the duration of our visit. And finally, I want you to lead all the negotiations and I will make it appear that I'm controlling everything. An Elf Prince would not play second to an ambassador."

"All are wise considerations Gatran, but you can lead the discussions."

"Possibly, but you have infinitely more patience than I especially if these Dwarves prove difficult."

"We could lead together."

"I have to ask this next question Dravel. Your answer will remain with me alone. I have wondered at your abilities, aware you're capable of more than demonstrated. Your manner of thinking alone suggests you have position above most High Elves. Your knowledge, your command of white magic, and your concern for others. Who are you Dravel, really?"

Dravel paused from answering but retained an impassive expression while he decided whether to share the truth. Time passed before he shifted position to one opposite Gatran. That one simple move told Gatran he was about to learn his friend had real position beyond an ambassador. He wanted to face him and make eye-contact. The truth was significant, and Gatran realised he would gain knowledge few others were privy to; the weight of sharing it, from Dravel's perspective, was enormous.

"The truth is difficult; there are several revelations, my friend. I share because of our friendship. There are few I trust more.

"Your words will stay with me alone Dravel, I promise."

"Your promise is not required; your word is enough. There is another reason, perhaps surprising to you. Should I die in the attempt to secure our mission I would seek your promise to find my mother and tell her of the Elf I became and the good I chose to do with my life. I have not seen her in over eight-hundred sun-cycles."

"That's not required, we'll finish this mission as we started, together. But you have my promise, regardless. Perhaps, after this, we could visit her together so I can thank her for the friend I've gained."

"I would like that, I truly would."

Again, a pause before Dravel continued and Gatran waited with consummate patience.

"My mother is a humble Elf who for a time worked at the royal dwellings of my King and Queen. She was content with her work and asked for nothing in return, serving with loyalty and a grace suiting her gentle personality. After some time in the position, she became noticed by my King. He fell in love with her, totally smitten and beyond self-control. You should understand he was married to a suiter of position; love played no part in their relationship. I was born from the loving relationship they had.

"Because of his position, I could never be accepted in High Elf Society, so I was secreted away with my mother, and we lived peacefully alone. After the first-hundred sun-cycles my father, the King, visited me and lay out a course of instruction from trustworthy individuals. It spanning the next six-hundred sun-cycles. All my learning came from them, while my gentle and peaceable nature came from her.

"Once my training was completed. I was again visited by my father and instructed to assume a position of ambassadorship; I have remained such ever since. I can never claim position as High Elf Royalty and could never address my King as father."

Dravel at last ceased talking. He maintained eye-contact with Gatran, seeking an indication of how this might affect them. However, this time, Gatran held the stare with his own, completely impassive. He made the High Elf wait before shifting position, as Dravel had, before speaking.

"That you have royal blood flowing through your body is of no real surprise. You hold yourself in manner and behaviour as royalty, you're probably not aware you do this. Not acknowledging your father must be difficult. If you are fond of him, painful."

"I have known him more these past years and admire the Elf he is. I am drawn to him, but absence caused by the diplomatic position offers much time away from him.

"I am saddened for your mother too. To lose position because of love. I assume their love was mutual, or you would never have been born."

"I live hoping circumstances might change and allow recognition of me in public, but I doubt that will happen."

"Change is coming Dravel, if we achieve our mission, you will be remembered in High Elf folklore for ever. Our two societies will combine, that cannot happen without change, who knows what doors will open, my friend."

"For every door that opens, another closes."

A realistic viewpoint keeps us balanced. Let's hope the right one opens for you, your father and mother."

Chapter 51:

"There is a dust cloud to the south of our position, Gatran. It can only be a sizable force. "

Gatran looked behind. "We're too far for it to be the Anurans, the Trolls don't command such numbers, which means it's either the Dwarf army or ours. It would be the answer to many of our problems and give us the final leverage we need."

"If it's our army, we must ensure they remain free from dark magic influence."

"Surely their numbers remain too numerous for magic to affect all."

"Affecting all is unnecessary, just Eckna and the Masters. Every Elf follows them without question. If not, then others whose sole mission is to make life difficult when possible and report our every move to their leader.

"True, and you're right we should ensure they are in the proper state of mind for what comes next. I can't speak for you Dravel, but I've had enough surprises already from this journey."

"I can check each of your commanders without their knowledge. If dark magic is present, I'll know."

"That's helpful, but another issue remains. We were convinced of a traitor, maybe more than one, infiltrating our ranks."

"I've said before, more likely another creature disguises self as an Elf, a Witch probably."

"Would you be capable of discovering the dark magic in them?"

"The answer is unknown; I can only attempt this. If it is our army then perhaps a meeting of those within the ranks is appropriate. We could search the entire army using the tactic."

"And if we find them?"

"Exposing them is a mistake, they provide opportunity to discover who commands the dark forces. With patience and guile, we could finally understand the point for the resistance we've faced."

"It could take all night?"

"So be it. An opportunity too good to refuse."

"That's if it's our army and not the Dwarves."

"They draw closer, we'll know their identity soon.

Moments later, the force was close enough to identify individuals. Eckna rode at the front of the force. Sitting tall and proud, an imposing sight, suggesting he was every part an individual to be aware of.

"It's them, Dravel, it's really them."

"They survived the sickness! I see the Masters and Eckna."

"I never believed I'd be grateful for dark magic, but I am at this moment. Go forward Gatran, meet your army, I'll join you shortly."

"The concession is appreciated, but we continue forward together. Eckna's pleasure at your presence will be clear."

They moved forward, side by side, and a smile broke on Eckna's face as he recognised them. He halted a short distance away to prevent them being consumed in the dust cloud and dismounted.

Despite wanting to rush forward and greet his prince, Eckna used every ounce of reserve and discipline he had to march forward as the soldier he was.

"It pleases my heart to greet you, my Prince."

"As it does mine, old friend."

Before Eckna could say another word, Gatran wrapped his arms around his commander and welcomed him further with a huge bear hug.

"I cannot believe an Elven Prince would greet a commander in such a manner, especially in front of his soldiers."

"You have always been more than a soldier to me my friend. I am content with every soldier knowing this."

Eckna lowered his voice to a whisper. "Know that your affection warms my heart like no other."

"So, tell me what happened, when did the dark magic release you?"

"A Dark Elf released us from its grip and explained what happened, and that you continued your journey. To keep things simple, we've ridden hard every day since to catch up with you."

"Your presence arrives at a perfect moment. Kudra and Sitara are prisoners of the Dwarves, and we were about to enter Xeltar Mountain."

Anger showed in Eckna's face. "Your feelings for Kudra have grown?"

"Yes, as has Dravel's for Sitara."

"Forgive me, Dravel. In my haste to greet my friend and Prince, I have neglected you. I am pleased that the journey has rewarded you with fine health, and I am convinced you have played a part in keeping both you and Gatran that way."

"Your words speak the truth, Eckna, but each of us have contributed to that. Differing strengths and abilities have been a positive factor."

Eckna moved forward and gripped Dravel's forearms in a formal greeting. "Know a friend of Gatran holds permanent favour with me. I am grateful for your presence Dravel."

"You could demonstrate that gratitude easily with a show of food. We haven't eaten for the past few days."

"I will have my soldiers prepare a feast to honour both of you."

Gatran interrupted. "Allow my army such luxuries, each can celebrate our return."

Eckna grinned. "Your consideration for our soldiers is always a pleasure to witness; it is why they respect you so highly. We shall prepare food and the Masters will join us to learn of the adventures of their Prince."

"There is much to share and unpleasant warnings to bring also."

Eckna turned away to issue orders and as Dravel and Gatran moved within the ranks, cheers of joy echoed around them. Even Dravel lost his serious demeanour and smiled at those he passed.

Chapter 52:

Kudra and Sitara were led resolutely toward Xeltar Mountain. Their four Dwarf escort said nothing during the entire trip and maintained at a relentless pace.

"Unsure If can hold pace longer. Food and rest necessary," Sitara moaned.

"Share needs. Let's stop, refuse further travel without food. So far, they refrain from hurting us. Let's sit, now."

Kudra sat down and Sitara followed. Immediately, the four Dwarves closed in on them. One indicated for them to get up, but Kudra shook her head defiantly.

"Food and water, before taking another step."

The Dwarves stared at them blankly. The Elven tongue beyond their understanding. Kudra raised her hand to her mouth and pretended to place something in it. Then she mimed drinking. There was no mistaking her actions, and the Dwarves understood immediately. They had not eaten either, basic needs forgotten while under the influence of dark magic. One spoke, and two Dwarves slipped away. It was an hour before they returned, one carrying a small deer. The two remaining, had sat unmoving, close to the Elves to represent a threat, reinforced by staring at them.

Kudra rose, immediately followed by her two guards, and started collecting dried brush carried by the breeze. Sitara walked further away and collected sticks and small branches. The remaining Dwarves followed her. Returning to where the deer lay, Kudra lit a small fire and one dwarf cleaned and prepared the deer for cooking.

Another slipped away again, returning after a while carrying fresh water in a skin bladder. He indicated for Kudra to remove her bladder skin and filled it from his. He repeated the action with Sitara's skin and then shared the remaining fluid with his fellow Dwarves. The meat was slow to cook through, instead of waiting they cut thin slices from the outer layers to eat.

Kudra had no intention of travelling further that day. Instead, she lay back and closed her eyes. She was surprised it brought no reaction from the Dwarves who followed her example, one remaining on watch.

Unsurprisingly, they slept through the night, waking shortly after dawn.

Kudra declared they'd reach Xeltar Mountain. A pointless remark since the mountain dominated the landscape.

"Our lives may have purposes unclear."

"Maybe, but Gatran and Dravel will journey for us. Our imprisonment is temporary."

"We should learn what we can, it will aid eventual escape."

"I agree, but also mood of King and subjects, to aid tactics during dialogue."

They fell silent as the Dwarves rose, indicating for them to follow and the relentless march to the Dwarf homeland continued. They reached it soon after midday.

Standing at the foot of the largest mountain they had ever seen; the door's location remained a mystery. Since huge numbers of Dwarves lived here, the cavernous tunnels within had to be vast.

"Where is the entrance?" Sitara asked.

"It eludes me."

The Dwarves stopped and rested their hands against the mountain side. They bowed their head and chanted something illegible. After pausing further, they started walking around it before spotting a narrow trail leading up the side. The leading Dwarf selected it and they followed.

"The entrance must be higher up." Sitara intoned.

Her comment was unnecessary but highlighted her increasing fear of her being confined within the mountain. Higher and higher, they travelled until the trail petered out onto a wide ledge. Still no obvious door. One Dwarf touched the wall and ran his hand upward. Kudra and Sitara watched, both curious and fascinated. The Dwarf's hand stopped moving and three fingers curled into small holes. He pushed and part of the wall moved. A rock door was evident, moving into the mountain revealing a gap wide enough for a Dwarf to enter a tunnel beyond.

The second Dwarf followed and the two behind the Elves moved forward, prodding them to follow. Sitara briefly looked around. Absorbing a last glimpse of the sky, she inhaled deeply before entering. Kudra admired her friend's bravery, knowing how much she was afraid of leaving the freedom of outside behind. She followed her in.

Inside, a tunnel illuminated by fire-torches contained dark and light areas created by the distance between them. It gave the tunnel an eerie feel. They said nothing as the Dwarves continued forward. The tunnel opened into a cavernous space before reverting to a tunnel after passing through. Not one exit though, multiple alternatives to choose from. Kudra realised finding an escape route would be difficult.

The Dwarves continued without hesitation, choosing a tunnel heading at a downward angle. Incredibly, they wandered through tunnels and caverns for ages. The Dwarves in front eventually slowed when they reached the largest cavern they witnessed so far. At the far end, a throne. A chair so large several Dwarves could sit side by side. An imposing figure sat upon it, adorned with gold trinkets that reflected light, like stars in the sky. An entourage of Dwarves with a wide range of purposes moved around their King, bowing every time they passed within his gaze.

"That's him Kudra, the reason for travel."

"Show respect Sitara, remain calm as breeze on summer day and hope to receive treatment worthy of position."

"He cannot know identity."

"Mistake assuming this. State truth about us, and mission, but offer nothing beyond answering questions. Everything expected from this journey offered issues beyond expectation. Wise to expect continuation."

"Words speak truth. We must insist staying together."

"We will request if needed, insist nothing. He is King here."

The Dwarves stopped a few yards shy of the King and bowed. Words that left their lips were unknown, but the King stood and moved toward them. They kept their heads low until he touched each on the shoulder, allowing them to look at his face. More words were spoken, and the Dwarves behind Kudra and Sitara pushed them forward. Their movement was stopped by strong hands on their shoulders. Kudra took the lead. She bowed respectfully.

"Greetings King Dughork. I stand relieved before you. For many nights, I worried my mission would fail; and the future of our kinds continue toward extinction."

"Greetings Kudra, Princess of the High Elves, and greetings to Sitara who no doubt shares your concerns."

Any doubt about what Dughork knew disappeared instantly, and Kudra and Sitara tried not to display their surprise.

Chapter 53:

"Your command of the Elven language is excellent. Are you also aware of our purpose here?"

"Your visit was foretold in Dwarven prophesies, written hundreds of generations before ours. It states four visitors will arrive to save the future of the Dwarven empire."

Kudra hid her surprise but remained quiet, encouraging the King to reveal more. He didn't hesitate in doing so.

"The prophecy states three High Elves and a Wood Elf would visit, offering inducements to encourage the future of our kinds. It states the Wood Elf is a Prince and two of the High Elves are of equal standing, one Princess and One Prince. The remaining High Elf has no position, but is crucial for saving the lives of the delegates gathered for discussing futures. I am speaking the truth, yes?"

"I am Kudra, a High Elf Princess and Sitara is the fourth individual you mentioned."

"What of the two you travelled with?"

"We became separated by Dwarves who captured us. They act under influence of dark magic and showed no interest in companions."

The King moved forward. "Speak no more of this momentarily. I will clear Kingdom Cavern so we may talk without fear of reprisal."

He ushered his entourage away and waited patiently for the last of them to disappear.

"Accusing Dwarves of being under the influence of dark magic holds risk to accusers."

"I speak truth, we visit at crucial time, speaking untruths disadvantages discussions and breeds distrust."

"Why should I believe this?"

"Our two friends will arrive to speak. Their words will carry same message as mine."

"Prince Gatran and Prince Dravel are expected."

Kudra and Sitara both failed to hide their surprise at his words, and the King continued.

"Few know true identity of Dravel, born secretly to a lover of the King. His identity was protected to allow the King and him to live unchallenged by others. Such matters would hold similar arrangements in Dwarven society."

"Do you have Dwarves who can sense dark magic in those possessed."

"I will arrange for this to happen. If your words are true those affected will be killed to protect the rest of us."

"They have not harmed us or attempted to kill us. We believe purpose was to spy on us and those around us. They do not deserve to die. We've encountered many under influence during our journey here."

"And what was their fate?"

"We tried not to harm them. Our mission is peaceable. May I ask how you knew our identities?"

"Your encounter with dark forces at Rag Dire pass released Dwarves kept under influence of dark magic for many sun-cycles. Gatran did not harm them, instead he freed them. I learned your identity from them."

"They are still alive?"

"They were free of the magic. They suffered enough through the actions forced upon them.

"You and Sitara were also released from the dark forces, retained for service longer than Dwarves. I cannot imagine how you feel about that. Your return to Elven Society would cause problems too?"

"Your words are accurate; I remain in no rush to return to Elven kind until I have proved worthiness."

"Do you wish to discuss words of mission?"

"We cannot, that duty is confined to Dravel and Gatran. We respect their right."

"This I understand and respect, but I remember tales from my younger times. I learned of an Elven Princess who commanded white magic to such a degree it was deemed dangerous. Are these stories true."

"I have stated I will not lie. It is true."

"You can make gold?"

"I can; controlling magic is difficult. Many sun-cycles passed under influence of dark magic. Practice for even simple tasks is required."

"While we wait for Dravel and Gatran, you will attempt this for us."

"I must wait for Dravel, he has been aiding my control. I could inadvertently harm those around me attempting magic unaided."

"The truth or merely diversional."

"I speak truth, but I can reveal we have much to offer to obtain agreement with Dwarves."

The King's eyes gleamed. "And this includes gold?"

"All will be revealed when they arrive."

"In that case, you can taste Dwarven hospitality. Food and water and comfortable accommodation, but you will not have the freedom to move around our chambers."

"Your generosity is appreciated King Dughork." Kudra bowed her appreciation and Sitara mirrored the action.

"Time for further discussion before your friends arrive is possible and would be pleasing Kudra."

He clapped his hands, and a Dwarf appeared from nowhere obvious.

"This Dwarf is called Finrok, he can speak the Elven language sufficiently to communicate with you. Ask your needs and he'll provide. Forgive the guards he will place outside your accommodation. It is a necessary protocol and one I must follow. Not every Dwarf is privy to the knowledge I retain of you, and many would assume responsibility for your demise if given opportunity. Distrust between our kinds is unsurprisingly non-existent."

"And yet you display trust."

"Knowledge often displaces distrust, so does truth. Situations are sometimes viewed differently when these are in evidence."

"I hope our future discussions bring such positive outcomes."

"Revelations alone will provide this."

The King turned away and Finrok indicated for them to follow him. Another maze of tunnels and caverns followed before reaching a smaller cave. Finrok explained it was theirs for the duration of their visit.

He left them after two guards assumed position at the tunnel entrance.

"The guards will call for me if you utter my name to them. I have been instructed to give you whatever you need to make your stay comfortable. I have also been warned to state, should you prove difficult, then I am to imprison you in less comfortable circumstances. Fetter you with chains, preventing movement. Your meeting with the King was productive, as introductions go, it is wise to maintain that."

With that said, he turned and left, leaving Kudra and Sitara alone.

Chapter 54:

Gatran was working his way around his army, greeting and welcoming everyone's return. Dravel checked for signs of dark magic. He could do this while mirroring the enthusiastic greetings Gatran gave to his soldiers. He had already checked Eckna and the Masters earlier and found no sign of evil present.

They discussed their thoughts prior to their walk around and had agreed to expect at least two, possibly more, with dark magic. Dravel remained resolute that whoever the traitors were, they would not be Elves but something else in disguise. Gatran accepted his opinions but was not totally convinced. If this journey had taught him anything, it was to expect the unexpected.

They had started their search before dark and it was already half way through the night. Word had spread that Gatran was greeting everyone. His soldier's loyalty was demonstrated, none retiring to their beds before their Prince greeted them.

The infantry were greeted first and Eckna guided them around each of the smaller units, introducing Dravel where he thought it necessary. They covered the entire numbers with no success. Gatran commented he wasn't surprised. These soldiers fought at the heart of any battle; the risk was higher. A disguised individual would not naturally choose them to hide among.

They were accompanied by each Master as they covered the encampment. Gatran instructed them to ensure all were present and none had opportunity to slip away for any supposed reason. Feren, the Master of

Calvary, had each Elf attending their horses. Anyone missing would be noticed by an unattended horse. All his unit were accounted for and one by one Gatran greeted them all. As they walked away, satisfied none had been missed, Dravel whispered there were two individuals under the influence of dark magic.

"Dopan and Ingaw are affected by dark magic. I am convinced they are true Elves and have no clue they are affected."

Feren whistled his surprise. "I have seen nothing to betray they're under control."

"That's the point, Feren. They're under the influence of someone close, I'm sure, and I'm guessing others in the other special units are affected."

"Possibly more than one controller, Dravel."

"I'm almost certain of it, no one individual could infiltrate all the units to wield his control."

"He could if he could change appearance," Feren suggested.

"Shape shifters are rare, few in the known world."

"It would only take one and they too are masters of dark magic," Dravel responded.

"So, it's possible there's only one here controlling my Elves?" Gatran pressed. "This makes sense."

"What about Dopan and Ingaw?" Feren asked.

"Nothing should alert they have been identified as unwilling traitors and are being watched. Watched is the key word here Feren. I want two Elves assigned position close to them. Your most trusted. They're to report to you directly with any strange behaviours."

"I'll see to it, my Prince."

Dravel and Gatran left the unit and joined Dorna the master of Swords. They greeted each soldier and Dravel identified two more individuals under the influence. Dorna was instructed to react as his brother.

Later into the night, they discovered four more. Two in Omati's stealth unit and a final two in Cagen's bow unit. All were real Elves under influence of dark magic.

Despite greeting everyone present, the controller remained unfound. Dravel suspected he had avoided meeting them effortlessly. If he was a Shape Shifter then he could simply change into something else as they passed by. Dravel also commented he had maintained a fair distance between them, as he had not sensed the infiltrator.

The search had procured both a positive and negative result. Those under influence being positively identified, while the controller's identity remained unknown.

"It is a start, Dravel. We could not have hoped for all the answer in one swoop."

"I guess not. But what really bothers me is how easily the controller has avoided us. We'll only find him through luck."

"Or perhaps a trap."

"That won't be easy. A shape shifter can change into anything. Stopping one, means killing it."

"If that's what's needed, I'll not shy from the tough decisions."

"Nor I."

"We should return to Eckna and report our discoveries. He'll not be pleased."

"Being deceived is painful, Gatran."

"We've been deceived by powerful forces; we should not be ashamed. We should learn from it, ensure it doesn't happen again.

"The reach of whoever commands this attack against us is huge. Probably the most powerful individual we've ever encountered, and his identity remains secret."

"Someone knows who he is, Dravel and all we have to do is force a mistake from his subordinates and he will become known to us."

"When we started uncovering this plot against us, I thought it would only involve us, but now I'm not so sure. Your brother and sister could be facing the same dark forces and they don't have an army with them."

"I hope your thoughts are wrong Dravel, for individually they are no match for dark magic."

"Are you suggesting what I think you're suggesting?"

"If you mean, will I ride to support them, then yes, the moment after sealing the peace treaty with Dughork."

"Finding them won't be easy, they may already be prisoners of some unscrupulous individuals."

"I will not think negatively. Both Manudan and Putraya are very capable individuals, and their companions would have been selected carefully."

"You're right to think positively, forgive my doubts."

"Nothing to forgive, your honesty and interpretations are what I need from you, always. You continue to illuminate the path I have to follow Dravel, and I am forever grateful for this. Now let's find Eckna."

They walked side by side towards Lord Eckna's position and Gatran suddenly dreaded the news he had to share.

Chapter 55:

Eckna was shocked at the revelations from Gatran. That there were eight Elves under the influence of dark magic, in his army, was beyond his belief. Like Gatran, he was more concerned with the suspected Shapeshifter. Revealing and capturing him would be almost impossible.

Gatran allowed his friend time to absorb and consider the issues. After a brief period, he announced they would march for Xeltar mountain imminently. Eckna gave the order to break camp, and they were ready to leave before midday. If they travelled at speed, they would reach their destination before nightfall.

While preparations to leave were underway, Dravel meandered through the ranks searching for signs of the Shape Shifter but found none. He joined Gatran for the march just before it commenced and rode alongside.

"A horse is a luxury," Dravel commented.

"A pleasant change, we should reach Xeltar with fading light. If we camp at a reasonable distance, we can walk to the mountain at first light. I do not intend to use the army as a deliberate show of force intent on intimidation."

"Your tactic is sensible, and consideration towards the Dwarves is admirable."

"I have to consider Kudra and Sitara's position. They might be being kept against their wills, but I don't believe they'll be mistreated. I'm sure the Dwarves will suspect potential gain from our meeting, even if unaware of the talks purpose."

"I believe the Dwarves will have more knowledge of our visit than we expect."

"What makes you say that?"

"Expect the unexpected. The unexpected has happened frequently throughout the journey. Whoever plots against us will have some plan to destroy the peace talks, I'm sure."

"You're right to expect that, Dravel. I'm hoping Kudra would have informed him about the influence of dark magic and its potential for intruding our talks."

"You place confidence in Kudra's ability to read the situation."

"I do, she is astute. She will not discuss the mission without our presence because she was not originally part of it. Being viewed as connected to us is reason to ensure their immediate safety."

"They might know her true identity. We released Dwarves at Rag Dire Pass and told them to speak kindly of our actions. They could have learned their true identities, names alone sufficient to make connections. Kudra was famous during her time and Dwarves live long. They might remember her."

"If so, they would know of her ability with white magic."

"Making her incredibly valuable to them."

"Discussions are going to be challenging."

"We have a lot to offer."

Gatran and Dravel discussed everything in minute detail, ensuring everything they thought, they shared. Their stance needed to be identical, with possibilities of being separated. They scarcely noticed the time pass until Eckna gave the order to cease travel and make camp. A stream passing by their position ensured they could replenish their supply, wash and bathe and whatever else they needed to do.

Gatran rode to Eckna and asked him to arrange a meeting for them with the Masters. Plans were required for when Gatran and Dravel entered Xeltar.

It was completely dark by the time the meeting started. Dravel scanned inside the small shelter, erected for privacy, for signs of dark magic, but found none. He searched outside the immediate area, covering a complete circle around it with the same result. When he returned Gatran brought the meeting to a start.

He started by stating what he was intending to offer the Dwarves for a peace treaty, and they gasped at the unbalanced nature of it.

"Why so much, we gain nothing except peace and our intention is to leave the region for a new home. What is the point of it all?" Cagen asked.

"We offer much because our Kings demand it. Yes, we are leaving everything behind when we leave, but the Dwarves carry the responsibility of maintaining peace in the region. They will never leave Xeltar Mountain. Considering the extent of population growth in mankind, and the increased amount of dark magic used across the region, believe me, we are getting the better deal.

"I will not share the details of our talks, that is for Dravel and I alone. You cannot reveal what you don't know. Of course, none of you would share, unless under influence of dark magic. We've faced so many instances of it already that none of us can assume immunity from it."

The Elves nodded their agreement.

Gatran continued. "I expect negotiations to be extensive, the Dwarves will attempt to wheedle more from us. My intention is to finish negotiations in three days. If I haven't returned by the evening of the fourth day you can assume we have either been killed or imprisoned. They will not wish to return Kudra; in terms of value to them, she is priceless. There could be a multitude of reasons to prevent our leaving, but if we don't return at the arranged time, you are free to infiltrate the Dwarf Kingdom and destroy it. If we can't arrange a peace treaty, nobody can, and I will follow the orders of my King."

"To annihilate a species is extreme, Gatran, and while I would follow my Kings orders without question, now is the time to raise doubts about it."

"You are right, Eckna. It's an extreme situation with few options. I will attempt to avoid it, search every other alternative before following those orders. If I don't return you can assume I've failed and take the required action.

"Finally, I need to share the location of their entrance, it is not where expected."

Gatran explained how to infiltrate the mountain. He warned about the difficulty of navigating the numerous tunnels and caverns.

"How do you know about this, Gatran?"

"My father, in his younger days, had a friend who was half Elf and half Dwarf and learned of the mountain's secrets from him."

Gatran had said enough. His words had affected them all, including Dravel. He understood their concerns only too well, they were his too, but orders were orders. He called the meeting to an end by stating he and Dravel would leave at first light.

Chapter 56:

The following morning, Kudra and Sitara were summoned to the King. Both were suspicious about the reasons for it and Kudra suspected unscrupulous motives. Sitara was unusually quiet, harbouring her own suspicions and fears.

"The reasoning for visit is of concern Sitara."

"I share agreement, experiencing similar worries."

"All will become apparent soon. Finrok appears distant, possibly holding knowledge of visit."

They fell quiet as they walked through the labyrinth of tunnels and caverns.

The King sat on his throne as they entered, and he wasted no time beckoning them forward.

"Greetings Princess Kudra, greetings Sitara. Gratitude for the swift arrival to my summons."

He smiled, but little warmth emitted from it. Sitara seethed inside. The greeting was hollow, she realised instantly. As if they were responsible for their prompt attendance. Kudra responded to the greeting and Sitara bowed hers.

"I've asked for your presence to discuss opportunities regarding your future."

"Plans for futures were set long ago by our Kings."

"You know as well as I do, a restrained welcome awaits you when returning to the High Elves. I have a proposal allowing an alternative."

"And what is this offer?"

"A gift of power and prestige to remain at Xeltar Mountain."

"And in return for this gift?"

"You are quick to assume a return. I would like you to create gold for us. With you adding to our accumulated wealth, there would be no need for my army to continue fighting. This will allow Dwarf numbers to grow again safely within the confines of our home world."

"I have already informed you my powers are weak and difficult to control. A guarantee of achieving your request is impossible."

"I would allow you time to practise and master the white magic required. Perhaps Dravel, when he arrives, can also be tempted to stay."

"Dravel's destiny lies beyond Xeltar Mountain. That is certain. His loyalty to Gatran will not waver or fall victim to temptation. Both remain committed to cause; peace talks represent first stage."

"Perhaps another could be of help?"

"Possibly, but guarantee is as stated before."

"Would you humour me with an attempt to make a small amount."

"What, now?"

"Do you need preparation time?"

"Despite time, achieving goal is doubtful."

"But you will try, the peace talks will carry more merit through your cooperation."

"So, this is not offer, more bribe?"

"My offer is genuine, but I need to witness your capabilities if I'm to sway members of my council. I will allow a period for contemplation before insisting on your cooperation. You may leave now until I summon you again."

Kudra and Sitara were led away by Finrok. Once in their quarters, he left them immediately, averting eye-contact and without attempting conversation.

"I knew Dwarves were untrustworthy, Kudra. Their insatiable lust for gold is legendary."

"I agree, but I'm conflicted in deciding action. I may have to agree, allowing Gatran and Dravel time needed before arrival."

"If you agree, they will demand more?"

"I know. If I don't, Gatran may be refused audience with King and peace talks halted before starting."

"You are sure no other choice exists? I believe our departure will be prevented once King learns your capabilities. We'll be imprisoned here. Already depressing darkness affects my soul, I lose self to it."

"If we're imprisoned, we'll escape. You will confine thoughts to optimism and fight depression this place invokes."

"I'll try, but my weakened mind persists and becomes worse the longer we remain."

An hour passed before Finrok returned. "I'm instructed to escort you to the King."

"Speak Finrok, your demeanour shows displeasure with instructions."

"To speak thoughts would be disloyal."

"Those words alone suggest true feelings. We are betrayed, aren't we?"

Finrok deigned to answer, but his silence was enough. Kudra tried again. "You are concerned for your kind, Finrok."

This time, he answered. "The future looks bleak. Our numbers decline fast, the focus of our efforts should be about securing Dwarven futures."

"Your words suggest King's attention lies elsewhere, on gold perhaps."

"I cannot comment."

"I understand loyalty and appreciate it, Finrok. From Elven perspective, we share sentiments, our concern is future of our kind."

"Hush your tongues, we approach the King."

Entering the cavern, the King was already on his feet awaiting their entrance. He stared into their faces and dismissed Finrok.

"You are ready to make the attempt?"

"Success will be limited and consequences must be paid for effort."

"What do you mean?"

"My efforts remove strength; weakened sufficiently to require rest for long periods."

"How long?"

"At least a complete moon cycle."

"That is unfortunate and unacceptable."

"Surely you understand demands of magic on body?"

"I have heard tales but have not witnessed it. However, should you be successful, we could work around the periods of rest.

"The periods mentioned are for sleep, body and mind take longer to prepare for magic again."

The King snapped his impatience. "You are lying, attempting to delay the inevitable."

"What inevitability are you speaking of?"

"The one stating you remain here until you've satisfied my demand for gold."

"Elven kind will not allow this."

"They're hardly able to stop it, are they."

"They arrive here with honourable intentions, if you dishonour the peace process they will react accordingly."

"So now you threaten me?"

"I do not. I state truth of outcome if mission fail."

The King seethed anger and could barely control it. He circled the cavern before facing Kudra once more.

"If your kind raise arms against us, I'll destroy them, know and understand this."

"If you raise arms against us, you'll not receive gold desired. Gold warps Dwarven minds, banishing sensible thought. I will not follow your requests to make it."

"Refuse me and you die."

"My life is inconsequential to future. You know."

"Your death will be painful, and you will watch everyone you care for suffer the same fate."

"Threatening me carries little weight, I have experienced death under dark magic for many sun cycles. No light or dark, thought or feeling. There is a peace within it, welcoming those it traps."

"You will make gold for me now."

"I will attempt it with hope for future peace talks, but will cease all attempts if talks fail."

Kudra decided to end the conversation there. Dughork's anger was fast approaching the limit of his control. She turned away and sat on the cavern floor, beckoning Sitara to sit opposite.

"Assist me. You will break trance if magic fails. Intervene at point where I cannot communicate with you. Do you understand?"

Sitara realised Kudra was speaking for effect and played along. "And if you attack those present?"

"Restrain me as required."

Dughork looked alarmed, his anger tempered, and he considered bringing a guard unit before deciding not.

Kudra started chanting, a long wailing chant that echoed around the cavern. It lacked rhythm, melody or any other musical quality, but its haunting nature permeated the souls of those present.

Chapter 57:

Soon after dawn had shed her welcoming embrace across the sky, Gatran and Dravel rode away from the army. He had reiterated his three-day time limit for completing his mission. Eckna watched them depart with an affectionate farewell.

They rode in silence, again enjoying the fact they were riding again instead of walking. Gatran realised they would reach the mountain by mid-afternoon. Pleased, it offered sufficient time to find the entrance to the Dwarf Kingdom before darkness; he saw it in his mind; the memory was clear. Although knowing the rock face concealed the opening, accessible only by hand, he was unsure how.

Dravel maintained a respectful silence. It was his way to remain quiet until his voice was sought by others. Gatran admired this quality so much. That he was a Prince of the High Elves was of no real surprise. His humble nature defied the normal dispositions of Elven royalty, and Gatran admired that even more.

"You worry about Sitara my friend?" Gatran asked.

"I do. My feelings are in contrast to the rationality of the mission, and I worry my concern for her will sway my thoughts and actions from mission."

"I share concerns regarding Kudra also. Achieving their freedom is as important to me as the mission itself. I realise I'm mortal and cannot control my feelings. I also question why I should. Much is forsaken in fulfilling my destiny as an Elven Prince. If I sought recompense, I would ask only to journey through life with her. You too have given up much, Dravel, perhaps even more than I."

"You are correct. Sometimes I considered being alone was acceptable. No others have affected me as she. Now, I too believe I deserve something as reward for my loyalty and patience."

"We should strive to achieve both, the mission and them."

"And if we are forced to choose between them and the mission?"

"I will not allow this to happen, nor will I even contemplate the possibility. They've been present almost from the beginning, displayed loyalty and are driven towards our cause. I will not abandon them for any reason."

"Your words are the gentle breeze bringing the warmth of the sun to my heart, Gatran. We must safeguard them from the Dwarves and any other seeking to destroy what we've started."

They reached Xeltar Mountain on time. Gatran felt uneasy because there were no Dwarfs apparent. Surely, there would be a lookout somewhere. He mentioned it to Dravel who simply said it was unnecessary since access inside the mountain was unknown to those other than Dwarves.

They followed a well-worn path along the base of the mountain, seeking a trail leading up. It was not apparent at first, taking longer to find than expected. Dravel spotted it, indicating with an out-stretched arm. Gatran grinned and altered course towards it. The path remained smooth but was incredibly steep and they both laboured during the climb.

The climb took an eternity before the path flattened onto a small plateau, sufficient to hold twenty men.

Gatran immediately moved toward the mountain face and searched for access. Nothing revealed the doorway; no crack revealed where a door met the permanent mountain face.

"I can't see any sign of it," Dravel commented not trying to hide his disappointment.

"It's here somewhere, I haven't travelled this far to be thwarted now. I'm trying to remember how they activated it, but I'm not even sure I have the memory to draw from.

"Since it's not obvious it must be small. Perhaps a spot to depress or a tiny protrusion to turn."

"We should take our time, Dravel. We have spent many days travelling here, a little longer is not an issue."

"Perhaps staring at the rock face is detrimental. I suggest closing eyes and relying on touch alone. The slightest protrusion or depression could be the access point. Maybe it's easier to find by touch than sight."

"That's a good idea, let's try it. You start one side and I'll start the other. We'll meet in the middle."

They spent the rest of the afternoon searching until Dravel finally discovered a small depression with his fingers. He pressed into it and the wall started to move inward before swinging open like a conventional door.

"Success is ours Gatran," he announced triumphantly.

"Time to enter then!"

Gatran glanced poignantly at the world below.

"You are hesitant, Gatran?"

"I love the outside world Dravel, the notion of no landscape for several days is not my choosing."

"The outcome of our journey is within our grasp, my friend. Once achieved you will view the world however and whenever you choose."

"And if we fail?"

"We will not, failure is unacceptable. Too much rests on our success."

"You'll soon assume the responsibility of lead negotiator. I welcome the respite from leadership."

"You've earned that, my friend, and I'll not fail you with my efforts."

"I have no doubts regarding your abilities, Dravel. Far from it, you have persistently shown you lack nothing a true and successful leader might have."

"I appreciate those sentiments, but even those are insufficient to relieve the burden I carry."

"Then know I share the burden and draw comfort from it."

Without waiting for an answer, Gatran turned and entered the darkness. He paused inside, waiting for his eyes to adjust and notice the feint glows from the fire torches at random intervals. Satisfied, he moved forward, following the twists and turns of the tunnels. He appreciated their height, more than generous considering Dwarves lived there.

The tunnels continued, interrupted by the occasional cavern, and each leading deeper into the hill on a descending path. Dravel commented on the depth and descent, stating he was unsure if he could remember the route out.

"Hopefully, we'll have a guide with us when we leave."

"I can't believe we've travelled so far without being intercepted by Dwarves."

"That's about to change, I can hear voices and footfall ahead."

"And so, it begins Dravel."

"It does, my friend."

Chapter 58:

Kudra maintained chanting for an overly long period before stopping. She ignored the King completely and spoke to Sitara.

"I will rest effort as achieving task eludes."

Sitara realised she was using a delaying tactic and played along.

"Words of magic fail, or perhaps not accurate?"

"Answer is unsure, but failure taxes strength equal to success."

"How long is required?"

"A few moments; time will increase with each failed effort."

Dughork interrupted the conversation; displeasure at being ignored evident on his face.

"What is the problem? There no gold!"

Sitara took responsibility for the response. "Kudra stated magic was problematic, but you failed to listen. She stated control was issue, and you failed again."

"Hold your tongue, Elf. How dare you speak to me like that. Think carefully about your choice of words. Your life can be ended with a snap of my fingers."

"Without help, Kudra will not create gold."

"There are others on route here, they can assume your role."

"Not without relevant training."

"Dravel will know how."

"Harm me and Dravel will never fill Dwarf King's needs."

"Finrok," the King shouted, and the Dwarf rushed into the cavern.

"My King," he answered.

"Take Sitara back to her quarters and chain her. I will not tolerate her words without recompense."

"I will see to it."

Kudra interrupted. "Our mission is peaceable, treating us this way is unacceptable."

"You're in my kingdom, I make the rules here."

"If your response is hostile, the gold you seek will not bear fruition."

"If that remains so, Sitara's time in the living is shortened."

Kudra was about to answer, but Finrok reappeared.

"She is secured my King."

"Escort Kudra back to her quarters so she can witness Sitara's plight and understand what it means to defy me."

He turned his back and walked to his throne as Finrok led her quickly away.

"This is not proceeding well, Kudra. Aggravating him will bring pain and suffering."

"I will not bow to greed and protestations of an egotistical tyrant."

"The walls have ears, Kudra."

"I don't care."

"You should, Gatran and Dravel travel here; their task has become more difficult for your actions."

"You sound genuinely disappointed."

"That's because I am. I seek a future for my kind, not a battle to end us all."

"You're preaching to the wrong person."

"Not preaching, just warning."

Kudra fell silent. Irritated, she did not wish to pursue a conversation with Finrok, but his words had interested her. Clearly, he didn't agree with the actions of his king.

He left Kudra in her quarters, shocked by how Sitara was fettered. Hands and feet were chained as expected, but also her neck had been placed into a chained collar. It was secured tightly not allowing her any head movement apart from turning sideways.

"You should not speak so freely, Sitara."

"I achieved aim."

"Which was?"

"To relieve pressure of making gold."

"But why."

"There is no telling length of time before Gatran and Dravel join us."

"And if longer than expected you'll be forced to suffer for extended period."

"The weasel annoys me."

"Me also, but I want to end mission with you by my side. There is another matter to share. Success at making gold was not through choice; I planned creation of the smallest amount to keep Dughork interested, but I couldn't. My white magic does not work here. I do not understand why."

"Maybe that knowledge should remain discrete to us. Without it, our use is negated."

"My thoughts also."

"I wonder if Dravel will suffer same predicament?"

"Since your magic is superior, I would assume so."

"It's not time for magic to fail. I fear appearance of dark magic soon; a last effort to destroy peace initiative."

"Our situation will improve when Gatran and Dravel arrive."

"In the meantime, avert thoughts to Dughork. He is not acting in the best interests of kind, even Finrok agrees. Could he suffer influence of dark magic already?"

"Instigated in distant past, if so. The Dwarves leave mountain for hunting or battle only. They have not battled for many moon-cycles."

"That we know of. There is possibility an individual infiltrates ranks, as with Gatran's army."

"That might explain difficulty with white magic."

"There is plenty to ponder. Rest tongue and use thoughts to occupy time. A more constructive use of time."

They fell silent. They had not previously considered the possibility of dark magic being present inside Xeltar Mountain and yet it made perfect sense. Their problems were compounding by the minute and Kudra longed for the two male Elves who could reason and remain calm beyond any others she had known. She wondered about their army; had they reached Xeltar mountain yet? A physical presence could boost the peace talks, reinforcing the likely result of a battle, the probable extinction of both species.

Sitara's thoughts were solely on her fetters. Her feet and hands could move less than an arms-length, very restrictive, her head less. Already she itched, everywhere, induced more by being unable to scratch. Her discomfort was increasing by the moment, and she was regretting speaking out despite her valid reasons.

Chapter 59:

Gatran and Dravel continued through the labyrinth of tunnels. How could he have travelled so far without encountering Dwarves? Their isolation ended abruptly when they entered the next cavern. A group sat at a table drinking ale. They were as surprised as the Dwarves were at seeing them.

The Dwarves reacted immediately, standing swiftly and drawing their battle axes from their belts.

"Do not fear our intent, Dwarves. We do not draw our weapons."

One Dwarf spoke a rudimentary Elven dialect, but it was difficult to follow and Gatran had to infer from the Dwarfs demeanour.

"You don't belong here?"

"I am Gatran, and this is Dravel. We're here to meet with King Dughork, our mission is to bring peace between our kinds."

"There's been no peace for centuries between us, why now?"

"Our kind faces extinction, yours too. Rest your axes, we mean you no ill-well."

"You do not enter our kingdom without invitation and tell us to rest our axes. You are arrogant Elf, and the sworn enemy of my kind. Prepare to die."

Instead of staying their axes, one Dwarf leapt forward, a surprising distance for one so small, swinging his axe. Gatran instantly drew his sword and parried the blow, aimed for his head. With lightning speed, he twisted violently, pulling the Dwarf's axe arm to his right and

300

forcing him off balance. He reversed his sword and clubbed him with his swords pommel. The Dwarf fell unconscious.

"I say again, stay your axes. I have not injured your friend, merely rendered him unconscious. I could have killed him if I had mind. We are here on a peaceable mission."

A second Dwarf leapt forward into the attack and a third moved against Dravel who was slow to draw his sword. Gatran rendered his opponent unconscious with the same ease as the one before, but Dravel lacked Gatran's level of skill. Parrying his attackers blow, he lost balance and stumbled backward. Seeing his disposition, his attacker moved in again, swinging the axe violently. Dravel saw it coming and still off-balance was powerless to prevent the strike. The shrill sound of metal rubbing against metal brought his thoughts of imminent death to an end. Gatran had intercepted the blow.

Dravel regained his composure quick enough to warn Gatran of an attack from the last member of the Dwarf group. Gatran turned to meet the Dwarf's charge while Dravel engaged the one who threatened to end his life.

Swift and deft strokes of his sword forced an opening and Dravel wasted no time delivering a sickening blow to the head. The third Dwarf rendered unconscious. In the heat of the battle, he turned towards the last Dwarf, already occupying Gatran's full attention. With his back to Dravel, the Dwarf never saw him coming. Dravel kicked the back of his knee, forcing him to slump, and swung the sword hilt to the back of his skull. He fell to the ground.

Gatran looked surprised. "I had him under control, Dravel."

"Sorry, the heat of the battle and self-preservation kicked in; I acted on instinct, rather than rational thought."

"Apparently! How was that?"

"Not exactly how I normally act, and very strange, but the result was pleasing."

Gatran laughed and grinned at the High Elf. "I'll make a soldier out of you yet!"

"Unlikely, but I appreciate your comments, and glad I could assist where I wasn't really needed."

Gatran laughed harder. "If I didn't know you better, I would say you were attempting humour."

This time Dravel grinned and Gatran slapped him across the back of the shoulder.

"Time for us to move before these Dwarves wake and sound the alarm."

They continued into the heart of the mountain, uninterrupted, until entering a huge cavern. At least thirty Dwarves occupied the space and immediately surrounded them. Gatran announced his intentions to meet with King Dughork and a Dwarf in fluent Elven suggested they should follow him and not veer from the course he set. To do so would invite immediate attack and death. He and Dravel followed, the entire population of the cavern's Dwarves following behind them.

More tunnels and caverns ensued before they entered a huge one, clearly the throne room. Dughork was seated there. The Dwarf leading signalled a halt a few yards away from his King and marched forward. He bowed, asking permission to speak. The King granted his request and a lengthy discussion in the Dwarven tongue ensued. Gatran and Dravel waited patiently for their invitation to speak, but the wait dragged on and Gatran began experiencing a lack of patience.

Orders were snapped suddenly in a loud voice that demanded an instant response. The Dwarven folk behind Dravel and Gatran retreated from the throne room, leaving them alone with the King and the Dwarf who had instructed them. Dughork addressed them.

"Forgive my Elven vocabulary. I understand more than I can speak and although communication between us will ensue, I do not wish to misunderstand anything you say. Hadran, my aid, will remain with us, his command of the Elven tongue is far superior to my own, potentially dismissing any confusion between us.

"The need for introductions is not required. I'm fully aware of your identity, as you are mine. However, I welcome you to Xeltar Mountain. Your mission is known to me and I accept your intentions are peaceable. I have met with Kudra and Sitara. They are in good health and have been treated as guests until earlier. I was forced to restrain Sitara, whose tongue became hostile and disrespectful. Before you appeal against this, understand your presence here is by my grace and you live by my command. Dwarves here would kill you on sight if they had the choice."

Gatran seethed inside, wondering what punishment Sitara had invoked and why. Dravel's anger stirred too; his normal unflappable restraint both weakening and shocking as he realised it.

Gatran spoke. "You should know King Dughork that we encountered resistance in the mountain on route here. Four Dwarves attacked us despite telling them of the peaceable nature of our visit."

"Your mission is irrelevant to some. You're an Elf and are sworn enemies of Dwarves, resistance and distrust is inevitable."

Dravel intervened. "We are unaware of Dwarven ways and do not wish to be disrespectful. You claim to know of the reasons for our visit; If so, I ask for time to discuss the possibility of ending hostilities between our kinds. We bring incentives and news of imminent departure of all Elves from these lands."

Dughork looked surprised at the last comment, it wasn't something he knew about. His informants either left out that detail or didn't know about it themselves.

"We would also like to visit Kudra and Sitara," Gatran asked, as politely as he could.

"I accept your request for an audience and will wait with interest and patience for the incentives you mentioned. I assume this will require concessions to gain them and, if reasonable, look forward to learning of our potential futures. Regarding Kudra and Sitara, you will be taken to their quarters shortly. Sitara will be released from her fetters as she has received sufficient time to cool her temper. I've assigned a Dwarf to attend their needs; the same Dwarf will attend yours. His name is Finrok, I'll send for him now."

He spoke a few Dwarven words to Hadran, and the Dwarf left the cavern.

"We appreciate the concessions you've offered King Dughork and will abide by ways of your kind during our stay here."

"Appreciated, understand away from my presence your lives will be under constant threat. Feelings against Elves run strong, fuelled by battles throughout history. It would be wise to stay in your quarters; leave only under the watchful eyes of Finrok who will take you anywhere you wish despite protestations against it."

Finrok appeared before Gatran could respond, and the King instructed him to take them to Kudra and Sitara.

They left immediately. Dughork dismissing them without further comment. Gatran bit his tongue.

Chapter 60:

Sitara was flexing her body when they entered, enjoying the freedom from the chains. At the sight of Dravel, her face broke into an enormous smile, and she moved toward the High Elf.

"Your presence pleasures tired eyes Dravel, I have been absent sunshine too long."

"I, too, have missed you by my side. I will endeavour to ensure a parting does not happen too often. I heard you were restrained, that you spoke words edged with hostility."

Sitara lowered her eyes to avoid him seeing a fleeting moment of shame. "It is true. I find the King difficult; I have no worth in his view."

"A mistake he'll learn to regret, I'm sure."

"He is interested only in accumulating wealth."

"An opinion shared by us and witnessed in our conversation with him."

Kudra had moved toward Gatran, but for once words eluded her.

"You are strangely quiet Kudra?"

"I'm sorry, I'm pleased by your presence, of course, but while in Xeltar Mountain, my thoughts are devoted entirely on surviving. Dughork attempted to procure gold from white magic and tactics to avoid were only stayed by Sitara's intervention; being chained, her punishment. I am certain her release without inducement was unlikely, had you not arrived."

"Dughork has offered the possibility of discussion, but his interest is focussed on gain. He appeared to know about our mission except us leaving the region."

"He claims prophesies from centuries ago foretell of our arrival."

"Unexpected but useful; he'll want the prophesies to be accurate, running their course; he'll gain stature for being the King during prophesy revelations. It could well prolong his reign."

"All this aside Kudra, tell me of yourself, you are otherwise well."

Kudra smiled. "I am relaxed and ready for task ahead. The mission is of utmost priority. I will do as required."

"I'm pleased, but not necessarily the answer I sought."

"You wish to know if I miss you as much as you missed me?"

Gatran smiled. "Your directness always makes our conversations so much easier."

"You deflected answer."

"No, merely prolonged the wait for it."

"You tease at moment when teasing is unrequired."

"I stand admonished. Yes, I missed you and I want to know if you felt similarly?"

Kudra's alert eyes softened, and she leant towards him and kissed him gently on the lips. Gatran hid his surprise, a display of affection in front of others unusual for her, but an intense pleasure flooded his every essence.

"Does that answer your question?"

"Actions can be stronger than words, although words would have been enough."

The four sat together, silent for a while, enjoying being back together again; their proximity as a group evidencing it. Finrok made an appearance, sensing the intrusion he made, but still acted friendly and offered food. Gatran and Dravel accepted readily having not eaten for somewhile. The food was strange but not unpleasant and they ate heartily.

Soon after Kudra removed the empty plates, Dravel broached the subject of the upcoming meeting with Dughork.

"We must decide upon a strategy, achieving our ultimate goals will not be easy."

"Especially as gold is interest dominant in mind. He will expect Kudra to evidence magical prowess," Sitara added quickly.

"Perhaps evidence of capability will be needed, but we will offer the cache she created before," Gatran offered.

"I believe that alone will induce the peace treaty, but leaving our homeland for distant lands will spice the deal. To be rid of Elves prevents further battles," Dravel continued, "even without a treaty."

Sitara leaned forward, "I fear gold cache falls short of meeting Dwarf King's greed."

"No deal, no cure from sickness. Even the absence of Elves is no guarantee of preventing extinction."

Kudra joined the conversation. "We don't have cure yet, Gatran, surely this is not bartering issue."

"It might be useful as a bluff."

"We need to learn of influence of dark magic. I'm certain it prevails, as it showed everywhere we travelled."

"You're right Kudra, Dravel have you sensed any so far."

"It has not commanded my attention since arriving. However, Kudra is right. If dark magic is present, it will poison all attempts to make a treaty."

"More individuals present here than in my army, the task is onerous, almost impossible. We'll never have total freedom to conduct a search."

"I don't believe that will be required, Gatran. Only those close to key players in discussions are likely under the influence. I will check those involved."

"Do I need to remind you those infiltrated in my army were not key players in terms of position."

"I appreciate that, but we had an entire journey ahead of us then. We are at the journey's end now."

"There's a key player involved here, an individual wielding enormous power, one who acts with improvisation."

"That makes sense. We must realise a threat constantly. He may choose to appear, influence any of us effortlessly."

"Is there no magic you can use Kudra to highlight the proximity to dark magic?"

"It's possible. Dravel might assist. If we combine knowledge, a spell might revel itself, but magic eluded my capabilities here."

"Make this a priority, if we have capability before speaking with Dughork we'll command an advantage."

Kudra acknowledged his wishes and fell silent.

With little else to discuss, Gatran moved away from the group and fell deep into contemplation. Kudra moved closer to Dravel and Sitara.

"Your help may also be useful Sitara."

She nodded, pleased at the inclusion and feeling more useful than Dughork had suggested.

Chapter 61:

King Dughork summoned them early the next morning. Without warning, Finrok appeared and escorted them to the council cavern. The route was lengthy, Gatran estimated its location as several times further than the throne room and deeper into the mountain.

The cavern was less spacious and with a low ceiling. Dravel could touch it with his head if he raised himself on his toes. It was featureless, lacking decoration or adornment and was dominated by the largest table any of them had ever seen. The top, made from solid timber was so large the tree it originated from defied belief. It's top polished with a shine so deep, it seemed to draw them inside it.

Finrok led them in and showed them to their places. Dravel asked about formalities during the proceedings, requiring honour and respect. He received a negative response.

"Discussions often become heated and sometimes threatening. It is the way of our kind to be passionate about whatever we seek," Finrok explained. "The King will keep you waiting, it's customary, and there will be four others present. The two highest ranked army Generals, and two of our most experienced ambassadors. A guard unit will also assume position behind the King."

"Gratitude Finrok, is there anything else we should know?"

"The King will make negotiations difficult, expect the days duration."

"And after negotiations, will we be free to leave the mountain," Dravel asked.

"I cannot answer with any certainty. It would depend on the results of the negotiations."

"I appreciate your candour, Finrok."

"I am present to make your stay easier and comfortable. Our ways differ. My King is powerful and dominating. The right to ascension here is through strength alone. Intellect is not a requirement, but greed often plays a significant part. In telling you this, I am not being disrespectful, it's simply necessary for you to understand the differences between us."

Dravel nodded. "I appreciate your counsel."

"There is wine, water and fruit on the table, indulge. I will be close by but not present during the negotiations."

"That's surprising since your command of Elven tongue is superior to other Dwarfs met," Kudra questioned.

"My position is too low to be present."

"Is your King to be trusted?"

"The answer is not simple. Power often corrupts common sense; greed overshadows needs of others. It's the same with each successive leader but by varying amounts."

Kudra nodded. "I understand."

They took their seats and Finrok retreated from the cavern.

Immediately after he left, Dravel turned to Gatran. "He is under the influence of dark magic. It was difficult to recognise it, but is definitely present. No Dwarf would speak of his King disrespectfully, with death the likely punishment."

"An individual under the influence has never positioned so close to us. His purpose won't be helpful, we must be on our guard. Why so difficult for you to read it in him, Dravel."

"I believe the power controlling him is weaker. I cannot be certain if he wields the power or is simply controlled by it. If controlled, I suspect the individual behind it is close by."

"I did not sense the magic in him. Dravel is correct the magic is weak to be so disguised."

"Any thoughts, Sitara?" Gatran asked.

"I'm not accustomed to feeling negatively, but for reasons unclear, I'm consumed with doubt and concern."

"I appreciate your direct and honest manner, Sitara. It's probably true we all feel a little like that."

"I used the word consumed with intent. The feelings are incredibly strong, and the weight bears down uncomfortably."

"I hear your warning, Sitara, know I heed it."

They fell silent, each awaiting the King's arrival and his advisors. Dravel picked at the fruit and sipped water from his goblet. Their wait soon ended.

The King entered followed by his two generals and two ambassadors. Gatran's group stood showing respect. None acknowledged their guests as they took their places. Once settled and with wine overflowing from their goblets the King used his knuckles on the table to draw their attention.

"Allow me to introduce my guests, he addressed his fellow Dwarves. This is Gatran, Prince of the Wood Elves of Graylen Forest. Kudra, Princess of the High Elves, thought to be long dead by her kind. Few know of her existence. Dravel, illegitimate Prince of High Elves. A diplomat foremost, only a few know his true identity. And finally, Sitara, also a High Elf but of no rank and assumes position as Kudra's hand maiden."

The Dwarves muttered in their own language, the generals laughing at a comment from one ambassador.

"My guests, please allow me to present my diplomatic team. This is General Tanga and General Kylav my two top ranked army commanders. Gatran, you have fought against them in the past. Also present are my two senior Ambassadors, Junavid and Klyac. All negotiations will include everyone here and are privy to no others. The guard team behind me have no tongues and cannot speak, which is why they are assigned to my personal guard."

Dravel replied, assuming the role of chief negotiator. "What we embark upon today, holds the potential for the betterment of our kinds. Creating opportunity for increasing our numbers and preserving both for an unlimited future. You honour us with the invite to sit at your table and discuss the issues at hand and we hope to work toward a common goal with a peaceable conclusion."

"For the benefit of my delegates, Dravel, could you make clear each of the issues you wish to address?"

"We wish to discuss the sickness, sweeping our lands with devastating loss to our number. The continuing wars between us, also result in loss to our numbers. The current search for the cure to the sickness is unknown to you. Overwhelming upsurge in dark magic, infiltrating our ranks, also warrants discussion. Finally, the withdrawal of Elven kind from the lands we are both familiar with."

"Issues of immense importance, Dravel, and commendable. The solutions you seek benefit both our kinds. Where would you like to start?"

"I believe the issues regarding the preservation of our kinds are of the most immediate importance."

"Then we should start there. State your proposals."

"My gratitude, King Dughork. It is of no surprise to you King Dughork, that the numbers of our kinds are diminishing with the passing of each moon-cycle. The reasons are two-fold, first those who fall victim to sickness sweeping our lands and second to the continuing war lasting for generations. The first is problematic. The sickness is of dark magic origins, formed by a witch and spread by birds controlled by magic. Despite our best efforts, finding a cure by normal methods has proved impossible, nothing is effective against it. So, our tactics have changed. We now seek the individual responsible to obtain a cure."

"If the sickness is indeed caused by dark magic, what makes you believe it is possible to find the individual and obtain the cure?" Dughork asked scornfully.

"Failure is simply not an option. This sickness will affect us all eventually, of that I'm certain. It alone will wipe out our kinds. The only ones not affected by it are those who spread it."

"But you are no match for the dark magic, surely."

"Even as we speak, Gatran's sister searches for the cure. Once successful, our intention is to share it with you and preserve what numbers remain of our kinds."

"Generous! But why, after generations of war, would you share a cure with your enemies."

"We have been enemies beyond memory, it is not our interest, or yours, to witness the demise of either of our kinds. All kinds are important to our existence, we balance the known world. If that balance is altered it will cause devastation; one kind gains in strength and another weakens. Consider the emergence of Human kind. They invade our territory to gain land for an ever-increasing population. The balance is altering and not for ours, or your betterment."

"This is true, humans have been deterred from our lands frequently."

"If not detrimental enough for the sickness and war to deplete our numbers, add the potential for war against Humankind. How many must die before our populations fall below what is required to replenish."

"The cure is a dream at present, no guarantee of discovering it; our numbers will continue declining."

"This is true, and that brings me to my second point. It is time to end the hostilities between our kinds. A peace treaty, ending hostilities and preserving numbers long enough to discover the cure."

"And what of Humankind? A peace treaty with them won't happen. Their appetite for land is insatiable."

"We must avoid contact with them; they do not appear afflicted by the sickness, although we don't know this for certain."

"They can be avoided for a while, but inevitably they must be thwarted from invading our lands."

"I agree; this can be done without battle. For example, magic. An invisible barrier they cannot pass through They have no control over any form of magic, unlike our kinds."

"Few Dwarves have abilities with magic and their control is limited."

A babble of unexpected voices outside the cavern rose to a pitch difficult to ignore. The King rose and shouted a command for those outside to explain the purpose of their interruption.

Two Dwarves entered the cavern and approached with heads bowed. One spoke in Dwarven tongue. The Kings demeanour changed, and he turned to the Elves.

"What treachery is this? An army of Elves waits outside the mountain."

"They are my army, King Dughork," Gatran spoke for the first time since the meeting had started. They are here for me; we were separated on route. No treachery, this group would have failed to negotiate the journey without their help. They offer no threat to you or your kind."

"This is an outrage; they camp just beyond reach of arrows and spears. I smell a trap set by Elves, a siege to starve my kind."

"I repeat, there is no treachery, King Dughork."

"Guards escort them to their quarters, they are no longer to be treated as guests but as prisoners of war. Take them away, now."

The guards moved in and ushered the Elves from the cavern. They offered no resistance.

Chapter 62:

They were escorted to their quarters and an armed guard unit was placed at the entrance. Unexpectedly, they weren't fettered. They sat close together scarcely believing the recent events.

"I believe Dughork is being influenced by dark magic. At first, I didn't sense it in him at all, but when he angered it was easy to read."

"He must be controlled from close by Dravel, surely."

"I believe so."

"Could it be any of his negotiating team?"

"Somehow I doubt it, yet it's possible."

"Did you sense magic in any of them?"

"No. but the ability to conceal it has increased since entering Xeltar."

"Kudra, Sitara, did you sense anything?"

"Not dark magic, but something amiss with team. Uncomfortable at table and yet opposite should be true, at home, holding advantage." Kudra answered first.

"I sensed it also, but believed it due to presence of Dughork. None made eye contact or attempted to speak. Not exactly normal behaviour for negotiation team."

"I had not noticed, and yet I believe you're right Gatran. One explanation might be the King is not acting normally. They should respect him, and his position, but, as his senior advisors, they should not fear him," Dravel added.

"Yes, Dravel is correct, uncomfortable and scared," Sitara agreed.

"Anything further to add Kudra?"

"No, I believe Dravel accurate in assessment."

"What this means is we're fighting for a cause Dughork won't accept, he won't be allowed to. We've failed before we try. There are two options. First, we wait for Eckna, or, we discover the origin of the dark magic and destroy it."

"Dughork will never concede to being controlled by dark magic," Kudra's face expressed her doubt.

"Maybe he won't have to. If his representative's sense something wrong in his demeanour, perhaps they are where we should concentrate our efforts. They may be open to the possibility and aid us in identifying the dark magic instigator."

"We cannot trust they'll not reveal our plan."

"We don't reveal more than necessary, Dravel, get them to conduct the investigative work while we action a plan resulting from it. Once convinced he is acting under the influence, I'm sure they'll favour us further in rooting out the culprit."

"And if not, Gatran?"

"If not, Sitara, we wait for my army to infiltrate. My instructions to them were clear."

They fell silent and were soon joined by Finrok. His demeanour suggested need, and an urgency and impatience about his movements. There was also concern, and he did not hesitate to speak.

"May I join you," he asked, indicating the gap between Kudra and Dravel and sitting down before they could answer.

"What is it Finrok? You can speak freely with us," Dravel invited

"Freely, but cautiously. I do not need the guards overhearing our words and betraying me to my King," he whispered.

The Elves remained silent, an unspoken invitation for him to continue. Despite his obvious impatience, he hesitated for a little longer.

"I overheard the negotiations. I was present just outside the council gathering. My King was not himself."

He paused, and Gatran encouraged him to speak further.

"We sensed something amiss, but the cause was unknown."

"The proposals you brought with you were enough to move forward and action, without the concessions you mentioned."

"There were more than mentioned."

"It does not matter. Protecting our kinds from extinction is a shared cause. Our numbers are at an all-time low. To fight would end us both. Your offer to share the cure, assuming you gain it, is of incredible generosity. I'm not convinced we'd offer it, if we had it."

"This we already understand Finrok. What is amiss with your King?"

"I believe my King is under the influence of dark magic, to where his decision-making ability has been compromised, Dravel."

"Do you suspect who controls him or how to prevent the influence?"

"Unfortunately, no. You are correct in assuming the negotiating team are aware something is amiss, but I haven't shared my conclusions with them. My position is too low to gain easy access to them."

"So, you want us to approach them?"

"It is the only way."

"Would they listen to us."

"They know something is wrong, but they fear his wrath and won't approach him directly."

"Well, the King won't listen to us!"

"I'm not suggesting talking to him."

Gatran voiced Finrok's idea, "You want us to remove him from the negotiations."

"Negotiations would continue in his absence."

"So, abduct and conceal him from everyone."

"The Dwarves will not act against him. With the negotiators help, we could arrange for you to become unguarded and show you where to detain him."

"The idea demands thought. Allow consideration before meeting again for further discussions."

"We will not have long, Gatran, I fear King Dughork may place you on trial for treasonous acts. A trial you cannot win and may result in your deaths."

"We must decide quickly. Leave us Finrok. We'll ask the guards for you when our deliberations are over."

Finrok rose and left the cavern. He didn't look back, the guard unit separated and closed again after he passed them by. At first nobody spoke; Sitara broke the silence.

"The man is treacherous, as any I've met. What game does he play? He is under influence of dark magic yet hatches plan as if not."

"He may not know he's swayed," Dravel countered.

"This is trap to capture all in act of treachery against Dughork, I'm convinced."

"Kudra, your thoughts?"

"I agree with Sitara."

"And you, Gatran?

"It is clear the talks will bring no peace among us. What Finrok suggests allows us opportunity to escape, if we follow his ideas."

"And escaping is your proposal?"

"No meaningful talks, no point in our presence."

"And the masterminds controlling dark magic?"

"We're outnumbered, we should leave and regroup."

Chapter 63:

They continued discussing every aspect of action but failed to decide on an agreed choice of action. Dravel wanted to pursue the talks with the Dwarf negotiating team. Gatran focussed on escape and regroup with his army, Kudra and Sitara sought to discover the identity of the dark magic instigator. Their sole area of agreement was not wanting to work with Finrok, suspecting his motives were less than favourable.

"We are at an impasse, Gatran."

"Yes Dravel, we are, but as leader the ultimate responsibility for deciding rests with me."

"Kudra and I are with agreement, if continuing in manner we are accustomed to, our choice should be favoured."

"I appreciate your opinions and honesty of thought Sitara. The situation weighs heavy; the future of all Elves rests on my shoulders and those of my brother and sister."

"The situation weighs heavy on all shoulders here; we are all committed to cause."

"You're right, I did not mean to undermine your commitment. To remain here risks our lives, the peace process would end with our demise."

"It might end when army enters mountain."

"Weight of numbers helps, though."

"Sometimes small groups can hold powerful armies at distance. Here tunnels are confined, only two can pass together. No similar advantage on the battlefield."

Gatran smiled at Sitara. "When did you learn to be so tactically minded?"

"I serve Kudra for many sun-cycles, her wisdom and way of thoughts have become mine also."

"Kudra, are you in total agreement with Sitara's arguments?"

"I am. She is right in assessment of situation and advantage here. There is another matter to consider, though."

"Which is?"

"How to gain freedom to move through tunnels without restriction."

"We need permission from the negotiating team."

"Which means we have to adopt Dravel's position too."

"And my army?"

"The order to infiltrate tunnel system already given, we must survive and route out culprit before they enter."

"So, we can cancel the order and leave without conflict?"

"Exactly."

"And finally, what about Finrok?"

"We explain we'll approach negotiating team, attempt to sway minds to our conclusions, that confining King is a risk beyond sense for now."

"Dravel?"

"Since no individual idea was agreed to, it makes perfect sense to combine all ideas, none were wrong, but all lacked the likelihood of success."

Finrok returned shortly after with the same sense of urgency as before displayed in his walk.

"You have discussed matter at hand and drawn a conclusion?"

"We have."

"And your answer?"

"It would be detrimental to hold King against his will. His followers are not understanding his actions are forced by dark magic. But we agree to approach the negotiating team. Since we are already prisoners here, we have nothing to lose. As you have already confirmed the Ambassadors and the Generals already suspect something amiss with their King, we'll start with them."

"It may not be enough?"

"We appreciate that, Finrok, as we appreciate your courage in confiding with us. My thoughts conclude you should remain unseen and unknown in helping us. If you are caught, we have no other aid to turn to. Time to reveal your part in helping achieve a peace treaty must wait. The likely reward would be to rise in position. Do you agree to this?"

"I can see why you were chosen to lead the negotiations, Gatran. I agree to this and will remain close but distant for the meantime."

"We will need you to arrange a meeting with the Generals."

"Not the Ambassadors?"

"The Generals hold position above most Dwarves and can sway opinion of army. If we cannot get them on side, all we are planning will fail. The Ambassadors will follow the Generals."

Finrok stood. "I will arrange the meeting but will remain distant from you for now."

Gatran nodded his agreement.

Chapter 64:

In the caverns, time passed without recognition of length. Gatran had no idea how long he waited, it just seemed an eternity. They remained silent while considering every aspect of what they hoped to accomplish. The actions would invoke the King's wrath if he discovered their intent.

Finrok returned with the positive news the Generals had agreed to meet with them. His persuasive attempts were tested to the limit in gaining an agreement; they threatened his life if the talks proved unproductive. He left immediately after sharing the news and stating they would be along soon, but he had not received an invitation to attend.

The group still wondered what his purpose was. Was the control over him so weak he could play both sides? It was confusing and Gatran knew he shouldn't trust him.

The Generals kept them waiting longer than expected and their patience was wearing thin. Sitara was considering they might have changed their minds. Eventually, they entered. They brought no guard unit with them and Gatran admired their confidence despite being outnumbered.

Tanga and Kylav sat before them and Tanga opened the dialogue.

"Finrok mentioned you believe King Dughork acts under the influence of dark magic."

Gatran answered immediately. "It is true, the High Elves can feel its presence in an individual."

"And you have felt this."

The High Elves nodded.

"Who could wield such power within Xeltar mountain?"

"He is not the only one. Since embarking on our journey here, we've faced it many times without discovering the orchestrator. I repeat, your King is not the only one under the influence. None of the individuals know the power governing their thoughts and actions."

He explained the encounters endured along their journey and the two Generals looked alarmed.

"You suspect more than one individual controlling?"

"Yes several, their power is immense and stretches over great distance. Many living in these lands command dark magic, and when combining, little we do thwarts them."

"You stated our King is not the only one here under the influence. Who else acts against us?"

"Again, before I share his name, I reiterate those under its control have no awareness of it."

"We must know."

Gatran nodded and dropped his voice to a whisper and said Finrok.

"This makes no sense. He speaks in favour of you."

"We believe the power controlling him is weaker than on your king. I suspect he acts as a messenger only, relaying information to those controlling him."

"If we end his life the control would be gone."

"If we did that, then we lose a lead to the controller. He must report to him sometimes."

"So, we should watch him."

"Seems a prudent choice of action. We cannot, but you can place a watch on him."

"I can make that happen."

"What else can you tell us."

"About the dark magic, nothing, except the power wielded varies in different individuals and there is no real pattern to it. When we passed through Rag Dire Pass the forces we encountered were of massive proportion. Dravel suggested many working together to achieve so much."

Tanga and Kylav stroked their lengthy beards, contemplating what they had learnt and the power they would have to face.

"If we were to combine our forces, Elves and Dwarves, could we defeat these powerful individuals?"

"The problem is not defeating them, but identifying them. We have fought and defeated beasts and have no idea who their leaders are. If we identify them first, then our armies fighting alongside each other would be momentous. The hostilities between us could finally end and the future of our kinds possible to maintain."

"Our prophesies predict this, so I cannot claim the idea as my own. Why are you interested in keeping your enemies alive?"

"It's like I said before, the Elves plan to leave the region, our numbers will not increase as quickly as yours. Your survival is necessary to maintain the equilibrium between the kinds remaining here."

"Are you suggesting we should rule them?"

"There is no need, we have been maintaining their existence through our presence. The constant battles between our superior forces us has kept the focus away from them."

"I understand."

"You mentioned concessions in our previous meeting. If we are to convince our kind to act against the will of our King, the concessions will help sway opinion," Kylav spoke for the first time since entering.

"Dravel maybe you could share this."

Dravel nodded, pleased to get involved. He had not expected Gatran to lead the conversation, but was pleased he had.

"We discussed the possibility of a cure to the sickness."

"Why would you give us this?"

"The sickness is painful, and death allows suffering before taking grip. No individual should die this way. There is no honour. If we cured our own kind and kept the cure for ourselves, risk remains. Inevitably, our kind would encounter Dwarves, Orcs, Trolls, Anurans and others carrying the sickness. It could establish itself again among my kind. The survival of all is the priority. My sister seeks the cure and will bring it to you after finding it."

"When we leave the region, the available food for Dwarves doubles, we eat similar foods. Hunting will be easier for you and feeding the new generation you'll sire will be guaranteed."

"We didn't consider this concession."

"Last is wealth. We know that Dwarves favour gold almost as much as meat. Your appetite for it is insatiable. We offer a cache of gold unequalled in any other single gain."

"This will please my King, his appetite for it is greater than any other. But he knows those commanding white magic can make gold to requirement. He has already attempted to force Kudra to magic some."

"Some High Elves command sufficient white magic to achieve this, it requires much power. The more power used, the weaker the individual, eventually losing ability to make gold."

"We did not know this. Where is this cache?"

"It is close by and will be given to you when we leave."

"And what of your army?"

Dravel leaned in closer. "Our army is instructed to infiltrate Xeltar Mountain should we not return within three moon cycles. Almost two of which have passed already. The resulting battle will decimate numbers and lead to our extinction."

"You would battle despite knowing what the outcome is?"

"We came here in peace, with a peace offering. We hoped to leave here in the same manner with a treaty between us."

"Such a battle is not in our interest," Kylav stated. "Tanga and I will leave to discuss this between us before deciding. Understand, should we back your plans, it could cost our lives."

"We will provide safe passage until you find a new home."

"It couldn't be home if away from our kind. Dwarves live with Dwarves, it's the way of our kind."

"We understand, it's the same for Elves."

"The offer is appreciated, though. Since time is shorter than expected we'll make our decision as soon as possible."

The Generals left the caverns. Dravel looked at Gatran. "The discussions proceeded beyond expectation."

"I hope so and hope they result in the action we need."

Finrok appeared and immediately sat with them, without asking for an invitation.

"How did the discussions go?"

Gatran answered. "It is difficult to know. Dwarves are hard to read, their faces remained impassive throughout the talks."

"But they listened?"

"They listened, but whether they heard us remains to be seen."

"I was hoping to hear more positive thoughts from you."

"I was hoping to give them to you."

"What is happening now?"

"They are considering our proposals."

"You'll need to escape Xeltar Mountain if they don't meet requirements."

"How will we manage that, and why are our lives of concern to you?"

"I know the prophesies. Our future depends on you, it is written."

"I don't think the dark magic of those against us care about your prophesies."

"I will do everything in my limited power to ensure they come true."

"We must hope the Generals decide in our favour because the chances of escaping here are minimal."

"Finrok left, and they considered his actions yet again."

Dravel commented. "The dark magic is still present in him, yet the words he speaks are sincere. He believes what he says. I don't believe he can be trusted at all."

"The simple answer is we cannot trust him. Everything is at stake."

"Let's wait to hear what the Generals decide."

Chapter 65:

What happened next was unexpected, scuppering their plans before they started. Kylav and Tanga did not reappear and Dughork entered instead.

"So, you conspire against me with my own Generals. They will face trial by combat. I have not lost a battle in the last five-hundred sun-cycles."

The Elves did not hide their disappointment and shock at the news of their failure. Their plans were good. How had Dughork found out? Had Finrok betrayed them? The unanswered questions burned inside but they didn't raise them to Dughork.

Gatran addressed him. "We have repeatedly told you we're here on a peaceful mission; we've offered incentives and are turning the entire region over to your control. Nobody could offer more."

"I'm here and you sit at my feet. At my feet, in a powerless position. I asked Kudra to make me gold, and she failed. Until she does, Sitara is now my prisoner and will be treated as one."

"Harm one hair on her head and I'll never meet your demands," Kudra fired.

"Your defiance has just placed you into chains as well. Another word and I'll sever Dravel's head from his shoulders. Guards."

Four guards entered and escorted Kudra and Sitara away. Dravel made to rise, but Gatran's hand on his shoulder prevented him.

"You will remain in your quarters to witness the suffering of the females. It will be in your interest to persuade them to my cause."

With that, he turned and left. Four more guards entered and escorted them to their quarters. Kudra and Sitara were already chained. Their movements restricted by the collars around their necks.

"What now Gatran?" Dravel asked.

"We must improvise, as we have done persistently throughout this journey. I suspect Finrok will be along soon. We must discover the whereabouts of the two Generals and free them first. They alone can guarantee our safety."

"We haven't got long before Eckna enters with our forces."

"We know, the Generals know, but the King doesn't, Finrok is also unaware. Dravel, why do you believe white magic isn't working in Xeltar mountain?

"There could be several reasons. A spell cast inside the mountain may be responsible. Being in the presence of dark magic may be enough to prevent it working. Perhaps... yes, I never considered this before, but perhaps it is a false conclusion, suggested rather than imposed."

"What are you saying?"

"Well, Kudra attempted making a small amount of gold but couldn't. Her failure prevented Dughork's greed dominating his actions. His obsession with it might weaken the dark magic hold on him."

"When she tried, a spell had been cast upon her. It would drain an individual's power to maintain it for the duration. The initial spell told her she couldn't use it. Kudra, have you tried magic since?"

"There has been no requirement."

"Try now, release yourself from these chains."

Kudra attempted it and the chains fell to the ground.

"Unbelievable. You're right Gatran. I have full power."

"Dravel hide the women in a veil of invisibility."

Dravel followed the instruction and the two females disappeared from view.

"I too command my magic."

"Excellent, that changes things considerably."

"Now what, Gatran?"

"Now we free the Generals. Dravel, cloak us all so we can travel unseen along the tunnels."

Dravel raised the cloak, and they walked out of their cavern, past the guards and journeyed toward the Kings chambers. They meandered through the myriad of tunnels and caverns for ages, passing numerous Dwarves. Eventually found the Kings throne cavern. He wasn't there!

"Something is going on Gatran. We've passed countless Dwarves, all heading in different directions."

"Any ideas what?"

"The trial by combat, King against Generals. It is a momentous event in Dwarf terms. The strongest Dwarf against the next two strongest. It's a spectacle no Dwarf wants to miss."

"A King would want it witnessed. A demonstration of his supreme power."

"How will we stop it with so many Dwarves present," Kudra asked.

"It's simple. I intend to challenge Dughork in front of the entire Dwarf population. He won't refuse, can't refuse. If he does, I'll ridicule him, make him angry. Anger blinds an individual from thinking straight."

"It's too risky, Gatran. He's under the influence of dark magic."

331

"And we have white magic. My purpose is not to kill him, just defeat him. He will lose face, lose respect and ultimately power."

"If you lose, our mission will end here and now."

"I will not lose Kudra. Dravel, follow the next group of Dwarves we meet, we must arrive before the fight starts."

"Already doing it, Gatran."

Moments later, they entered a huge cavern, the largest they'd seen so far. With hundreds of Dwarves present, the air was warmer than inside the tunnels. Dravel worked his way forward, circumventing the crowd by keeping close to the wall of the Cavern.

The King stood before his kind, his battle regalia gleaming in the flickering light from a hundred firelights. The Generals stood without their armour. Their hands and feet were chained. They were going nowhere. Dravel finally stopped a few metres behind the King. A small outcrop of rock offering a small recess for them to hide behind. Dravel lifted the veil of invisibility and they waited for the proceedings to commence.

The buzz of Dwarf voices drowning the sound of their own whispered voices and thoughts.

"You need to be careful, Gatran."

"Do not worry Kudra, I cannot lose with you by my side. If the need to use magic arrives, don't hesitate, but wait for my command. I must gain respect with the Dwarves in their traditional manner, by show of strength. That is my goal. His death will serve no purpose. After his defeat, I will invite the two Generals by my side to relate the true situation confronting us all. Most Dwarves are unaware of the truth."

"I understand Gatran and will wait command. To make it less obvious, use a word within a taunt to Dughork nobody will suspect use of magic."

"And the word?"

"Weakness!"

"After the battle Sitara, cloak yourself and leave the mountain. Greet my army and instruct them not to enter."

"But..."

"No buts, we'll be safe I promise. Can you do this?"

"I can."

"Thank you, Sitara. Know after all this is finished, I will ensure you gain in status. It's the least you deserve."

Sitara dipped her head, and Gatran turned to the King.

Chapter 66:

Satisfied his audience was large enough to start proceedings, the King raised his arm in a signal for silence. Many responded immediately, raising their arms in response, and demonstrating their obedience. The buzz of conversation ceased gradually, and the silence became deafening.

"Fellow Dwarves, you're here to witness Dwarf justice. Two of my most trusted Generals have been sentenced to trial by combat. They were witnessed conspiring with Elves; attempting to deceive Dwarves into a peace treaty we neither need nor want. The event is imminent, and justice will prevail."

A cheer started deep in the crowd and spread through the gathering. Again, Dughork raised his hand to gain the silence he needed. He was exercising his power, demonstrating to all how powerful and influential he was, and was enjoying the focus placed upon him.

"After punishment has been administered, the charges against the Elves will culminate with sentencing. Further trials by combat will follow."

Another cheer. This one did not linger as they became impatient, wanting the battles to commence. Gatran emerged from hiding and stood a short distance away from Dughork. An invisible shield had been raised by Dravel to prevent anyone reaching and attacking him. The shock on Dughork's face too obvious for any to miss. He composed himself to speak when Gatran prevented it by starting his own rhetoric.

"Dwarves, hear my words. I am Gatran, Prince of the Wood Elves of Graylen Forest. I have faced many of you in battle during a lifetime of encounters with your kind, and I hold no greater respect for an enemy. You fight with honour, respect and for the future of your kind, as I do for mine.

"I came to Xeltar Mountain on a peaceful mission to seek a peace treaty between our kinds. The time for fighting has ended. Our numbers dwindle at an alarming rate, as do those of Dwarves. The lives spared in battle face another problem, a sickness affecting all but humans.

"Your generals have committed no treasonable act and were discussing the issues we face. They agreed with the solutions I suggested and the incentives I offered. Your King does not. As I stand here your King is under the influence of dark magic. His responses and failure to consider the needs of his kind results from the influence. He is not the only one altered by the effects of dark magic. There are others moving freely around you who suffer the same affliction.

"I have faced many challenges during my life. This one, however, represents the greatest I've faced. Dark magic is everywhere. Its current purpose is to cause the demise of all Elves and Dwarves. You can imagine the chaos, without Dwarves and Elves to maintain the equilibrium between all kinds, our demise would cause."

Dughork had heard enough. It was testament to his surprise appearance that Gatran said so much. He interrupted to prevent any further comment.

"Did you hear his claims, his treasonous words. He lies. He's here only to wipe out our kind. His army sits just beyond the reach of our arrows. No doubt already preparing for a siege.

"Our Generals have swallowed every word from his treacherous lips and have agreed to act against the will of your King and all Dwarves. Their weakness for Elven lies, reveals they're unfit to lead our army. Guards detain the Elf."

A group of Dwarves moved forward, surrounding Gatran but unable to move closer to him than a body length. Dughork recognised the use of magic and attempted to use it for his own cause.

"The magic used in Xeltar comes from Elves. The dark magic controls and guards him."

"You would already be going to the afterlife. Dark magic is mostly used for evil purposes. What I use now is white magic. Your King's words are untrue. Those knowing the ancient prophesies are aware your kind will be saved by four Elves. This is what your King and his controllers fear. He wants the credit for himself."

"And what do you propose to do Elf Prince?"

"Instead of fighting your Generals I challenge you to fight me. You boast of your prowess, believing there are none in Xeltar strong enough to challenge you, and yet here I am. A solitary Elf who will stand for your Generals and support them against the unjust punishment you placed on them. Are you Dwarf enough to meet me in battle, or will you cower away and focus your discontent on your own kind?"

"I promise you, Elf, you'll not find me lacking. I'll deal with you and then carry out the sentence I gave the Generals."

"So, you accept my challenge."

"Gladly."

"Then choose a weapon. Whatever you choose, I'll choose similarly."

"That's a mistake Elf. I have no equal with the battle axe."

"If that is so, prove it."

Dughork selected his axe and instructed another Elf to part with his to Gatran, who took it and tested the weight and balance of it.

"Am I to face magic as well?" Dughork asked scornfully.

Gatran strode forward, grabbed the King's arm and placed it on his shoulder. "No magic surrounds me now."

The King snatched his hand away and retreated a body length from him.

"The rules are simple Elf. An arena will be constructed around us, leaving ample room for us to fight. Attempt to leave the ring and the Dwarves closest to you will kill you instantly. Dwarves hate cowards more than anything else. The fight will continue until one is rendered incapable of fighting or dead. In your case, understand my intention is to kill you."

"That all sounds very civilised, but actions speak louder than words and I have no intention of dying today. Look carefully into my eyes for signs of weakness Dughork. You can't see any because weakness does not inhabit me. I do not fear you."

"Brave words, but misguided. We'll see if you remain so confident when my axe swings to sever your head."

"Enough with these claims of your prowess. I grow bored with the sound of your boasts. It's time to fight."

The Kings anger started to overflow, and he bellowed to his personal guard to form an arena. The crowd opened up in front of him and the arena was formed. The King strode towards it with Gatran following immediately behind.

Chapter 67:

Dughork strode around the arena, battle axe held high, swinging through the air at lightning speed. Kudra's voice spoke beside Gatran. He turned immediately, ignoring Dughork's attempt to whip up support from his followers.

"You will fight carefully; it is better to render Dughork incapable of fighting. Killing him gains nothing. If I sense problem during fight, I will lend assistance unnoticed by others. Know I dislike choice of action and risk to one I hold favourably in heart."

"Action is needed to gain respect from all Dwarves."

"I am aware of reasoning, but thoughts remain same."

Kudra left the arena. Gatran watched for her safe retreat as she pushed by the Dwarves.

The Dwarf crowd were gaining in volume as they cheered for their King, inflating his confidence and belief. Finally, he ceased his strutting and turned to face Gatran.

"Are you ready to die, Elf?"

Gatran smiled at him and raised his eyebrows. His lack of respect encouraging anger.

Dughork spat on the ground. "I'll enjoy making you suffer."

The crowd hushed, waiting for the first move, almost certain it would come from their King.

Dughork strode towards Gatran, swinging his battle axe high above his head. His arrogance encouraged him forward a little too far. Before he could bring his axe down, Gatran jumped forward and jabbed his stomach with the club side of his own axe. Dughork bellowed and reeled backwards.

"Too much strutting, Dughork, made you over-confident. Look what it got you."

Dughork was fuelled by pure adrenaline now and attacked, swinging his axe lower to prevent receiving a repeat blow. Gatran moved easily and lightly on his feet. His lack of armour allowed this, but he was also unprotected. As Dughork moved closer he parried one swing with his own axe, shocked by the power it carried. He leapt away from the following blow, pivoted and swung his own to Dughork's back. The blow connected and Dughork stumbled forward again bellowing, more with anger than pain. Gatran used the club side of the axe again.

"You've no idea how to use the axe at all Elf, and you'll pay for your ignorance."

"Consider yourself fortunate you're not suffering from two open wounds, then. This is a training session, not a battle, you cannot break my guard."

Dughork bellowed again. Gatran was getting to him, and he was rising to the taunts. His anger threatened to spill over and force mistakes in his attack. Gatran waited with the patience of a predator cat on the hunt.

"Can't imagine what your kind are thinking right now, Dughork, watching their King humiliated by an Elf."

"It's just a matter of time, Elf, until I remove your head."

"I've heard this before, but you've come nowhere near."

Gatran laughed, fuelling Dughork's anger further. The Dwarf was close to losing any kind of composure. One more humiliating strike and his anger would explode. He decided to change tactics and launch a surprise attack. Jumping high in the air, he almost flew over the Dwarf. He landed and quickly jumped again before the Dwarf completed his turn. Dughork realised he had been outmanoeuvred, he faced only his kind. Gatran was behind him; He wasn't quick enough to turn again. A blow to his skull, insufficient to render him unconscious, but caused his vision to swim. He teetered on the brink of collapsing, but just held himself together.

The audience were stunned into silence. Dughork turned to find Gatran waiting patiently.

"Dughork, you're simply incapable of hitting me."

Dughork roared and swung his axe towards Gatran's stomach. He expected the Elf to move back, but that didn't happen. Gatran stopped the axe's momentum with his own and then pushed back. Dughork was still semi-dazed from the blow to the head and quickly realised his strength had deserted him. A look of fear crossed his face as Gatran pushed harder. Their bodies met, and Gatran suddenly dropped his axe. In a blur of lightning-fast movements, he struck Dughork's chin with his fist several times and the Dwarves knees buckled. Still, he clung to consciousness as Gatran picked up his axe completely ignoring the one still in Dughork's hands. He swung it above his head, round and round at such speed it appeared he held several. Then, with a battle cry, he brought the axe down towards Dughork's neck and stopped it close enough to shave the beard from his face.

"Do you wish to live or die Dughork."

"I live to die in battle."

"It's not going to happen today, Dwarf no longer King. By Dwarven law, I assume the rank of King of Xeltar Mountain. You will become my prisoner until the magic consuming you, leaves your body."

"Kill me Elf, allow me to die with honour."

"There's been too much killing between our kinds. It's time to stop it."

He turned his back on Dughork and addressed the gathering.

"Dwarves, hear the words I speak and know they are true. I have fought your King, defeated him and assumed his position. Understand this is temporary. I have no desire to remain your King for longer than it takes to secure a peace treaty. The words I spoke before are true, both our kinds face a bleak challenge to secure our future. I have spoken with the Generals your King challenged to combat. They are fine Dwarves, each worthy of becoming your King, but your future would be secured more easily if several such Dwarves led your kind.

"Release the Generals," Gatran commanded, and their guards unlocked their chains. Gatran beckoned them forward and called Dravel, Kudra, and Sitara to his side. The crowd gasped as three more Elves revealed themselves and stood by his side.

"As soon as the negotiations are concluded I will pass my Kingship to these two Generals. By my reckoning, they have the future of Dwarven kind at the forefront of their minds. During my conversations with them, they agreed to end hostilities to preserve what remains of the Dwarf empire. The opposite to your previous King who was more concerned with the gold he could gain. Let me iterate gold has no value to a dying race, you cannot buy a cure to the sickness or an end to those using dark magic against us."

Gatran took the shouts from the Dwarf gathering as discontent to his words. Others joined in and Gatran realised their voices held a warning. He turned to see Dughork, axe in hand. Movement at both sides of Gatran threatened to turn his head, but he focussed his eyes on Dughork who swung the axe backwards and then forwards. To Gatran it seemed to happen slowly, yet he

341

could not move away. A flash in front. At first, he failed to recognise what had happened. Dughork stopped moving. His hands dropped the axe, and he slumped to the ground. A second axe was buried deeply into his side. Gatran looked away as Tanga moved forward and retrieved his axe from Dughork's body.

"It appears Gatran, as if there was no weakening of his treachery. His actions were not in the best interest of Dwarves, and he acted cowardly, he stated grimly. The crowd became silent again and Tanga addressed them.

"Fellow Dwarves, a peace treaty will be negotiated immediately, as you return to your stations. It will be swift and lasting. I tell you now, there will be no further raising of battle axes towards Elves."

Gatran stood by his side. "I can promise you no Elven weapon will be raised against Dwarves. Peace between our kinds now exists and all our efforts should concentrate on protecting our numbers. Our futures are still not secured until we defeat the dark magic that threatens us all."

The Dwarves cheered and started to leave the cavern.

"Perhaps you could join us in the council cavern and help formulate the treaty." Tanga suggested.

"It will be our pleasure, General."

The Elves followed the Dwarves.

A hand reached out and closed over Kudra's mouth. At the rear of the group, nobody witnessed her being dragged away in a different direction.

Sitara slipped away, concealed under a cloak, to find her way out. Her journey made easy by following the departure of a Dwarf hunting team.

Chapter 68:

Dravel led the forming of the treaty details along with the two Dwarf ambassadors. Agreements were easy, due to the willingness of the participants to ensure its success.

Gatran found his thoughts wandering and turned around to speak to Kudra. Her absence shocked him. A feeling of concern coursed through his every pore, making his skin itch. She rarely left his side, at any point during their journey unless it was by agreement. He turned to Tanga and Kylav who were focussed on the proceedings.

"General Kylav, have you seen Kudra, she left the arena with us but has vanished? It's unlike her to leave without warning."

"She is likely in another cavern, but I sense your concern."

"My concern is due to the individuals here commanding dark magic."

"I will raise a search party, worry not Gatran, we'll find her."

Kylav left the cavern to raise the search party, but Gatran could not shake the feelings of worry. He wanted to discuss it with Dravel, but couldn't interrupt the proceedings. Forced to wait, all sorts of potential scenarios permeated his thoughts, none favourable.

Sitara followed the hunting party from Xeltar Mountain as discretely as she could. Keeping her distance in the tunnels, she only just reached the exit door before it closed. Discovering how it opened from the inside could have proved difficult.

The view from the plateau stretched for miles and she felt her spirits soar as she soaked in the daylight. She could see Gatran's army camped close by. Several thousand Elves, moving about, appearing like ants from this height. She stayed where she was, allowing the sun's rays to warm her body, causing an upsurging sense of positivity. Then she started the trek down the slope. She slipped several times, sliding on the loose gravel; it had been easier to climb up the steep slope than down. Reaching the ground, it was only a short distance to the camp. The Dwarf, sounding the alarm at the army's presence, had been accurate, they were just beyond an arrows flight distant.

Entering the camp, several soldiers smiled or nodded a greeting and for the first time in many moon-cycles Sitara felt safe. Eckna's shelter was easy to spot, it was larger than anyone else's, and she head straight for it. He was outside, sitting at a table and drinking water when she reached him. Her movements caused him to look up, and he grinned a welcome of delight.

"Sitara, wonderful to see you, what news of Gatran and the peace negotiations?"

Typical of Eckna, no fuss, and straight to the point. Quickly, she relayed the recent events in Xeltar and Eckna listened without interruption. When completed, he asked after Dravel and Kudra. He was pleased with her response and confident his Prince would return soon, after successful negotiations and no battle.

"The individuals commanding dark magic, did you discover them?"

"Unfortunately, we did not. Dughork was definitely controlled by magic as was gaoler, Finrok, but to lesser amount. Whoever controlled them remains mystery. And those hiding in your army under influence?"

"We watched them closely and one day they simply vanished. We are unsure if they remain in a different form."

"When Dravel returns he'll walk encampment and seek those under influence again."

"Better if they've left. Are you returning to Xeltar or staying with us?"

"Little point in returning. I will stay."

"There are some High Elves among the ranks who would enjoy your company. They have integrated well and are popular amongst the Wood Elves. In view of our potential future together, the signs of a peaceable co-existence seems positive."

"I witness same, within our group. Gatran is like us, and we are like him. Same peace is evident."

"Are you hungry, Sitara? I would enjoy your company over a meal."

"Elven food is good, even army food, after eating Dwarven meals; while acceptable it was different."

Later that evening, Gatran paced the cavern. The treaty was completed a while ago. All efforts concentrated on locating Kudra. Tanga spread the news of her disappearance to encourage all Dwarves to seek her location.

Kylav reappeared after instigating teams of searchers. "There is no sign of her. The upper cavern searches are completed; the lower caverns are being searched now. There is something else to share. There is no sign of Finrok either."

"Finrok is missing? I wonder if his disappearance is connected to hers. Dravel what do you think?"

"He is under the influence of dark magic. The treaty is finished and signed, and I suspect those with dark magic have realised they've failed to stop it. Surely, their goal has failed. If they have Kudra, and it makes sense, they might use her to destroy what we've created."

"If they're no longer in Xeltar Mountain, where have they gone?

Our route from here is home. We will travel directly and safely. We worked out that the extinction of Elves is the ultimate purpose for everything that's happened. Perhaps they see a circumstance where Kudra can help their cause."

"She wouldn't help them willingly."

"No, the likelihood is she's now under influence of magic. It makes sense, she would be easier to control."

"But where would they take her?"

"Anywhere an attack on us would have the most damaging effect. Five or six places, on our route home, are likely; consider where we had difficulty, the likelihood is it will be difficult again."

"The journey was tougher than gaining our goals."

"Are you suggesting our gains only appear reality."

"We could second-guess possibilities for days. It would only add frustration and anger and possibly force us into making mistakes."

"What do you suggest?"

"My thoughts are simply based on circumstances. If Kudra and Finrok are not in Xeltar then we'll encounter them on route somewhere. They'll be used against us, I'm convinced. So, let's leave here, start the journey home, and wait for them to appear."

"And if you're wrong?"

"If I'm wrong, then I've potentially lost Kudra forever. I'm not wrong, I can't be wrong. If she's not here, she's somewhere else."

"If I were in your position, I would act similarly."

Gatran nodded. "We'll leave as soon as the search is finished."

"It saddens me your visit ends sourly."

"Thank you, Kylav. Know I do not harbour ill-feelings towards Dwarves because of this. The forces of dark magic conspire to thwart our achievements. Never have we faced an enemy so powerful."

Tanga brought the news they expected. Kudra and Finrok were not present in the lower regions of Xeltar. The Generals guided them to the mountain exit and, after farewells and conveying of good wishes, Gatran and Dravel stepped into the early evening.

"You know, I lost all sense of day and night inside the mountain."

"I did too. I experienced the same fall in spirits as Kudra and Sitara. Daylight has a new significance in understanding myself."

"I feel similarly at losing Kudra."

"We will find her again, I'm certain. Her destiny remains incomplete. You've achieved a peace treaty, with Dwarves. That accomplishment defies the expectation of most Elves."

"We achieved a peace treaty Dravel. Do not understate your own involvement."

"What now then, Gatran."

"Now, we join with Eckna, start the journey home, and find Kudra on route."

"It shouldn't take too long, then?"

"Another attempt at humour, Dravel and successful too."

"I learn from an expert, despite his height disadvantage."

Gatran laughed but his heart weighed heavy...

C. S. Clifford has always been passionate about stories and storytelling. As a child, he earned money singing at weddings in the church choir; the proceeds of which were spent in the local bookshop.

As a former primary teacher, he was inspired to start writing through the constant requests of children he taught. Now he writes for four different age groups. He lives in Kent where, when not writing or promoting and teaching writing, he enjoys carpentry, sea and freshwater angling and exploring the history of his local countryside.